SOMEBODY LIKE YOU

Also by Candis Terry

Any Given Christmas
Second Chance at the Sugar Shack
For Love and Honor (anthology)

SOMEBODY LIKE YOU

A Sugar Shack Novel

CANDIS TERRY

AVONIMPULSE

An Imprint of HarperCollinsPublishers

Excerpt from *Second Chance at the Sugar Shack* copyright © 2011 by Candis Terry.
Excerpt from *Any Given Christmas* copyright © 2011 by Candis Terry.

SOMEBODY LIKE YOU. Copyright © 2012 by Candis Terry. All rights reserved under International and Pan-American Copyright Conventions. By payment of the required fees, you have been granted the nonexclusive, nontransferable right to access and read the text of this e-book on screen. No part of this text may be reproduced, transmitted, downloaded, decompiled, reverse-engineered, or stored in or introduced into any information storage and retrieval system, in any form or by any means, whether electronic or mechanical, now known or hereinafter invented, without the express written permission of HarperCollins e-books.

EPub Edition JUNE 2012 ISBN: 9780062105257

Print Edition ISBN: 9780062202079

10 9 8 7 6 5 4 3 2

This one's for you, Mom,
because you always believed in me and told
me I could do anything I wanted.
Sorry if I sometimes took that literally
and ended up on restriction.
Love you.

ACKNOWLEDGMENTS

A special thank-you to Rachel Gibson. For seventeen years you've been my friend, my confidant, my mentor. How can I ever thank you enough? Lifting my glass to many more martinis, laughs, and good times!

A heartfelt hug to my readers, who took on the challenge of a new author. You gave the Sugar Shack life, and you are what keeps me going on those long, solitary nights at the keyboard.

Once again I need to thank my family, who has been so patient with my busy schedule. Especially my husband, who never reads anything except the newspaper and hunting magazines. Yet he devoured my first book in just two days and became an advocate for not only *my* books but all romance novels. You are a king among men. And, yes, you may keep your man card.

CHAPTER ONE

Kelly Silverthorne despised killers.

Especially the type who possessed the charm of a movie star that belied the icy heart of the snake that beat in their chest.

"I think it's dead."

Jarred from the dark images in her head, Kelly looked up at her fellow Chicago prosecutor, Daniel Bluhm. A streak of sunlight shot through the window of the deli and glimmered in his golden hair. While they awaited word that the jury had reached a verdict in the Colson murder case, lunch had seemed a good idea. The nerves coiled in her stomach said otherwise. "Excuse me?"

"Your potato salad." Daniel pointed to her plate. "Or maybe I should call it lumpy soup."

Kelly glanced down at the fork in her hand and the mess she'd made of what had once been a tasty side dish. She dropped the utensil to her plate and glanced around the old-fashioned restaurant and the retro decorations that adorned the walls. "Sorry."

A smile crossed his mouth before he stuffed in the last bite of his patty melt. "Nervous?"

She nodded.

"You did a hell of a job with closing arguments."

"Daniel?" Kelly sipped her Diet Pepsi and wiped her mouth with the paper napkin. "I don't know if I mentioned this or not, but this murder case we've been working on for more than a year? The case in which I pushed for an arrest and prosecution against the state attorney's better judgment? The case I swore we had enough evidence to get a conviction?"

"You mean the case that's been plastered all over the real *and* entertainment news networks?"

"Yes!" Her eyes widened in feigned surprise, and she pointed at him with the straw in her soda. "*That* one. In case I forgot to tell you, it involves a popular movie star–like senator and a glamorous cast member of *The Real Housewives of Chicago*. By the time I wrapped up, the jury looked at me like I'd kicked their dog."

"Don't be so hard on yourself." Her partner chuckled. "We went in prepared. We had forensics, motive, and—"

"No body." She shrugged. "Bottom line, Bluhm. No. Body." Kelly grabbed a french fry off his plate and shoved it into her mouth.

"Hey. No fair eating my food because you trashed your own."

"Partners share."

He reached across the table and covered her hand with his. "Some partners would like to share even more."

Kelly playfully poked his hand with her fork. "Not gonna happen, Romeo."

"You're killing me, Silverthorne." He leaned back in his chair. His sharp blue eyes focused on her face, much the way they focused on a defendant he intended to break. "I've been asking you out for two years. When are you going to cut me some slack and let me take you on a date? I promise dinner, a movie, the whole shebang. I'll even be a gentleman, even though it might kill me."

She laughed at the exaggerated whine in his tone. "Daniel. You are a really nice—"

"*No.*" Comically he covered his face with both hands. "Do *not* give me the *friends* speech."

His reaction sent her into a fit of laughter, which helped to ease the tension churning the tuna-salad sandwich in her stomach. Her phone chimed. She and Daniel looked at each other before she picked it up and checked the text message. "Jury's in."

One golden brow lifted. "Two hours to deliberate?"

Kelly nodded.

"Shit."

"Yeah." She tossed her napkin on the table and grabbed the check. "Let's go."

It took another two hours for the media to be notified and for everyone to reassemble in the courtroom. Kelly had stood outside in the warm June sunshine until the last possible moment. Praying. Searching for a lucky penny on the ground or a stray rabbit's foot. Heck, if it meant a conviction, she'd haul a whole danged bunny into the courtroom.

Her high heels clicked on the marble floor as she passed

through security, headed toward the elevator, and pressed the button. She reviewed the trial in her head while the floor numbers lit up like Christmas lights. With the exception of admitting two questionable exhibits into evidence, she'd done everything possible to nail Andrew Colson for the murder of his wife, Alicia. Over the past year Kelly had given meticulous consideration to the evidence. She'd role-played. She'd spent hours and hours at the law library looking up comparable cases. She'd interviewed dozens of character witnesses. By the time she and Daniel had the case packaged and ready to present, she'd been confident they'd get a conviction.

Two hours to deliberate.

An icy chill shot up her back as the elevator doors slid open.

She wished she felt that confident now.

Inside the courtroom she set down her expandable briefcase and returned the anxious regard Daniel gave her when their gazes met. She sat down and busied herself with collecting her notes and her thoughts. Minutes later the defendant in his Armani suit and expensive haircut strolled in with his high-powered attorneys. He cast an arrogant glance toward the already seated jury then sat down and leaned back, as though he was in a bar waiting for his scotch.

Geez, couldn't the guy even pretend to be human? After all, this was a trial for the murder of his wife. A woman he had pledged to honor and cherish all the days of their lives. His two children were now motherless, and, if Kelly had done her job, they would be fatherless, too. In a moment of sheer compassion, she felt bad about that. Not for the defendant, but for the children who would grow up forever wondering what had really happened to the woman who poured their cereal every day, taxied them to soccer practice, and tucked them into bed at night.

Kelly slid her gaze across the courtroom to where Alicia Colson's family sat together, holding hands like linked chains. They would be there for the kids. Thank god for that.

Judge Reginald Dawson entered, and the courtroom stood until he was seated. Kelly gripped her pen in her hand and mentally began her customary chant.

He is guilty. He will pay. He is guilty. He will pay.

"Has the jury reached a verdict?" Judge Dawson's deep voice boomed through the packed room.

The jury foreman stood and sweat broke out on the back of Kelly's neck.

"Yes, Your Honor."

"Has the jury signed the appropriate verdict form? If so, please provide them to Deputy Southwick who will then present them to me."

As Judge Dawson opened the envelope and silently reviewed the documents, Kelly crossed her ankles and squeezed them together. Her heart pounded.

The judge passed the papers to the court clerk, who then began to read, "We, the jury in the above titled action, find the defendant . . ."

CHAPTER TWO

Defendant not guilty.

They were only three words. But for Kelly they were three words that had taken all the wonderful things she believed about life and made them hideous.

Surrounded by the scent of caramel, and chocolate, and cinnamon-raisin bread warm from the oven, Kelly propped her head up with one hand and shoveled another bite of chocolate chip cheesecake into her mouth with the other. When the golden retriever at her feet begged for a taste, Kelly guarded her plate like security at Fort Knox.

"Dream on, pooch."

The smooth dessert melted in her mouth while she studied the small office in which she'd sequestered herself a little over an hour ago. A calendar on the wall designated "Sweet Sale" days at the Sugar Shack, the bakery established by her parents, now run by her kid sister, Kate. On the dinged-up desk sat a faded photo of her parents' wedding thirty-six years ago, and a photo of Kate's wedding to Matt, the new sheriff of Deer Lick, Montana, taken just seven short months ago.

Ceiling-to-floor shelves lined the back wall where a rainbow of sugar sprinkles, edible sparkles, and candy crunches lined up cap-to-cap next to an array of both PG- and X-rated cake pans. Enormous differences existed between the Silverthorne women. While her mother had once created basic cakes with buttercream icing, her sister Kate's creations reflected her imaginative and often racy specialty cakes. Kelly, though she had a talent for making kickass fudge, couldn't fashion a buttercream rose to save her life.

She glanced back up to her parents' wedding photo and studied the faded print of her mother, who'd died suddenly last fall. Mixed emotions rumbled around inside her heart as she thought of the last time she'd spoken to the woman who'd given her life. Well, the last time she'd heard her mother's voice. Kelly had placed her scheduled weekly call expecting their conversation would go as usual. *Fluff calls* she'd come to name them, because they'd contained little more than generalities.

On that last call her mother had been too busy to talk. Several days later she'd returned the call, but Kelly had been in court and unable to talk. It seemed like that had become the pattern of their relationship. Mom was always too busy, and when she'd find time Kelly would be unable to connect.

Kelly shoveled in another bite of cheesecake, closed her eyes, and swallowed her guilt. She'd worked in this bakery beside her family from the time she'd been old enough to hold a mixing spoon until the day she'd left for Northwestern University. Today, the place felt foreign, and isolation echoed in her soul.

Her fault.

Like the inexorable loss of her mother, the events of the past month slammed through her head as if she still stood on that courtroom floor fighting for a piece of justice that would be denied. Fighting for the rights of a woman whose life had been ripped away by a monster. A fiend now able to roam free because *she* hadn't convinced the jury of his crime.

Her fault.

She'd pushed for that arrest. Pushed for an indictment with the grand jury. Pushed for a homicide case without a corpse.

Nausea and half a mountainous slice of cheesecake roiled through her stomach as she visualized the disbelief on the faces of the victim's family when the verdict had come down. The family she'd promised a conviction.

In her mind she could still hear the collective gasp echo across the chamber walls. She heard the grief and torment in the family's voices when they'd pointed their fingers at her and her fellow prosecutor and accused them of incompetence. Of failure.

She'd been so sure.

But she'd been wrong.

She'd never been wrong before. Never lost a case. Never led so many innocent people into such a clusterfuck of bad judgment, poor execution, and weak evidence. Not once since she'd been an intern with the state attorney's office had she ever been doubted. Until that verdict had come in. The eyes that followed her out of that courtroom and back down the hall to her office had been teeming with accusation and disappointment.

She'd failed each and every one of them.

Horribly.

She'd lost her touch. Lost her confidence. And she had no idea where to go from here.

Her sister's monstrous golden retriever pup curled around Kelly's feet and groaned as though he could read her thoughts.

"Nice try, Happy."

The pup looked up at her with big, understanding brown eyes, but no one could imagine the agony and guilt that spun a toxic web around her heart. Not even the man who'd stood beside her in that courtroom for months. When the verdict came down, he'd shrugged as if it didn't matter. For him, maybe it hadn't. She'd been the one who'd had to face the family, the media, the critics. She'd been the lead on the case.

Her fault.

The office door opened, and her sister with her shiny auburn hair and clashing pink apron barged into the office. The dog got up to greet her, and his long furry tail swept the floor in a happy wag.

"When you said you needed to hide out, I didn't think you meant literally." Kate used her foot to scoot a chair out from the wall, and she plopped down. She leaned her forearms on her knees, and she studied Kelly for a good long moment. "You look like hell, big sister."

"I imagine that's an understatement." Kelly leaned back against the rickety chair in which her mother had sat to order flour and sugar for over three decades. "I haven't slept much since the verdict came in."

"You did your best, Kel."

"Did I?" The pressure between Kelly's eyes intensified.

"Yes," Kate insisted. "You used every bit of evidence you

had. Your arguments were clear and concise. You led the jury down a path where they could visualize the timeline and the crime. It's hard to win a murder case without a corpse." Kate leaned forward and wrapped her arms around Kelly's shoulders. "What more could you have done?"

"That's what I keep asking myself."

Kate gave her a squeeze then leaned back. "Well, you're home now. And if anybody in the press shows up to harass you I will personally kick their ass." Kate's brows lifted. "It wouldn't be the first time."

"It feels good to be home."

"You say that now, but wait until you're tucked into that lumpy twin bed tonight and you hear dad snoring from down the hall."

Kelly smiled for the first time in weeks. "Icing on the cake."

"Speaking of . . . I hate to impose, but would you mind giving me a hand out front? I've got a few orders I need to box up, and I still have to ice two dozen cupcakes for Mary Clancy's baby shower. Dad's busy with a batch of dinner rolls."

"You *don't* hate to impose, but I'd be happy to help anyway." Kelly shoveled the last bit of cheesecake into her mouth, stood, and grabbed an apron off the hook on the wall.

"Good thing you came home wearing jeans and a T-shirt instead of your usual lawyer regalia."

Kelly draped the apron over her head and nodded. She didn't think now was the right time to tell her sister she had doubts she'd ever wear another Brooks Brothers suit. Her colossal failure had led to a murderer's freedom—and there was no doubt in her mind that Andrew Colson had murdered his wife. She couldn't afford to screw up again.

Someone's life may depend on it.

She followed Kate out of the small office tying an apron around her waist and preparing herself to dive back into life in Deer Lick. She'd taken a leave of absence to attend her brother's wedding. But she'd also come home to hide. To lick her wounds. To overcome her guilt. If that was even possible. She hadn't quite planned to shovel cookies and cupcakes into white boxes, but that's exactly what she was about to do.

As she passed him in the kitchen she gave her dad a quick kiss on the cheek then headed toward the front counter. A glance over the top of the glass display case indicated a number of patrons reading the menu or pointing out sugary delights they intended to take home. Kelly's gaze skipped over the fresh Neapolitan ice cream colors of the shop, the vintage photo of her mom and dad on the Sugar Shack's opening day, and came to a sliding stop near the door. Back turned toward her, a wide set of khaki-clad shoulders blocked the summer's glare off the patrol car parked outside.

She sucked back a groan.

Apparently karma wasn't done playing *gotcha*.

Her hands stilled on the apron ties. Her heart knocked against her ribs. The knot in her stomach pulled tight. On the other side of the lunch counter stood another of her monumental screw-ups.

As if she'd called his name, he turned his sandy blond head. His brown eyes brightened, and a smile tipped the corners of lips that were sinfully delicious. She knew. She'd tasted them.

She took a wobbly step backward.

In her thirty-two years she'd been struck with accusatory

scowls from a judgmental mother and murderous glares from convicted felons, but nothing had ever hit her below the belt like a smile bursting with sexual promise from one of Deer Lick's finest.

Deputy James Harley.

His intense gaze perused her body like he was on the cruise of a lifetime and enjoying the trip. He'd looked at her that same way just a few months ago—braced above her on arms thick with muscle while the rest of his hot, hard body did the talking.

A tingle ignited from her head, sizzled like a fuse down the front of her shirt, and detonated beneath the zipper on her jeans. Her skin turned hot and a flush crept up her chest. All thanks to the memory of one night in James Harley's bed.

As a deputy sheriff he'd sworn to serve and protect. During the hours she'd spent rolling in his sheets, he'd done both. At least from what she remembered.

The night of Kate's wedding reception, Kelly knew she should have stayed focused on carrying out her maid-of-honor duties. But one too many glasses of exceptional champagne had dislodged a few of her bolts and screws and she'd completely given herself over to whim and mind-bending orgasms. Afterward, she'd made a promise to herself to get a serious handle on the sometimes uncontainable urges that never ceased to embarrass the hell out of her. Even if they did provide a real jolt of excitement.

She blinked away the sweaty memory of the hot, sexy man on the opposite side of the counter, sucked in a breath, and stepped up beside Kate. "What do you need me to do?"

"Could you box up that chocolate cake and then fill James's lunch order?"

Crap. "Sure." *Kill me now. Please.*

Her hands uncharacteristically trembled as she opened a pastry box and lifted Dr. Robinson's double chocolate birthday cake from the display case. She didn't know why her stomach was so keyed up. She'd spent the last seven years in the heat of the spotlight, prosecuting some of the dirtiest criminals in the state of Illinois, and she'd never once been nervous.

So why did taking a lunch order seem so damned intimidating?

With a smile she handed the pastry box over the counter to Dr. Robinson's nurse and rang up the bill on the register. She closed the cash drawer and wiped her hands down the front of her apron, leaving a streak of chocolate. When she looked up *hot cop* was standing at the lunch counter. Muscled arms expanded from beneath his short uniform sleeves while the fitted shirt hugged his wide chest and slim waist. Kelly knew that beneath all that khaki fabric was a talented body of pure strength and muscle. A *very* talented body.

God, her thoughts were a train wreck.

She grabbed the pencil and order pad. "Can I help you?"

A smile crinkled the corners of his brown eyes and a slow blink swept long, dark lashes across his cheeks. "You're back."

"Apparently."

He chuckled. "And you're not happy to see me."

"I'm not *not* happy to see you."

"Okay then. I'll take that for starters."

Oh, no. His days of taking from her were over. She was on a *save your soul and sanity* mission. No boys allowed. "And what would you like to eat?"

The spark in his eyes guaranteed she wouldn't need a Geiger counter to detect what he was thinking. "Sandwich, Deputy Harley. What kind would you like?"

"I'd like two tuna subs. No tomato. Two iced teas." He settled a lean hip against the counter. "And your phone number."

A laugh escaped before she could stop it. "That will be nine fifty-six."

"Is that a no?" He reached into his back pocket, withdrew a worn leather wallet, and handed her a twenty.

Her fingers curled around the money. "I'm sure you have all the numbers you can handle."

James held onto the cash, just to be able to touch her for half a second. "I'd be willing to throw all those numbers away in exchange."

Since she was a pro and could read a lie a mile away she probably thought he was bullshitting her. But he'd never been more serious.

One night with Kelly Silverthorne hadn't been nearly enough. Once she'd hightailed it out of town he'd tried to discount the hours he'd spent with her in his arms but it had been impossible. Now here she was again. And everything inside of him was buzzing with awareness.

As expected she looked up and studied his face like he'd been named a prime suspect. He knew that look. On the job he'd used it himself once or twice.

"Without all those phone numbers what would you do on a rainy day, Deputy?" Her head tilted just slightly and her ivory hair fanned like silk across her shoulder. "I'd hate to be the cause of your ultimate frustration."

"Nice jab, Counselor." James steadied his breath as he watched her delicate fingers punch the amount into the register and slide the cash into the drawer. Kelly Silverthorne was the most beautiful woman he'd ever laid eyes on. And he'd seen plenty. From the second grade he'd watched her, admired her, and had probably had a crush on her even though the only glances she'd ever returned had been rife with warnings to keep his distance.

The night she'd ended up in his bed? No one could have been more surprised. Oh, he wasn't about to complain. No way. The counselor was hot. And sweet. And way out of his league. Though he knew he'd had his one and only shot with her, he craved her like a decadent dessert or a fine wine. One taste was just not enough to satisfy.

He watched as she grabbed the sandwich rolls, cautiously sliced through them, and spread a thin layer of mayonnaise across the surface. She topped the bread with perfectly rounded scoops of tuna salad and carefully placed leaves of crunchy lettuce on top. Every movement was smooth and calculated, as if she'd be judged on her placement and presentation.

In an attempt to gain control over his body and all the odd stirrings around his heart, he looked away. A quick glance at the two sisters revealed the vast differences. Kate, his best friend's new wife, was a bit taller and looked as if in a scrap she could hold her own. Her straight auburn hair displayed a meager reflection of her fiery personality. Whereas Kelly, a few inches shorter, teetered on the more delicate side. She looked like a woman a man would jump to protect. Her long ivory hair had a soft curl that made her glow like sunshine.

He smiled.

At least she'd lit up his world. For a night.

"So what made you leave the Windy City and come all the way back to our little town?" he asked as she wrapped each sandwich in white paper as carefully as if she'd been swaddling a newborn.

"Just needed a break." She slid the packaged sandwich into a crisp white bag.

"Most people who need a break hit a tropical beach. Not some dusty back road to nowhere."

"Maybe *nowhere* is exactly where I want to be." She shoved the second sandwich into the bag a little less carefully.

Whoa. Was it his imagination or was he detecting some underlying aggression?

"Well, I'm sure your family will be happy to have you around for a little while," he said, watching her graceful fingers fold down the top of the bag.

She gave him no response as she set the bag on the counter, grabbed two paper cups, and began to fill them with iced tea.

"So . . . exactly how long of a little while will that be?" he asked.

The glass pitcher thunked on the counter and tea sloshed up the sides. "The length of my stay is really no concern of yours, Deputy Harley."

"True. But I'm more than willing to change that if you are."

A smile tilted her soft, full lips. "You really are incorrigible."

He mirrored her expression. "It's a cross I bear."

She set the cups of tea down in front of him and pushed plastic caps over the rims. "I hope you enjoy your lunch, Deputy Harley. Please do come again soon."

"Is that an invitation?" *Say yes, Angelface.*

Her delicate brows pulled together over sea-green eyes. "Are you serious?"

"As a tortoise trying to cross the road."

"I'm sorry, Deputy—"

"I think we know each other well enough to be on a first name basis, don't you?" Her slight hesitation gave him hope.

"Like I said, I'm sorry, *Deputy*, I'm not here to engage in anything other than some rest and relaxation. I need a break. Not an opportunity to . . . lose control," she whispered.

James smiled. He knew exactly how loudly Kelly lost control. And exactly what made her lose it. Then again, he was more than willing to invent new techniques to make that happen too. Even if it took all night. *Please God, let it take all night.*

If Princess Prosecutor imagined him as a man who gave up easily, she'd be very wrong.

"You know . . ." He leaned closer and spoke low, for her ears only. "If you give me your number you might just have a little fun losing a little control for the little while you're here." He lifted the bag and cups from the counter, stepped back, and gave her a good long appreciative once over. "Or is that what you're afraid of?"

CHAPTER THREE

Whether she'd intended to or not, Kelly found herself immersed in the high-energy swing of things. She didn't mind helping out her family, but she hadn't come home to push pastries. Yet, in a matter of minutes after she'd stepped through the door of the Sugar Shack, Kate had her packaging up cakes and taking orders from a certain tall, sexy, smart-aleck customer who made her want to reconsider all those stringent rules she'd imposed on herself.

Eventually she'd found her escape and slipped out the back door of the old red brick building and into the alley that ran behind Buck's Gun Shop and the Once Again Bookstore. She flipped through the minivan keys on the keychain she'd snagged from Kate's purse and tried to soak in the oddity that her sister had traded in her BMW for a minivan. If there was a single person on the planet who did not fit the minivan mold, it had to be Kate.

Behind her, a low rumble bounced off the walls of the surrounding buildings. Kelly turned as Dean, her ex–NFL superstar brother, pulled up into the alley, rolled down the window of his SUV, and flashed her a *gotcha* grin.

"Car theft is against the law, you know."

She held up the cupcake-shaped charm on the ring and jingled the contents. "Not if you have the keys."

"I know a good attorney who could prove otherwise."

Yeah, and that would be one of the easier things she'd ever have to do in her career. "Are you stalking me or did you really just happen to be driving by?"

"Emma sent me down to the True Value to pick up some new gloves. She wore a hole in hers planting the garden."

Kelly leaned her arms on the SUV's window sill. "Wow. It's really weird to see you so domesticated."

"Tell me about it. And I don't even have the ring on my hand yet."

"You're loving it. I can tell."

"Seriously loving it." His handsome face broke into a grin. "To think just four months ago I was sweating it out, wondering what I was going to do with the rest of my life. Today, I've barely got time to think about football."

"So you don't miss it?"

"Every once in a while. But then I look at Emma and everything we're building together. Honestly, I wouldn't want to be anywhere else."

"Congratulations, big brother."

"Thanks." He reached across the seat and moved a bag and stack of papers from the passenger seat. "Hop in. I'll give you a ride."

"What about Kate's keys?"

He laughed. "Just open the back door of the bakery, toss 'em inside, and run like hell."

Kelly did just that and within seconds they were out on Main Street whizzing past the Blue Moon Café. Her stomach rumbled. During her visit, she promised to treat herself to one of the restaurant's to-die-for Monte Cristo sandwiches they served with homemade huckleberry jam.

If she thought Dean was just being a good brother and giving her a ride home, she'd be wrong. As crafty as he'd been with a fake pass on the football field, he sneaked past the street that would take them to their parents' house.

"Where are we going?"

"I'm kidnapping you." With a laugh that fell short of evil, he headed straight to the Clear Creek Lodge, the beautiful mountain resort home he and Emma would share once they were married in a few weeks.

When they arrived, Dean gave her a tour of the place and showed her the recent changes they'd made to the guest cabins. The Letty Silverthorne Sunshine Camp had already had two groups of special needs campers come through. Dean told her both had been successful and that they had a third group coming in a few weeks after he and Emma returned from their honeymoon. From there he ushered her into the huge house where he proceeded to corner her in his office with a Diet Pepsi and a stack of organizational documents. One of the things she admired most about her brother was the passion he'd put into the camp for special-needs kids he'd created in honor of their late mother. As an attorney *and* a board member of the Letty Silverthorne Sunshine Camp, Kelly was more than happy to give the documents her professional once-over. Tomorrow, after a good night's sleep, would have been better. But today would do.

"So things have been pretty rough lately in the Windy City," Dean said, leaning back in his executive leather office chair.

"Well, there's an understatement if I've ever heard one."

"What happened?"

She shrugged. "It's possible to get a murder conviction without a body, but not probable. Everyone knows Andrew Colson is guilty. We just didn't have enough solid evidence to go beyond a reasonable doubt. I don't think the jury found him innocent, just not guilty beyond a reasonable doubt."

"There's a difference?"

"For a jury that's been instructed to follow the rules? Yeah. A big difference."

Dean ran his hand through his hair. "Just doesn't seem fair."

"It's not." Anger and guilt coiled inside her stomach. "There's now a killer running free while Alicia Colson's body is God-knows-where and her children are without their mother. As you know Andrew Colson is a high-profile politician. So all we can hope for now is that somehow he'll slip up and we can get him on another charge. But we'll never be able to try him again for Alicia's murder."

"Double jeopardy."

"Yeah. Whoever thought up *that* rule was crazy." If it was up to her, she'd try the bastard ten times over until she could get a conviction.

"If it's any help, I know how you feel. Like you've let everyone else down." He paused. His expression darkened. And

Kelly knew he was thinking about the shoulder injury that ended his NFL career. "Like you've failed."

"Exactly."

"Don't let it take you down, Kel. Life is big. And sometimes control slips through our hands. But that doesn't mean you failed. And that doesn't mean there isn't something equally as important for you to do."

"Like what?"

He shrugged. "Stick your hand in the bag and see what you come up with."

Frustrated, she lifted her glass of soda from the coaster on her brother's desk.

"You want something a little stronger in that drink?"

She sipped, crunched a chip of ice between her teeth, and shook her head. "I just need some sleep. Maybe indulge myself in a really good book, and relax a little before I have to go back to the mines."

"Well, don't get your hopes up for too much R&R. I thought the same thing and look what happened to me."

True. However, this was Deer Lick—a place where she'd spent eighteen years of her life. A place she'd always viewed as little more than a journey down a gravel road to complete and utter tedium.

Strangely, she couldn't wait to get started.

Three hours later, as the sun hovered low over the ancient pines, Kelly had finally wrapped up the document review. Her eyes burned. Exhaustion tangled around her spine. And drowsiness spun a web around her brain. She may have dreaded crawling into her old twin-sized bed, but now it sounded like absolute heaven.

La-la land was far away as she stood inside her brother's English country kitchen and glanced out the huge windows that overlooked a wood deck and the lake beyond. While she'd offered to go inside and grab another bottle of Cabernet, the rest of the clan stood outside where thick slabs of sirloin sizzled on a huge stainless grill. An impromptu party atmosphere had begun to take hold and it appeared she wasn't about to get those much needed Z's anytime soon.

Kate and Matt stood arm-in-arm, while Dean and Emma took turns flipping the steaks. Tonight wasn't the first time in her life Kelly had found herself the odd girl out. It was a role she'd become accustomed to over the years. Not that she always liked to be the spare tire, but more often than not her relationships never seemed to gel. Since most of her dating selections came from the legal pool, conflicts in time management and opinionated incongruities often put a big spike in the middle of her ability to find Mr. Right. Or even Mr. Right Now.

In any case, *right now* all she wanted or needed was to find a little peace of mind. To find a way to overcome her guilt. And to spend a little time with the people who meant the most in her life, but with whom she seemed to spend the least amount of time.

Finding Mr. Right couldn't be further down her to-do list.

Pushing away from the counter, she went to the built-in wine rack and pulled down a bottle of Beringer Private Reserve. Then she went on the hunt to find a corkscrew.

"Third drawer on the left."

Kelly jumped at the deep voice. She turned to find James Harley standing just inside the door of her brother's kitchen. He'd traded in his khaki uniform for khaki cargo shorts that hung low on his lean hips, and a black T-shirt that fit snug across his wide shoulders, nicely defined chest, and narrow waist. He'd also traded in his spider-stomping boots for flip-flops. His thick sandy blond hair ranged somewhere between wind-blown and finger-combed. And from across the kitchen, Kelly caught the fresh clean scent of his recent shower. He smelled good enough to eat. Or lick.

The female part of her shot into sensual overdrive—until she noticed the Kim Kardashian clone clinging to his arm.

"You startled me." Kelly backed up and met the cabinet with her behind.

"Sorry." His brown eyes softened. "That wasn't my intent."

"What are you doing here?" she asked, not meaning to sound bitchy but probably failing.

"It's Friday night."

"And that means?"

"I usually get together with your brother and sister and their significant others on Friday nights for either a beer or a barbecue."

"Oh." Shoot. There went any chance of relaxing tonight. Everything about James Harley woke her up. "Well, everyone else is out back."

"Great." His smile lit up his eyes. "Kelly, this is Brianna."

Brianna the bombshell brunette gave a finger wiggle and a beauty-pageant smile.

"Nice to meet you," Kelly said, although something territorial inside of her wished *Brianna* had a wart on the end of her perfect nose.

James turned to his date. "Why don't you head out back. I'll finish helping in here."

"Okay." Brianna went on tip-toe in her sparkly blue flip-flops and kissed James's cheek. "Don't make me wait too long though."

James watched the woman's ample booty leave the room with an appreciative smile on his face.

Kelly frowned. And to think, just a few hours ago he'd been asking for *her* phone number. *Player.*

He set the brown paper bag he'd been holding on the granite counter and came toward her in a relaxed gait that boasted confidence with every step. He reached into the drawer next to her hip. "Here you go." He held up a corkscrew and flashed a smile like he'd discovered gold.

"Thank you." She reached for the metal tool.

"On second thought," his warm palm curled around her hand and electricity snapped. "How about I just take care of that for you?"

"I'm perfectly capable," she said, untangling their fingers.

"Of course you are." There came that grin again. "But how about you allow my chivalrous side pretend to help a lady in distress?"

"Have at it." She backed away. "Who am I to wound an ego?"

He tore off the seal and stuck the pointed end of the tool into the cork. "I'm sure you've crushed a few in your day."

Hardly. The only thing she'd ever crushed was the ability

to put a murdering psycho behind bars. She watched James wind the opener down into the cork. With each twist, the muscles in his biceps tightened and flexed in a fascinating way. Geez, she had to find something else to occupy her thoughts.

Apparently he and his *date* planned to stay so she reached into the cupboard and took out additional wine glasses. "What's in the bag?" she asked, steering to a safer subject.

He opened the bag and peered inside as if he didn't know, then shrugged those wide shoulders. "Steaks. Bread. Beer. These get-togethers are usually a BYOBB."

"BYOBB?"

"Bring your own beef and booze."

"Ah." She lifted the wine bottle from the counter and juggled it in her arms with the glasses and the napkin holder. "I'm sure your *date* is waiting. So you should probably get outside."

"There's no hurry."

When he remained immovable Kelly looked up. "You aren't actually hitting on me when you have a woman waiting outside for you? Because if you are, it's a complete waste of your time. I don't associate with multi-daters."

He looked surprised instead of insulted. "I am proud to say I have never dated two women at the same time."

"Then I stand corrected." She bowed her head.

"You don't know me well enough to judge, Counselor." The hint of a smile pushed at his sexy mouth. "I do have principles."

"I'm sure you do." She laughed. "Somewhere."

"I didn't know you were going to be here."

"Obviously. But don't worry, Deputy. I won't rat you out

that you asked for my phone number just a few hours ago. Your questionable scruples may remain . . . undamaged."

He plucked the bottle and glasses from her arms, poured a splash of wine, and handed her the glass.

"No thanks."

"Loosen up, Counselor. Just because I asked for your number doesn't make me a bad guy. God knows I've never claimed to be a saint. But you and I, we had something—"

"We had *nothing*. I was drunk and—"

"Horny?"

Ouch. "Obviously."

"Otherwise you wouldn't have chosen *me*. Right?"

"I don't know. All I do know is that will never happen again."

He grinned. "You sure of that?"

"Absolutely." *Not.* She folded her arms. "Enough to bet money on it."

Loaded down with the wine and glasses he grabbed the bag off the counter and headed toward the door.

Good. He'd finally gotten a clue.

When he reached the door he stopped, turned, then came back to stand in front of her again. His warm brown eyes glittered with mischief. He leaned in, bringing his freshly showered, sexy male scent with him, and grinned.

"I'll take that bet, Counselor. How much are you willing to lose?"

"Not going to happen, Deputy."

"How much?"

She searched his face and the anticipation she found there started a fire burning at the base of her spine. "Fifty. Think you can afford to do without?"

"Fair warning, Angelface." He leaned down and spoke very clearly. "I never lose."

The BYOBB dinner conversation spanned the gamut from fantasy football to wedding flowers to cake pops. With the chairs gathered around the fire ring, James leaned back in the Adirondack on Dean and Emma's deck. Above them the stars winked in a calm velvet sky and danced off the gentle ripples on the lake.

It was a perfect night.

He'd only made one huge error.

Bringing Brianna.

He glanced over at the pretty brunette he'd dated off and on for a few weeks now. He'd invited her last week after they'd had a nice time together at Matt and Kate's turn to host the BYOBB, but there was nothing more there than a physical attraction. With only a few hours warning that Kelly Silverthorne was back, he'd been unable to cancel. In his book, breaking a date at the last minute was rude and unacceptable. Even if his heart was not in the game.

During the robust discussion he had plenty to contribute to the dialogue of legendary quarterback Peyton Manning's career turns, but he was clueless on whether the scent of the star iris might be too overwhelming for a bridal bouquet. Or if the idea of cake on a stick sounded like a profitable bakery item. But even if he had nothing to say at all he was content to sit and watch Kelly Silverthorne try to pretend he didn't exist.

To his dismay the prosecutor was doing a damned fine job.

"So what made you decide to have the wedding here by the lake instead of a church?" Brianna asked Emma, who seemed perfectly comfortable perched on the lap of one of the NFL's greatest quarterbacks and stroking her kitten, Lucky. "I've always dreamed of a big church wedding with at least ten bridesmaids," Brianna said, shifting her hopeful gaze to James.

James took a well-timed slug of his Sam Adams.

"Who wouldn't want to be married out here? In fact," Dean said to Emma, "we might want to put that on our list of possible uses for the lakeside meadow. We could loan it out for weddings."

Emma's eyes widened. "Great idea. We could even build a gazebo." She pointed toward the lake where the sliver of moon reflected like a beacon off the water. "Right there."

"Do *you* want to be married in a gazebo?" Dean asked Emma.

"That would be really nice, but the wedding is only a few weeks away."

James laughed as Dean gave his intended a *look*.

"If you want a gazebo, honey," Dean said. "You'll have a gazebo."

Emma gave Dean a countering look filled with so much love that even James's romantically stunted heart took an unexpected leap.

"Aren't you guys worried about all those people tromping through your property?" Kelly asked, while her thumb absently stroked the glass globe of wine. "You're going to need to up your liability coverage. I mean, you've already got the risk of kids here for the charity camp several times a month."

"The more the merrier," Dean said.

"Don't be such a party pooper, Kel. It's so much more beautiful out here," Kate added, as she took her husband's empty beer bottle and replaced it with a full one. "The only reason Matt and I were married in the church was because we would have gotten frostbite if we'd tried to have an outdoor wedding in December. Things don't always have to be so stringent. Sometimes things are better a little . . . messy."

"Yeah," Dean teased. "Lighten up a little."

"Easy for you to say." Kelly glanced away, her next comment a barely audible mumble. "Neither of you screwed up your job and let a murderer walk free."

Curious, James sat up straighter. He hadn't heard anything about this case. Not that he followed what Kelly did in Chicago. But he definitely listened when Dean or Kate mentioned something.

James watched Kelly's shoulders stiffen as she sheltered her remaining thoughts behind a mask of indifference. He imagined she used that same façade in the courtroom when she became the bug under the microscope. When everyone watched her for a reaction. Judged her for a wrong move. Here in the mountains of Montana, that façade had no place.

An unexpected wall of protectiveness fell over him.

"Wow. That's awful. How did she do *that?*" Brianna whispered. Loudly. James wanted to choke her even though she didn't say it in a malicious way.

Unfortunately the damage had been done. Kelly clearly heard the comment and the smoothness of her forehead disappeared behind a chain of worry lines. She stood and went to the deck rail, pushed her curly blond hair behind her shoulders, and looked out over the lake. "You guys act like I don't know how to have any fun."

Kate looked up. "Maybe it's not that you don't know *how* as much as maybe you've forgotten to make time."

"Leave her alone, Kate," Matt said.

James was happy to see someone take her side before he jumped in to defend her.

Kelly turned to face her sister. "My kind of fun is probably just different than yours."

"Then give me a for-instance." Kate scooted to the edge of her Adirondack chair. "You know I love you. I'm not trying to be nasty. I'm concerned."

"Well . . . for starters . . ."

From James's point-of-view, the long pauses indicated Kelly was waiting for her wheels to start turning. Not a good sign.

"I jog along the lakefront every chance I get," Kelly finally said.

"Running is a great way to clear your mind," James said.

"It is." Kelly smiled as though she realized he'd just rescued her from a sinking ship. "Of course, it's not a year-round activity. Sometimes it's just too cold or too hot."

"What other *fun* things do you do?" Dean asked.

"I belong to a book club." Kelly's delicate brows came together. "We meet once a month. Usually at a nice restaurant."

"I'm not much for reading, but restaurants can be fun," James added, knowing it sounded lame but wanting to take the heat off her. He may not like the way her siblings were ragging on her so-called *fun* activities, but he was definitely on their side. The pastimes that seemed so hard for her to come up with sounded a little lackluster. He knew from experience she had a whole lot of good time wrapped up in that curvy, petite body. She definitely could put a lot of pop in the fire. He'd seen for himself what the woman was like when she let go.

He thought of her in his arms, and in his bed. She took what she wanted, gave back in spades, and opened up like a treasure chest bursting with sparkling jewels. She'd smiled. And sighed. And even giggled. Of course that could all have been from the champagne bubbling through her system at the time, but he doubted it. She'd just become a pro at restricting that delightful part of her personality.

He took another long draw of his beer and studied her over the top of the amber bottle. She gave him a tentative smile that opened a small window into her soul.

Tonight she seemed wound tight. Closed off. Stressed. Worried. Exhausted. A completely different woman from the one he'd made love to back in December. She'd come home for her brother's wedding and a little R&R. To cut loose and maybe learn to have a little fun.

He set his bottle down on the table beside his chair. Forget about just wanting the gorgeous prosecutor in his bed again. If she needed a little instruction on the finer joys in life, James figured he was the right man to teach her.

With clothes or without.

CHAPTER FOUR

Close to midnight Kelly finally had the keys to her escape in hand, and she climbed into her mother's ancient Buick. The beast of a car had been used by both Kate and Dean upon their arrival back in Deer Lick. Now it was hers for the duration of her stay.

Why no one had sold the heap of junk after her mother died was anyone's guess. Sentiment probably. Then again, who'd want to buy the rusty old thing? As she cranked over the engine, waved to her brother and Emma, and drove away, she wasn't even sure she'd make it home. The fuel tank read full, but there were other things that could go wrong in a more than twenty-year-old car than just running out of gas.

The headlights lit up the rows of pine trees bordering the road while Kelly yawned. She imagined her head hitting the pillow of the twin bed she'd slept in as a kid in the room she'd shared with her baby sister. The same sister who'd managed to torture her as much then as she did now. As a kid, Kate had been somewhat of a loose cannon. Her relationship with their mother had been contentious, to say the least. Moving back home and falling in love again with her high school sweetheart had seemed to take the snap out of Kate's sizzle. Then again, their mother had dropped dead of a heart attack almost a year ago, so Kate really didn't have anyone around to ruffle her fighting spirit.

The interior of the car still smelled like vanilla—her mother's scent. The woman could shower and splash on ten dollars worth of Avon, but she'd still end up smelling like the baking extract.

Sadness pinged around Kelly's heart and stole her breath.

She'd never had a chance to say goodbye to her mother. Of course, if she had, her mother probably would have corrected her on the way she'd spoken the words. Or better yet, she would have ignored the words altogether. Sadly, Kelly knew she hadn't had any better of a relationship with her mother than Kate.

No better. Just different.

As a diversion from her thoughts she turned on the radio and found the oldies station they'd all been brought up on. If she and her siblings had wanted to listen to metal, pop, or rock, they'd had to do it outside the home, because her mother insisted they'd quit making good music in the sixties. So while Elvis sang "Suspicious Minds," Kelly continued down the road, taking in the darkness that sucked up the exterior of the car. If she'd been anywhere in Chicago by herself on a dark road like this, she would have been petrified. But she was in Deer Lick, where even the crickets knew nothing exciting ever happened.

After commercials for Big Pop's Popcorn and Buffalo Bill's Funeral Home, the song on the radio changed to Tom

Jones's "It's Not Unusual"—her mother's favorite. A wave of nostalgia swept over her tired brain. She laughed, thinking of the times her mother would watch the Welsh singer perform on TV then get up and mimic his moves. Kelly found herself singing along, if only to keep herself awake.

Unexpectedly a light flashed in the rearview mirror and nearly blinded her. She flipped the mirror to night vision but it didn't dim the glow.

"Geez, go around if you're in such a big hurry." She eased off the accelerator to give the car behind plenty of room to pass, but the light remained. Kelly's stomach jumped. She dug into her purse for her cell phone in case the person tailgating her car wasn't just some innocent driver sharing the same road at the same time. Maybe Deer Lick had changed after all.

Tom Jones gave a whoa-whoa-whoa and Kelly pulled the iPhone from her bag. She wasn't one who believed in texting or dialing while driving, but the hell if she'd pull over with the mad tailgater kissing her bumper. She slid her thumb across the display and tapped *Contacts*.

"Put the phone away. You have no reason to be afraid."

The voice from the backseat startled Kelly. The phone fell from her hand and she swerved to the side of the road in an abrupt stop. She pushed open the door and jumped out. Then she realized she may have just put herself in more danger. She turned to look for the car that had been tailgating her, but there was no car. She looked in all directions and saw nothing but darkness. She was completely alone on the dark and deserted road. Alone except for the blinding golden glow that filled the entire backseat of her mother's beat-to-shit Buick.

Keeping her distance, she ducked down and peered through the window. Nothing there except the glow.

What the hell?

She grabbed for the door handle as if it was flaming hot and yanked the door open. The glow disappeared. Her eyes scanned from the floorboard to the roof and found nothing out of the ordinary. All that remained in the car were an array of pastry cookbooks, a box of quilting fabric, and a knitting tote with super-sized needles poking out of the top of a ball of red yarn. All objects that had been left there by the car's now-deceased owner.

Crap.

She really should have taken a leave of absence much sooner.

She slammed the car door and took a deep breath of clean mountain air to clear her head. She'd gotten up at the break of dawn, climbed into an airplane, and flown halfway across the country. Once she'd arrived, she'd put in several hours at the Sugar Shack and another couple of hours going over legal documents for her brother's charity organization. It was now past midnight. She was just . . . exhausted.

There could be no other explanation.

She needed to shake off the heebie-jeebies, climb back in that car, drive straight home, and crawl into bed. Screw putting on her pajamas. Screw washing off her makeup. She was plunging face first into the pillow, and she didn't plan to wake up until noon tomorrow.

With another quick glance into the backseat and finding it gloriously empty, she climbed back into the car and put the gearshift into Drive. She'd gone a few uneventful miles when Tom Jones began to sing.

"It's not unusual . . ."

"Wow. Again?" she said to the radio and poked at the buttons to find a new tune. "Better hire a new DJ with a more extended playlist." But with every button she punched, old Tom continued to croon away. Kelly sighed and returned her hand to the wheel. She blinked her tired eyes. When they reopened, the golden glow in the backseat reappeared.

"Don't put your panties in a pretzel. It's only me."

At the sudden voice from nowhere, Kelly slammed her foot on the brake and turned in the seat. Her jaw dropped. Her heart stuttered. And a cold chill sliced down her back.

There, in the backseat, amid the cookbooks. Amid the balls of yarn. Wearing her traditional overalls, white Tee, and red plaid flannel shirt, sat her dead mother wiggling her fingers.

"Surprise."

Kelly froze.

"Shoot." The smile on her mother's face fell and her glow dimmed. A long chilly sigh of exasperation whipped through the interior of the car. "You're going to be the difficult one, aren't you?"

"Difficult?" Kelly clasped her hand to the front of her shirt. "Me? *You're* supposed to be dead."

"I *am* dead." A lopsided smile tipped Letty Silverthorne's colorless lips.

The blood drained from Kelly's head. Her ears buzzed. Her throat got tight. "I'm going to puke."

"Oh boy. Here we go." The figure in the backseat scoffed. "You are *not* going to puke. You *always* say you're going to puke when things get a little iffy. Like the night before your biology report on genetic testing was due. You said you were going to puke. The night before you took the LSAT, you were going to puke."

"I was just working myself up to the big time." Kelly turned back around in her seat and tried to ignore the freakish likeness of her mother in the backseat. She gripped the steering wheel. "I'm going to get out of this car, puke, then go home, and pass out. I am way too tired to be driving. I should have called it a night hours ago. But noooo."

"Kelly Grace, who in the world are you talking to?"

"I'm not talking to a ghost. That's for sure. I am a logical person who bases everything on facts. *If* I were talking to a ghost, they would lock me up with some of the crazies I've put away over the years."

"What did I ever do to discourage you from expanding your beliefs that the impossible may be possible?"

If that truly was her mother's ghost in the backseat, she would know what she'd done to discourage her middle child from expanding her views. In fact, her mother had been the creator of Kelly's "Sister Serious" moniker. Back then she'd thought the only way to grab her mother's attention had been to be a straight-A student. Which meant that any fun and games to be had would be enjoyed by her two siblings.

Kelly squeezed her eyes shut then opened them again, thinking the glow and her passenger from the other side would disappear. They didn't. She turned around again and looked at the *person* in the back who looked like a perfect replica of her mother minus the whole opaque thing.

"Mom? Is that really you?"

"No, it's the stinky cheeseman."

Kelly pulled her head back. "Well, that little bit of snark is unnecessary."

"You can get away with a lot when you're dead."

"Apparently."

"Don't you want to know why I'm here?"

"No."

"Seriously?"

Kelly inhaled a big breath of air. "Seriously. Because if you tell me why you're here it might make sense, and then I'd have to rethink the whole life-after-death thing. And right now I'm so tired I can barely think straight, let alone try to solve the mysteries of the universe."

"Exactly."

"Exactly, what?"

The lines on her mother's transparent forehead curled together near the center of her brows. "That's exactly why I'm here. Because you can barely think straight. And if you ask me—"

"I'm not."

"Gonna give you my two cents' worth anyway."

"You always did."

"No sense stopping now, right?" Her mother grinned.

"Sure."

"I think you need to reevaluate your whole life."

"Wow. Really? My *whole* life?"

"Yep." The tangled gray knot of hair at the top of her mother's head wiggled when she gave a curt nod. "The whole danged thing. I thought Kate's life was a mess, but you—"

"Please don't compare me with Kate. We are two entirely different people."

"You're not as different as you'd like to think," her mother said.

"Of course we are." Kelly folded her arm across her chest. "That's what made it so easy for you to ignore me half the time."

"I never ignored you."

"Really?"

"No."

Kelly shrugged. "Okay."

"That's it?" Ghostly hands flew upward. "You argue for a living, and all I get is an *okay?*"

"What do you want me to say? Because right now, quite honestly, I'm thinking I need more than a brief leave of absence. I think I need some serious therapy and maybe a hiatus of, oh, a decade or so." Kelly clutched her hands together to steady them. "*You* are dead. You are *not* here sitting in the backseat of your crapper of a car."

"Uh-oh. I think we might have unresolved issues." The backseat voice sounded mystified.

"Of course we do."

"Then I'm so glad I'm here." The mother image thing leaned forward with a big smile. "Isn't this amazing? That even after I'm long gone, we still have the chance to patch things up? Oh, we are going to have so much fun!"

Kelly didn't want to hear anymore. Her imagination had gone into slug mode, and she just needed to stumble into bed and have a good sleep. Still . . . she turned again, and whatever or whoever it was that had been in the backseat had disappeared.

Not for a minute did she think she'd actually seen a ghost.

Then again, if you'd asked her three weeks ago if she'd ever consider walking away from the career she'd worked so hard to build, she would have told anyone they were crazy.

As things stood now it looked like the real crazy person might very well be sitting behind the wheel of the world's biggest clunker.

The clock hit 1 a.m. as James opened the front door and stepped into his living room, where a pizza box, dirty napkins, and empty soda cans cluttered the surface of the coffee table. Sofa pillows were strewn about the floor, and, in their place, gamer controls sat in the middle of the sofa. He picked up the pillows, tossed them back on the leather couch. and sighed.

"Hello, girls, I'm home."

Yips and yaps and the scrambling of tiny toenails on a hardwood floor commenced from down the hall. As the sounds grew closer James knelt to receive the impending assault. In a flash of silky fur, the two dogs he shared his home with launched themselves into his arms. Slick pink tongues slurped him up one side of his face and down the other. It probably wasn't the welcome home most thirty-two-year-old men received when they walked through the door at night, but it felt good to know someone cared. Even if they had dog breath.

He captured Poppy and Princess, his two inherited Yorkshire terriers, in each arm and chuckled. "Did you miss me today?"

Poppy's small body wiggled like a wind-up toy, whereas Princess, the decided diva of the two, played a little harder to get. He gave them equal adoration time then played fetch with their favorite dog-slobbered toys for a few minutes, before he got up and went into the kitchen to feed them.

To his dismay the kitchen was in no better shape than the living room. As much as he tried to make the house a home, someone else always managed to unravel his good intentions. Dirty bowls filled the sink, and empty packages of cookies and chips cluttered the counter. Disgust curled up his spine, and he marched toward the back of the house to have yet another confrontation. He opened the bedroom door—or at least he *tried* to open the door. Something behind the panel prevented him from doing so, and he had to give it a good shove with his shoulder. When the barrier broke free he stepped into the chaos that was his little brother's domain.

With the exception of the clothes and other teenage boy objects scattered about the floor, dresser, and bed, the room was empty.

"Shit."

James ran a hand through his hair as he surveyed the disaster. How could one person make such a mess? Then he thought back to when he'd been seventeen—Alex's age—and knew he probably had no right to judge. In those days he'd been a walking tragedy of a human being. Danger and disrespect had been his game.

Until it had nearly killed him.

Princess strolled into the room, took a look around, and sneezed so hard her pointed ears jiggled.

"Yeah. It's a mess all right."

One half of the doggie duo he'd inherited from his ailing mother looked up at him with her big brown judgmental eyes.

"Don't look at me like that," James said, imagining what was going through her prissy little head. "I know you love him. But he's a pain in my ass."

Princess sat back on her haunches and gave him a look of complete and utter understanding. He reached down and lifted her into his arms, stroked her silky head, and held her close to his heart. "What am I going to do with that boy?"

The dog in his arms gave a little shudder.

He hadn't asked to take on the responsibility of his younger sibling. Hadn't wanted any part of it. Had proven time and again that he was the last person who should be counted on. But he owed it to his mother. Big time. With the stroke she'd suffered, caring for the little dogs she adored became impossible. For her, raising his unruly teenage brother had become monumental. Aside from his mother's deteriorated health, and aside from James's own past recklessness, he knew he owed it to the little boy who'd once looked up at him with such adoration. Neither of them had ever had a father for more than a blink of the eye. Alex's bio dad had stuck around only long enough to remind a then-teenage James that he wasn't wanted, needed, or liked.

After their mother's debilitating stroke, they'd all switched positions. Alex had become the hard-headed teen, and James had become the parent in charge. And as long as he'd been appointed to that position, he planned to kick Alex's rebellious ass all the way to a good life. No matter how hard the task. For either of them.

James took another look around the room before he closed the door and grabbed his truck keys. Alex may think he was smart and knew all the best places to hide and create havoc, but James wrote the book years ago.

CHAPTER FIVE

On Saturday morning, Kelly forced herself from her lumpy twin bed at the crack of dawn. Exhaustion and some explicitly erotic dreams kept calling her back. But when she'd heard her father moving about, she knew she needed to get up and spend some time with him before he went off to the bakery for the day.

After a quick trip to the bathroom, where she washed her face and gave up on the idea of taming the hair sticking up like she'd gone through a wind tunnel, she joined him in the kitchen.

For a moment she just watched him going about his routine. Sunshine beamed through the window, and tiny dust motes floated about his balding head like glitter. His work clothes, which consisted of white pants, a white shirt, and spotless white apron, had been freshly laundered and smelled of fabric softener. His grayed brows were pulled together over a faraway look in his eyes. His movements were stiff and slow, as if he had to focus on every single, painful joint—no doubt created by the tremendous amount of hours he'd spent kneading dough and scrubbing pots. When he heard her approach he turned, and his warm smile lit her up inside. She'd always had a much better relationship with her father than her mother.

Robert Silverthorne was a loving man with a generous heart. He was a competent provider, and there had never been any question that he would protect his own until his dying breath. He was exactly the type of man a woman with any sense would look for in a mate. Her mother had chosen well.

"Good morning, beautiful girl." He opened his arms and gave her a long hug as they rocked side to side.

"Morning, Daddy." A sense of calm washed over her, and she wished she could stay right there in her father's arms forever.

With a kiss to the top of her head, he drew away and reached into the cupboard for another ceramic mug. She laughed at his choice.

World's Best Pop.

"Didn't I give that mug to you for Father's Day when I was like . . . ten?"

He filled the mug with steaming coffee then grabbed the sugar bowl and slid it to her across the counter. "I think it was somewhere around that time."

"Wow." She dunked a spoonful of sugar in the mug and stirred. "I'm amazed it survived all these years."

"Your mother and I tried to take care of all the stuff you kids gave us. We have boxes full of your art and homemade cards out in the shed."

The thought warmed her. "You do?"

"Sure. Who knows, we might have had the next Picasso living in our midst."

Kelly laughed.

"Your mother refused to get rid of anything." Her dad's expression turned wistful, and her heart squeezed. "Gosh she loved you kids."

A shiver sped up Kelly's spine as she thought of the drive home last night and her hitchhiking ghost. Kelly knew her mother had loved her children. Kelly also knew her mother had loved some children more. And *she'd* never been Mama's favorite.

"How long you plan on staying, sweetheart?" her father asked.

Forever? Kelly shrugged. "I'm not sure."

"You look tired."

"I am."

"Then stay as long as you want. Or need." He stirred his coffee and looked up. "I like having you around."

She smiled. "Thanks, Daddy."

He sipped at his coffee. "Maybe you could do me a favor while you're here?"

Please don't say come work at the bakery. "Sure."

"You think you could help me go through your mom's things?"

"Oh, Dad." The finality of the mental images those words brought were just miserable. "Are you sure?"

His barrel chest lifted on a heavy sigh. "I think it's time."

Kelly set her mug down on the counter and crossed the room. She put her arms around her father and laid her head against his chest. His arms curled around her, and they stayed like that for several long moments.

"I'll do whatever you need me to do," she said. "I'm so sorry I had to go back to Chicago right after mom died. But I'm here now."

"That's all that matters."

The words were simply spoken. But the grief overshadowing their meaning made her wonder if she could ever do enough to make up for her father's loss.

She may not have had the best relationship with the woman who'd given her life, but her mother had been her father's true love. His soul mate. His *till death do them part.*

And it did.

Summers in Montana tended to be brief. The warm sunshine barely had enough time to bask on the fields of corn, alfalfa, and home gardens to get the red on a tomato, let alone a tan on a Chicago-based prosecutor. Kelly intended to soak up every golden ray of sun she could capture before she had to go back to her small, windowless office in the suffocating heat of the Midwest. Not to mention her enormous failures.

After making a quick omelet for her father before he left for work, she shoved her hair into a ponytail, sank her legs through a pair of running shorts, and stuffed her feet into the barely worn tennis shoes that had beckoned to her from the closet all last winter.

She stepped off the small front porch and did a few stretches before she took off down the street at a slow jog. The branches of the sugar maples overhead filtered the morning sun and cast fluttery shadows against the sidewalk. Kelly breathed in the clean mountain air and paced herself for the several miles she'd decided to run. She made it past the cute little cabin-like homes on her block down to Main Street and into the center of town. She passed the Sugar Shack, where a bouquet of sweet smells teased her nose and tempted her to stop for a calorie fix. Next came the Yee-Ha Trading Post with its silly tin can totem pole outside the front door. She made it beyond the row of downtown storefronts, then she broke into a longer stride and headed toward the lake.

Once she hit the bend in the road the teens had dubbed Deadman's Curve, the rumble of an engine came up behind and paced her for longer than comfortable. Her big-city defenses sprang to attention and prickled along the back of her neck, as if she'd just stepped through the doors of a haunted house. After last night's ghostly episode in her mother's car, she wasn't about to take any chances.

A quick glance over her shoulder revealed the big black truck on her heels. Kelly knew of an easy way to fix the problem. She moved over to the dirt path on the side of the road— out of the way and out of grabbing distance. For a moment the truck remained a step behind, then slowly it eased up alongside. The passenger window rolled down, and the guitar riff from Jason Aldean's "My Kinda Party" blasted through the window.

Irritated and prepared to unleash some girl power, Kelly stopped, turned, and came face to face with—who else?

"Seriously, Harley?" Trying to catch her breath, she propped her hands on her hips. "You've resorted to stalking?"

"No stalking intended, Counselor." He smiled, and a perfect set of ultra white teeth brightened the mischief in his brown eyes. "Just appreciating the view."

"Oh, my god." She dropped her head back and sighed. "You are impossible."

"I can be. But you caught me on a good day." He leaned across the seat and opened the passenger door.

Kelly allowed her gaze to travel over him and the Stallions ball cap he wore backward. Some men looked ridiculous in summer clothes. They were either too milky white or flabby. But dressed in a blue tank, black workout shorts, perfect tan, and a really outstanding tribal tattoo banding his bicep, James Harley defined the word *sizzling*.

His widening grin verified that he knew she was checking him out. And he didn't mind. "Hop in."

"In case you haven't noticed," she said, "I'm out for a jog."

"Oh, I noticed." His eyes cruised what he could see of her body from his angle. "But aren't you a little tired of sucking in exhaust fumes?"

She glanced at their surroundings. "Um, in case you haven't noticed, we're in the middle of nowhere. I haven't even seen another car since I left Main Street."

"I know a better place," he said, bracing his long, muscular arm across the back of the seat like he had all the time in the world to sit there and gab.

"I'll bet you do."

One dark brow lifted. "You don't trust me?"

She shook her head, and her ponytail swung across the back of her tank top. "Not even a little."

He leaned back like she'd just insulted him. "You trusted me the night of Kate's wedding."

"I was drunk the night of Kate's wedding. And I'm pretty sure *trust* had nothing to do with it. So how about we just try to forget that ever happened?"

"Forget it?" His head moved slowly back and forth. "And ruin all those nightly fantasies I have of you? I don't think so."

He had fantasies of *her*? *Nightly*? She doubted it.

"You'd do me a big favor if you'd just let that thought trickle from your mind," she said. "I'm ashamed to admit that in those few-and-far-between, inebriated moments I've been known to completely surrender to a severe case of the crazies."

A slow smile curved his sensuous mouth. "I like your crazy side."

"I've also been known to not repeat a mistake twice."

"Now that's just a darned shame." He patted the seat beside him. "But I still plan on winning that fifty bucks. So why don't you get in, and we can talk about it. I promise you won't regret it."

Of course she would.

"There's a big pay-off at the end," he teased.

Well, didn't that just sending her mind screeching back to the erotic dream she'd been having when she'd woken up that morning. "What kind of pay-off?"

"Wet." A grin broke across his handsome face again.

Did this man never stop smiling?

"A little wild." His long fingers curled around the steering wheel. "And definitely satisfying."

"Deputy Harley, if you think you can just stop on the side of the road and talk a girl out of her running shorts, you'd better think again."

He leaned back. "I honestly don't know where your head

is at, Counselor. All I'm talking about is a nice little hiking trail."

Her head tilted. "That's all?"

"That's all."

"Are you serious?"

"As a hungry squirrel opening a nut."

"If you say *Aw Shucks, Ma'am*, I'm out of here."

"Hop in, Counselor. What have you got to lose?"

Everything?

She drew in a lungful of air and expelled it slowly, all the while studying his face. It was a great face even with a little morning stubble, but there was nothing trustworthy in those dark eyes. And the smile tilting the corners of that really sensuous mouth looked like it could tell lies all day long. Before her thoughts took her any deeper into the paranoia zone, she found herself walking around the truck and getting in.

"Buckle up, Angelface."

Angelface?

"This is going to be a bumpy ride."

Kelly sighed. Unfortunately she'd heard that one before.

James pulled the truck into the trailhead parking lot and cut the engine. He glanced over at his new running partner who looked great in the little pink tank top and black running shorts. Better than great. Almost as great as she looked without them. The worry lines crinkled between eyes as green as the forest had him baffled. It wasn't like he was a scary kind of guy about to take her into the woods and make her disappear.

His gaze dropped to her lips.

Damn. Kelly Silverthorne had the most amazing mouth. Soft. Full. Perfectly bowed. And she could kiss like nobody's business. When the woman put her mind to it, she could fill him with enough inspiration to keep him stocked up on fantasies for a while. Then again, he had a short memory. Frequent reminders were much preferred.

He gave her a smile and reached into the backseat for a couple bottles of water. "You ready?"

She glanced through the windshield at the surrounding forest. "Sure."

He laughed at her hesitation. "Don't be such a Tinker Bell. I'm not Marvin the Masher." He opened the door and stepped out. "I like my women willing."

After a second or two she got out and stood across the hood from him. "I guess I don't have to ask if there are more than just your Kim Kardashian look-alike waiting in the wings."

"More women?" He shrugged, walked around the front bumper, and handed her the bottles of water. "A man doesn't share that kind of information."

"Since when?"

He started his warm-up. Bent to stretch. Anything to keep his eyes off the front of Kelly's tank top and to keep his mind from straying beneath. "Since we realized that if we talk and get caught, we don't get invited back."

Since her muscles were already warmed up and ready to go, she leaned her weight on one enticing hip and watched him. "Ah. So you're a man of conviction *and* command performances."

He grinned, grabbed a bottle of water from her hand, and

took off at a jog. He could feel her eyes on him as he started the gradual incline of his favorite trail. Here, in the summer, the trees provided enough shelter from the sun to make it a cool run. In the winter, those same trees made an awe-inspiring tunnel to pass beneath on a snowmobile. He loved observing the outdoors almost as much as he loved looking at the woman bringing up the rear.

Several seconds later she caught up. "What?" she asked in a slightly breathy voice. "No cocky caveman response?"

He turned his head to look at her, watched the way her blond ponytail swung behind her back, the way her breasts moved and her toned muscles flexed with each step.

"Why are you so interested in my sex life?"

Her chin came up. "I'm not."

"Sounds like you are." He picked up the pace. "Maybe you're interested in a repeat performance after all."

She made a cute little snorting noise. "In your dreams."

"Don't you know just dreaming about something is no fun? You've got to roll up your sleeves. Get your hands dirty." His gaze strayed to the moisture glistening on her chest. "Get a little sweaty."

"Right."

He laughed. Her frown failed to conceal how hard she was thinking of *that* night and wondering just how sweaty they got.

"Very," he said.

Her head came up. "What?"

"Just answering your question."

"I didn't say anything," she said, looking confused.

"You didn't have to." He laughed again. Something he seemed to do a lot when he was around her. "For a professional prosecutor I have to say your poker face lacks depth."

A chunky chipmunk suddenly flew across their path, paws stretched out like he was diving for the end zone. James dodged. Kelly squeaked and jumped into his arms. Not that he minded.

He held her warm body against him and smiled. "You really aren't an outdoorsy kind of girl, are you?"

"Far from it."

"Have you even ever been on this trail? Or any trail in the area for that matter?"

"Mmmmm." To his dismay she extricated herself from his embrace and glanced at their surroundings as if they hadn't just had a close encounter. "Probably not."

"Probably not? Or definitely not?"

"The latter." She took off again at an easy pace.

How could she not know these mountains? These rivers and lakes? They were the sole reason hoards of people had moved into the area during the real-estate boom. He glanced up as she jogged by a small yet remarkable waterfall without even looking. Jesus, he had his work cut out for him. He put on the skids. "Stop."

She ran ahead a few steps then whipped her head around. "What?"

"I said stop." He walked the few feet toward her where she now stood motionless. "This is a mistake."

Her eyes darkened and narrowed. "You're the one who dragged me up here so I'm not sure I understand."

Of course she didn't. Because even he was having a hell of a time figuring it out. "Close your eyes and give me your hand." He reached out his hand, waiting for her to take it.

"Why?"

"Because you're missing the point of being here."

"But—"

"Take my hand, Kelly. I'm not going to bite you, or molest you—unless you ask. I just want to show you a different side of the place you grew up in. And missed."

She glanced at his hand and like any good lawyer, calculated the risks. He exhaled when she finally closed her eyes.

She did not trust easily.

He planned to change that.

Even if it killed him.

Kelly inhaled a breath, and for a moment she stood there feeling foolish. Ready to change her mind, turn around, and run back home. But then her hand became engulfed in his. His grip was strong and warm, yet amazingly gentle as he gave her a little squeeze. For a moment he held her palm in his without saying a word. She began to feel squirmy and was tempted to open her eyes.

"Relax, Counselor." His deep, calm voice came amid a rush of quiet. "Take a few deep breaths and just relax. There are no jurors here to judge you. No dream defense team. It's just you, me, and a couple of rodents."

"Rodents?"

"Squirrels. The cute furry kind like you see in cartoons. I promise."

After several minutes of silence she asked, "What are we doing?"

"Just giving you a few minutes to clear out all the garbage crowding your mind so you can see better."

"How can I see if my eyes are closed?"

He sighed. "Is that the lawyer side of you asking all the questions? Or are you just being a pain in the ass?"

"It's the lawyer."

"Then tell her to shut the hell up and listen."

"There's no need to—"

"Ah, come on."

"Okay. Okay." She did as he asked. Once she got past the idea that she was standing in the middle of the forest, next to a man she'd had sex with but barely knew and didn't exactly trust, she decided to just go with it. Open herself up to the whole Grizzly Adams experience.

Several breaths later, as if on cue, she heard the sound of a gentle breeze pushing through the pines. The screeching call of a hawk circling high overhead. The chirping of birds. The chatter of chipmunks. She even heard a pinecone drop to the ground and roll. It was the most peaceful sound she'd ever heard.

"Wow." She opened her eyes and found him watching her. "That's amazing."

He nodded. "Mind if we venture off the trail for a minute? I'd like to show you something."

"Sure."

He took her hand and held it as they dug their heels into the pine needles blanketing the ground and started up the incline across the rocky terrain. It was a peculiar sensation to hold a man's hand while walking through nature. Even this man whom she knew intimately. Though the details were a little sketchy.

At the top of the ridge, James stopped. "Okay, close your eyes again."

"You must have been a huge fan of pin-the-tail-on-the-donkey when you were a kid."

"No. I developed a proclivity for handcuffs instead." He gave her hand a little tug. "Follow me."

She did. Up a cascade of rock where the sound of rushing water grew as loud as a bass drum. When they reached a plateau he said, "Keep your eyes closed, Counselor."

She blew out an exaggerated sigh. "Yes, *Deputy*." Kelly realized she was being far more compliant on the top of this mountain than she'd ever been in the courtroom. She wasn't sure what that said about her. Or him.

"Okay." His warm palms cupped her shoulders as he turned her around and led her upward a few more steps. "Now open them."

She did. And gasped. They were at the top of the world—literally standing at the mouth of an enormous waterfall. The rock beneath her feet rumbled, and the soles of her tennis shoes vibrated. From their position she could see tree tops and wildflowers, puffy white clouds, and the sparkling waters of the lake below. "Oh, it's—"

"Gorgeous."

She turned to find him looking at *her* instead of the view. Her heart picked up a little speed. Not the first time today that had happened. Although she was pretty sure it had nothing to do with hiking. "Yes, it is."

"And you swear you've never been up here before?"

She shook her head. "Never."

"Well, that's an inspiration," he said, giving her that grin that was beginning to become all-too-familiar.

"Why's that?"

"Because I like knowing I'm the one who showed it to you first. I have all kinds of amazing things up my sleeves to show you, Angelface. Like my favorite swimming hole."

Again with the Angelface? Still, his tone didn't sound condescending the way defense lawyer Marshall Goodrow's did when he called her "little girl." Maybe James Harley was just the kind of guy who picked up pet names for people. She studied his strong chin and assessing eyes. Nope. He definitely had other motives.

"Maybe I don't want you to show me things."

"You sure about that?" He spread open his arms. "Because I'm all yours for the taking."

Kelly turned her attention safely out over the incredible scenery. Thirty-two years of experience identified that the tingles moving from her chest downward had nothing to do with the mountains and trees and lake and everything to do with the man offering himself up like a pupu platter on a tropical vacation.

Chapter Six

Monday morning Kelly found herself strapped into the Buick and on her way to the Sugar Shack. Once again, she'd tried to sleep in. Once again, the moment she heard her father in the kitchen, guilt prodded her from bed. She'd ended up offering to help bake three hundred cupcakes for the celebration during the Founder's Day parade. Her mother had started the ritual over thirty years ago when the bakery first opened. Kate had every intention of keeping the tradition alive, and Kelly could hardly refuse.

As a kid, she'd always been able to gauge the time of year by the treats going out the bakery door. Pumpkin pies for Thanksgiving. Fruit cake and sugar cookies for Christmas. Heart-shaped cookies and pink cupcakes for Valentine's Day. The Sugar Shack desserts were a staple in Deer Lick, and their designs had always followed their mother's traditional style—butter cream roses and white icing. Then along came Kate, who upended the party cruise by adding her more creative flair. However some of those designs tended to be a little on the racy side and had to be kept out of the display case. There were no guarantees that Kate wouldn't roll up her wicked little sleeves and come up with a design that would mortify her newly elected sheriff husband. Then again, he was probably used to that by now. Kate was nothing if not unconventional—a trait Kelly admired even if it often made her cringe.

Looking for some tunes to wake her up, she reached forward and turned on the radio. An old Smokey Robinson and the Miracles song segued into Tom Jones's "It's Not Unusual." Even with the warm summer air rolling through the open windows, the interior of the car turned icy cold.

Uh-oh.

The hair beneath Kelly's ponytail sprang up and crackled with electricity.

"You've been expecting me."

Kelly jumped at the voice coming from the back seat. She glanced up into the rearview mirror. "Mom?"

"Yep. It's still me."

"Why can't I see you?"

"Well, it is daylight. And I am dead, so . . ."

Right. "Sorry."

"Not your fault. Gotta blame that little situation on too many cream puffs and only armchair workouts."

Kelly glanced up into the mirror again and almost took out the light pole at the corner of Reindeer and White Tail.

"Honey? How about you pull over? I'm really not in any hurry for company up here."

Kelly edged the big car to the curb and turned in her seat. "Mom?"

"Still here."

"But the question is *why*, don't you think?"

"Gosh, you're so much like Kate. She questioned everything. What? Why? How? Now, Dean? He was just happy to see me."

"Kate and Dean know about you?"

"Do they ever."

"Why didn't they tell me?"

"What would you have thought if either of them had told you about me?"

"That they'd lost a screw."

"Exactly."

"Then why am I the last to know?" Just more proof she'd never really mattered. "Why didn't you appear to me when I drove all the way to the airport to pick up Kate the day after you died?"

"Certainly not because you're any less important, if that's what you're thinking. And I'm guessing you are." The straps of her transparent overalls lifted in a shrug. "You've always been the brightest, honey. I kept hoping you were going to work things out on your own."

"Like what?"

"The panoramic version of the big picture."

"I've been a prosecutor in Chicago for a long time. I think I've seen the big picture."

"Don't kid yourself. Even I'm just starting to figure things out. I might be dead, but I guess I'm not done learning."

Kelly folded her arms across the back of the seat and rested her chin. She couldn't see a thing except the pastry books, scraps of quilting material, and the other mom paraphernalia no one had bothered to clear out. "What have you learned so far?"

Her mother let out a whoop of a laugh. "That you have to live your life right, so people don't have to lie about you at your funeral."

"You think the community lied about you? Mom! You were a saint to this town. They loved you."

"Not the community, dear. My children."

"We didn't lie." And there went one more.

"Yeah. You did. But I think I understand now. And I've been trying to do something about it."

Kelly felt a squeeze in her heart. Was this what the afterlife was about? That you had to go around making up for the mistakes you'd made in your past? If so, she was exhausted already. Where would she even start?

"Mom, are you sure you're not just supposed to go into the light or something?" Kelly sat in total silence. Suddenly the chill lifted and the heat rolled back in through the window. "Mom?"

The car started on its own, and Kelly about jumped out of her skin. She guessed the conversation was over. For now. But if she wasn't certifiably wacko and her mother really *had* risen from the grave, she appeared to have plenty to say.

Lucky her.

Minutes later Kelly pushed through the back door of the Sugar Shack. She couldn't shake the experience she'd just had. And since she examined facts for a living, she knew she needed to find out more.

Kate stood over the mixer, adding chocolate to the batter swirling inside the big stainless bowl, and singing along with Miranda Lambert on the radio. After Kelly dropped her purse inside the office and grabbed an apron off the hook near the door, she joined her sister in the kitchen.

"Hey." Kate stopped scraping the chocolate from the bowl and looked up. "What are you doing here?"

"Guilt." Kelly tied the apron strings around her waist and went to the sink to wash her hands. "The idea of you and dad making all those Founder's Day cupcakes wouldn't get out of my head."

"Nothing we can't handle. You should have seen us over Valentine's Day. I swore I never wanted to see another red heart. Until Marta Bingham decided she wanted red hearts on her wedding cake. *And* she wanted that cake to look like a creation right out of a Tim Burton movie. Which turned out totally awesome if I must say so myself."

Kelly shook the water from her hands and wiped them dry. "Yeah, well, I'm used to getting up early anyway. And I didn't have anything planned."

"And?" Kate dumped the empty bowl into the stainless sink and gave her the stink eye.

"And what?"

"She's already shown up hasn't she?"

"If by *she* you mean our mother, then yes. And I'm going to consider the fact that you know about her and you seem relatively sane, I don't need to rent myself a room at the funny farm."

Kate laughed. "No, you're not crazy. Or maybe you are. But then so are Dean and I."

"Why didn't you tell me?"

"What? And ruin the surprise? No way, José."

"A little warning wouldn't have hurt. I almost took out a light pole."

"Would you have believed me?"

Kelly shook her head. "I would have arranged for a very nice suite at a local hospital."

"Well there you go. In any case, what did the meddling mischief-maker have to say this time?"

"She's being vague."

"Ha! Status quo."

"What does she want?" Kelly asked, as though this was an ordinary conversation about an ordinary mom.

"Well, that's different for each of us. And it's not my place to tell you what she has planned."

"Holy crap." Kelly stuffed her hands into a pair of latex gloves. "That sounds ominous."

"Eh. Depends what kind of mood she's in."

"I don't like this," Kelly said, pulling cupcake pans from a rolling rack. "It doesn't make sense."

"Maybe that's the point, Kel. Maybe you try to make sense of everything. And maybe you're supposed to just go with the flow for once."

Kelly turned and faced her sister, who looked to be highly entertained. "You do realize that I've been trained to compile facts and make a solid case? All of the sudden I'm expected to just accept something I can't see? Something that no longer exists?"

"You've seen her, though. Right?"

"Ummmm."

"It's okay. I don't think you've lost your marbles." Kate disappeared into the office and came out carrying a large pack of red, white, and blue paper baking cups. "In fact, I'm rather looking forward to the show."

"Gee, thanks. I can hardly wait."

Kate laughed and grabbed Kelly into a hug. "Welcome home, sis."

"I'm only here for a short visit," Kelly protested.

"Right." Kate patted her on the back. "Been there. Done that."

"I'm serious. There are some things coming down the line, and after Dean's wedding I have to get back to Chicago."

"I understand." Kate's eyes sparked with mischief. "Your real life calls. But just an FYI, sister dear, mine came in through a bullhorn. And look what happened to me. Besides, if you don't mind my saying so, you don't look all that happy."

"I'm happy."

"Yep. That would explain you hiding out in the office when you first came home. Shoveling cheesecake into your mouth like there was no tomorrow."

"The long flight and drive from the airport made me hungry."

"So, I'm guessing you've forgotten the conversation we had in which you expressed your feelings of total incompetence and regret at having lost a really impossible case to win?"

"No." Kelly blew out a puff of air. "I didn't forget. But I was hoping you had."

"Me? Ha!" Kate handed over the cupcake baking cups. "Mind's like a rubber band. Snaps back every time."

"Lucky me." Kelly moved her attention away from Kate's intense gaze.

"Time to move forward, sis. Expand your horizons. You never know what will come your way."

"Looks like that includes our dead mother in the backseat of her Buick. No disrespect intended."

"Oh, yeah." Kate laughed. "She isn't going anywhere anytime soon. You can count on that."

Four hours and two sore feet later, Kelly refilled the pitcher of homemade sun tea and wondered why she wasn't out basking in the sunshine. The bakery door swung open, and the bell above gave a happy jingle as Matt and James strolled in looking hot and hungry.

For all intents and purposes, Kelly meant weather-related hot. But there was something about a man in a uniform that just called to a woman's basic senses. Especially when that woman knew beneath that oh-so-proper outer layer of khaki the man was made of pure, defined muscle, and he used that body to weave a spell like a master seducer.

"Hi, Matt."

He gave her a smile. "Where's my wife?"

"In the back conjuring up some really naughty cake designs for Millie Johnson's retirement party." Kelly wanted to laugh at the eager look on his face. Maybe she needed to run interference to keep their dad from going in the back for a few minutes. Give the newlyweds a little *alone* time.

A twinge of envy tightened her stomach. Matt and Kate

had been destined to be together from the start. Even when for a decade they had lived in different parts of the country with entirely different ways of life, there had been some crazy sprinkle of destiny that tied them together.

Kelly had never even had a high school boyfriend. Since then she'd been too busy to get involved. She guessed she should be amazed that she'd ever lost her virginity. Not that men didn't seem interested. Just that she'd been so immersed in creating a career for herself that she'd kind of missed all the opportunities. Or most of them, anyway. Few of her relationships had been memorable. Some had been prompted with liquid courage. And then there was . . .

James stepped up to the lunch counter. His smile came quickly, sincerely, and full of promise.

Opportunities.

Hmmm.

She *was* looking for something to take her mind off her colossal failure in the courtroom. Something that tasted yummy without the liquid courage. Maybe her entire problem was that she'd been way too uptight. Maybe that had been her reason for making so many errors on the Colson case. Maybe all she really needed was to rediscover life's simple pleasures. Would it be so wrong to take what James openly offered? Even if there was fifty bucks at stake? Kelly had never regarded herself as the wham-bam type. Then again, on deeper consideration, she wasn't altogether sure she even had a type. Maybe she'd been looking at everything all wrong. Maybe instead of needing some*thing* to take her mind off things she needed some*one*.

She picked up a pencil and slid the notepad beneath the lead. "What can I get for you today, Deputy?"

His wide shoulders leaned in as he studied her. "Two tuna subs. No tomato. Two iced teas."

"Isn't that the same thing you ordered the other day?"

He nodded slowly as his eyes assessed her from her head to where her pink apron disappeared beneath the counter. "When I like something, I tend to want to enjoy it over and over again."

A memory of his hot mouth and exploring hands flashed through her mind, and she swallowed. When he *enjoyed* something, he took his time and savored every moment. That little slice of information she'd experienced first-hand. Several times. Happily.

Before she made a complete and utter fool of herself by drooling or something equally as heinous. Or before she took him up on his not-so-subtle offer, she took his money then slipped on a pair of gloves and grabbed two lunch rolls from the bin. She sliced both right down the middle and slathered on equal amounts of mayo.

"You make up your mind yet?" he asked.

"About?"

"Me showing you things."

"Jury's still out."

"Well deliver those closing arguments, Counselor. Because I've got something I want to show you Friday night."

"Like?"

"If I told you, it wouldn't be a surprise."

She looked up, waving the knife in her hand. "Have I mentioned that I don't like surprises?"

"Then you're cheating yourself."

"Are you still talking about that bet?" Kelly packed the sandwiches in the bag.

"Nope. Something better."

Better than sex? He definitely had stirred her interest.

At that moment Matt and Kate came out of the back—a little rumpled and smiling.

James grabbed the lunch bags from the counter. "I'll pick you up Friday at eight," he told her. "Be ready."

"For?"

He grinned. "Anything."

On Founder's Day the entire town turned out for the celebration parade. Warm afternoon sunshine glinted down on an array of observers and the various hats worn to keep the heat at bay. There were bands, and dance groups, and the Deer Lick Destroyers' cheerleaders on top of a flatbed truck decorated with streamers in red, white, and blue. A rodeo queen in a sparkling blouse rode by and waved while the Crafty Critters 4-H group led their cranky sheep down the route on red halters. The sheriff's patrol had blocked off all the paths that led to Main Street. Somehow James, in full uniform, had pulled duty across the street from the Sugar Shack. Which is exactly where Kelly stood beside her family and Edna Price serving up the Founder's Day cupcakes as the parade marched by.

Edna had been her mother's dearest and oldest friend. And when Kate had been going through her *should I stay or should I go* crisis—before she admitted she was in love with Matt—Edna had been the one to point out to Kate that one shouldn't just take love for granted. Edna—much like their mother—called them like she saw them.

Across the street James stood in a wide stance. Arms folded across his khaki uniform. A pair of Ray-Ban aviators covering his eyes. Even behind the shades, Kelly could feel his gaze on her with every move she made. Or maybe she was just imagining things. She decided to test the theory and *accidentally* dropped a paper napkin. When she bent to pick it up, his head tilted just slightly, and a slow smile curved his sensuous lips.

In reality he could have just been watching the kids on scooters passing by. She chose to believe that that head tilt had come in appreciation of the dip in the bodice of the white sundress she'd chosen that morning.

In the spirit of the celebration she'd also put her hair up in a ponytail and wrapped it with a sparkly red scarf. Not so much because it was a hot day and it felt good to get the heavy hair off her neck, but to tease the man across the street. On their hike he'd commented that he liked her hair up so that he could picture himself taking it down. While nothing outrageous had happened between them that day, she found flirting fun. Even if she wasn't entirely sure she welcomed his attention. He had heartache written all over him. Then again, when had she let that stop her?

She handed a cupcake with white icing and blue sprinkles to a little girl with red hair and freckles, as a hay wagon decorated with balloons and pulled by two huge black horses rolled by. "Here you go, sweetheart."

"Thank you." The little redhead slurped her tongue across the top of the icing.

Kelly laughed. "Hope you enjoy that cupcake."

"That's Sarah Littleton," Emma whispered as she handed

over a cupcake to an elderly gentleman in a straw hat. "I'll have her in my class this fall."

"She looks sweet."

"She is." Emma's shocking blue eyes darkened. "Her family is really struggling right now."

"Finances?" Kelly asked.

"Sarah's little brother." Emma pressed her lips together and shook her head. "A beautiful two-year-old with copper curls and a smile that could stop your heart."

As they chatted an old Volkswagen painted like a mouse, with rubber tubing whiskers and a spring tail, sputtered past the cupcake display table. Several clowns took their turn dancing toward the kids in the crowd and handing out candy and balloons. The sorrow on Emma's face stopped her from laughing.

"What happened?" Kelly asked.

"Leukemia." Edna Price leaned across the tale and handed cupcakes to a teenage couple in matching flip-flops.

Kelly swallowed a harsh gasp of air. "He died?"

Both Edna and Emma nodded.

"A two-year-old?" Everything Kelly had eaten for lunch threatened to make a sudden reappearance. "Oh, my god."

While Emma restocked the cupcakes, Edna curved her arm around Kelly's waist. "See that group of folks in the silly outfits?"

Kelly looked up at the clowns through misty eyes and nodded.

"His mother said they brought a lot of joy to her little boy near the end when it got really tough. He left this earth with a smile because of them. Just breaks my old heart every time I think about it."

Over the heads of those observing the parade, Kelly watched the clowns continue their funny wiggle-walk toward the end of the street. To know they'd given a dying little boy his last smile certainly put things in perspective. Kelly had been so focused on her solitary failure. Maybe her mother was right. Maybe she wasn't seeing the big picture. Because one thing was certain, her own inadequacies could never compare to the loss the Littleton family had suffered.

"Do *not* do anything stupid tonight." James held his ground against the obstinate teen slumped on the couch playing *Call of Duty* and giving him a look that made him feel very uncool. "I have plans and I don't want you to ruin them. Again." James was only thirty-two with a lot of cool left in him. But there he was, being a straight-laced caretaker to the kid brother who seemed to try every trick in the book to make him crazy.

Since he'd become the legal guardian for Alex two years ago there had been friction. Fifteen-year-old boys weren't usually the most rational. They thought they knew it all. As a whole they were self-conscious, argumentative, easily offended, and disrespectful. With Alex you could add lazy, sneaky, and rebellious. James understood these things. He'd been there, done that. Hell, he'd made some of the poorest decisions of his life when he'd been that age. Deadly decisions. But *being* a fifteen-year-old boy and knowing what to do with one were entirely different matters.

In two years things hadn't improved. Thanks to Alex's choice of friends, they'd gotten worse. Not that James could put all the blame on the group of rebels his brother hung out with, but they didn't help.

James continually reached inside himself to find the right path on which to lead Alex, but growing up he'd had little guidance himself and absolutely no role models. His mother had worked hard cleaning houses, and in her spare time she searched for husband number three. Luckily she'd never found him. James and Alex did not share the same father. James didn't even know who his father was, although his mother swore they'd been married. A lack of wedding photos or documentation left James with the truth that he'd been a bastard in more ways than one.

Lately, the situation with Alex had deteriorated. The more stressed James became, the more Alex rebelled.

Alex ran a hand through his long blond hair and gave him a half-cocked grin. "Just plan on playing a little Xbox tonight, bro."

"That's what you said last weekend, and I ended up having to rescue your ass from the drunk tank."

"Nobody asked you to rescue me."

"That's what I mean, Alex. You're too damn stubborn to realize when you're in too deep."

"Don't you mean I'm too stupid?"

James barked a laugh. "You are far from stupid. You're too clever by most counts." He shoved a frozen pre-made lasagna into the oven, slammed the door shut, and cranked on the heat. "I figure you'll be a damned genius by the time you're thirty. *If* you live that long."

He studied the defiant kid sitting on the couch, surrounded by two little dogs who thought he walked on water—as long as he petted them. James wondered if his little brother would have to go through the same hell he had before he'd finally wised up. God, he hoped not. It had taken him until nearly his last breath to figure out that life was a gift you did *not* take for granted. He shook his head, strode into the living room, and sat down on the couch. Poppy and Princess lifted their pointy ears and reluctantly moved aside to allow him room.

"Don't you ever think about what your behavior does to Mom?"

Alex looked at him. "Did you?"

"Exactly. I didn't." James folded his hands together and dropped them between his knees. "And I paid heavily for that. So did mom. But in those days mom was healthy. These days, she's not. And believe me, little brother, there is going to come a day when you'll regret your actions."

"Sure." Alex did double-time with his thumbs on the game controller.

James sighed and pulled his reluctant charge into his arms for a hug and a noogie. "If I didn't love you so much I'd totally kick your ass."

Alex squirmed away. "As if."

"What? You don't think I could?"

That got the smile James had been looking for.

"I'm willing to go one-on-one," Alex said with a lift of his chin.

James returned the smile. Mostly because Alex's were few and far between. Life had never been an easy road for any member of the Harley family. Sadly he couldn't imagine it smoothing out anytime soon.

He glanced down at his watch with a mix of enthusiasm and regret. He really should stay home and play night watchman. Something in Alex's eyes tonight spelled trouble. But he'd made a date with Kelly, and true to his code of honor, he would not break it at the last minute. Even if it meant he would pay heavily later.

"Lucky for you I have a date. Or I'd take you up on that."

Alex gave a rare laugh as James walked into the bathroom to take a shower.

"Don't forget a condom," Alex shouted.

James shut the bathroom door, looked in the mirror, and ran his hand across his five o'clock stubble. He'd shower, shave, and be prepared. But as much as he'd love to follow his brother's word of caution, tonight would not be that kind of night.

Tonight he planned to show Kelly a different side of Deer Lick.

Of course, if she happened to get really turned on by what he'd planned, who was he to tell a pretty lady no?

CHAPTER SEVEN

She had a date.

Kelly flipped through the pants hanging in the closet and decided denim did not make for good first-date material. Okay, maybe it wasn't an *official* first date, but the promise of one was there, and she planned to make good use of the practice if nothing else. Maybe after she went back to Chicago she'd change the way she ran her personal life. More leisure time. Less stress. Less guilt.

Wow. When had she ever been that big of a dreamer?

As if on cue, her text message alert chimed. She picked up the phone and read the brief text message from Daniel.

Jury selection begins in 3 weeks for Oganthaler case. You'll be back by then. Right?

Without responding, she deleted the message, tossed the phone on the bed, and continued to look through the small selection of clothing she'd brought for her *brief* visit. With every slide of a hanger, the sinking in the pit of her stomach verified she'd have to return to Chicago at some point. At the moment she felt like a coward—afraid to go back and face the reality that a killer walked free because she had failed to do her job.

Stop it.

She grabbed a summer dress from the wire hanger.

She wouldn't think about work *or* failure tonight. Tomorrow morning would come soon enough to let remorse reclaim control.

Tonight she planned to be open to whatever Deputy Harley had in mind when he'd told her to be ready for anything. He was a gorgeous man, and he made her laugh. Even if common sense advised her to steer clear, she chose to ignore the warning bells. At least for one more night.

What was a little fifty-dollar bet anyway?

She reached into the drawer and pulled out a brand new pair of pink Victoria's Secret panties and tossed them on the bed. Then she went into the living room where her father sat in his well-worn recliner speeding through channels with the remote control.

"Hey, Dad? Do we have any wine?"

"Wine?" Robert Silverthorne froze the channel on a rerun of *Chopped* and looked up. "I think there might be a box in the refrigerator."

A box?

"Can't say how old it is, though. You might want to check for an expiration date."

An expiration date?

Wow.

"Okay. Thanks." Kelly went into the dated 1970's-style

kitchen and opened the fridge. Yep. On the bottom shelf there was a box of wine. White. No fancy description. Just white. Fortunately the box had never been opened, so Kelly didn't bother to look for an expiration date. *Dear God.*

Unable to locate an actual wine glass, she reached into the cupboard for a mason jar then stopped and retracted her hand. On dates in the past she'd relied on liquid courage to stuff Sister Serious in the closet and let her hair down. Although tonight her nerves were doing a Mexican hat dance inside her stomach, she intended to let things happen as they were meant to.

She had a date.

With a man who promised heaven.

And delivered.

T he summer night proved to be perfect. Just the right temperature. A slight breeze that carried the scent of pine and wildflowers. A few fluffy clouds that would create a colorful sunset. James smiled. A guy just couldn't ask for more.

Well, he could. And he probably would. But first things first.

He rang the bell at the Silverthorne home and stood back. Anticipation rocked him on his heels while he waited for the door to open. When it finally swung wide, he had to step back and catch his breath.

Just inside the entry stood Kelly with a smile, looking like she'd just stepped from his fantasies. Her curve-hugging floral dress was simple—little more than a tee that hit her mid-thigh—but that simple little dress screamed money. And sexy. His appreciative gaze traveled from her pink-painted toenails and strappy high-heeled sandals, up her shapely legs, to the top of her shoulders and the thin dress straps.

He wished he could afford a woman like her, but he'd never been one to kid himself. A guy like him, who'd chosen a job in community service, lived a paycheck-to-paycheck existence. Sure, he managed to take care of his sick mother, and he'd saved up enough to buy his small two-bedroom house and some nice transportation. Someday he'd even be able to afford a nice retirement, but he'd never have the funds for extravagance.

Kelly Silverthorne deserved indulgence.

That didn't stop him from mentally removing that silky fabric and covering her breasts and body with his hands and mouth. An inescapable moan of admiration lifted from his throat, and the action inside his cargo shorts got a whole lot of happy.

As soon as he rolled his tongue back up into his mouth, he smiled. "You look amazing."

"Thank you." Her green eyes scanned his casual attire, and tiny little lines crinkled between her brows.

"But you might want to go back and change," he said.

"Seriously?"

"As much as I hate to have you take off that incredible dress—on your own—I don't think it will work well with our mode of transportation."

Her head tilted slightly and her hair fell across her shoulder in an ivory cascade of soft curls. "Which is?"

He stepped back and extended his arm toward their ride parked at the curb.

Her green eyes widened. "An ATV?"

"Your chariot awaits."

"Oh. Ummm . . . okay." She stepped back.

"Are you disappointed?" he asked, concerned that everything he was about to throw at her would be too much.

"No."

Yes. She was. "I did tell you to be prepared for anything."

"That you did." She gave him a brief smile that was unusually timid for a woman who commanded a courtroom and put away bad guys.

"Tell you what. Since I've obviously thrown you for a loop, I'll give you the chance to back out." *Please don't back out.*

She looked him up and down, then smiled. "I wouldn't dream of it."

He wanted to act cool, but that huge sigh of relief he'd just expelled pretty much blew any chance.

"Do you want to come in while I change?"

Can I help you change? "You bet." He stepped into the living room where Mr. Silverthorne rose from his recliner and shook his hand while Kelly disappeared into the back of the house.

"So you're taking my daughter on a date."

"Yes, sir."

Kelly's father scrubbed a hand up the front of his shirt. "What do you have planned?"

"Probably nothing your daughter had on her radar. Dinner. Cooked on a campfire. Next to Fawn Creek."

"Excellent choice." The man gave him a sharp nod then returned to his recliner and kicked up the foot rest. "Got the other two taken care of. This is her time."

Something moved within James's chest. "Mr. Silverthorne, I'm not sure what your expectations are but—"

"Just show her a good time, young man. Treat her kind. And we'll have no problems." He lifted a pair of glasses from the table beside the chair and slipped them on. "I know you were a bit wild when you were younger."

An understatement if ever there was one.

"But," the man continued, "you've more than proven yourself around here. My wife—God rest her soul—liked you. She was a good judge of character, and I always trusted her one hundred percent."

The compliment surrounded James like a warm hug. "Thank you, sir. I promise I'll treat your daughter well. But—"

"Call me Robert. And no buts. No expectations. She's had a tough time lately. Make her smile. That's all I ask."

James knew he could *and had* made Kelly smile. Though he didn't think her father would appreciate the details on how he'd gotten the job done. "You have my word . . . Robert."

"Is this better?"

James turned to find Kelly behind him, dressed in a pair of snug jeans and a shrunken down version of the dress for a top. She looked sweet and sexy. But to him she'd look just as sexy if she was dressed in an old robe.

"Perfect."

With a goodnight to her father, he opened the door, took Kelly's hand, and led her to his yellow ATV.

She chuckled as she climbed on the back. "Well, at least its not camo."

"Too many of those around. I like to be different."

"I'll bet you do."

He settled in front of her and put his hands on the handlebars, when he'd rather put them on the gorgeous woman pressed against his back. He'd do anything to touch her, he realized. When he'd been younger he'd had many weaknesses he'd had to overcome. *She* was his weakness now. "Hang on."

Her slender arms slid around his waist.

"Tighter."

He smiled as her small hands hooked around his shirt and her breasts pressed against his back. "Perfect."

Their individual expectations of the evening's events might be on complete opposite sides of the coin, but as he angled the ATV away from the curb he planned to make this a night to remember.

For both of them.

As the warm, pine-scented wind whipped through her hair, Kelly held on tight to James's hard body. Once they'd left the paved road behind, the ATV began to climb into the mountains on rough and uneven trails. Several times her butt bounced off the seat and she had to hold on tighter. Their method of transportation might be unusual, but Kelly wasn't about to complain. From where she sat the scenery was breathtaking, the air was fresh, and with the setting sun in her face and the wind on her cheeks she felt alive. That she also had her arms wrapped around an extremely gorgeous man, and an up-close-and-personal vantage point that offered some really good opportunities to catch his warm, clean, manly scent? Well, she wouldn't complain about that either.

Dusk swallowed up the light as they rode through the

forest and everything took on a different appearance. The higher the elevation, the more dead trees and limbs littered the forest floor and jutted out over the trail. One particular section looked menacing and scary. As though any moment the wicked witch would appear from behind a tree, wave her magic broom, and flying monkeys would appear. Kelly snuggled closer to James and several times she even closed her eyes. If she was a kid she would totally count on having nightmares.

Moments later James announced, "Here we are."

The ATV engine settled into a low hum as the vehicle slowed, and James parked it beneath the canopy of an enormous Ponderosa. The forest around them had grown thick and blocked out the sky. With night falling quickly, it was difficult to see. A shudder ran up her back.

"And *here* would be where?"

"Fawn Creek." James swung his long leg over the seat and held out his hand. "I still can't believe you lived here for eighteen years and you don't know about any of these places. They're legend."

She took his hand and slid from the seat. "Not everyone is outdoorsy. Some of us were meant to stay indoors and study."

"Bullshit. God didn't create all this so you could miss it in exchange for four walls and a set of text books."

"Didn't you ever study?"

He laughed. "Only if I had to." He unhooked the bungee cords holding down an enormous duffel bag that had been tied to the front of the ATV. "Come on." He heaved the bag over his shoulder. "Follow me if you dare."

"Is that a challenge?"

He turned quickly and she bumped into his chest. "Would you take me up on one?"

"Depends what it is. We already have a bet going. One which you will lose, by the way. I am *not* going to sleep with you again."

His lips curled into a smile she remembered well. The one that verified he knew what made her shiver with pleasure. He gently took her hand and his calloused thumb lightly caressed the backs of her fingers. "Told you, Angelface. I never lose."

"We'll see." She was so *not* going to sleep with him. But that didn't stop her from really, really wanting to.

"Actually, now that I think about it, a challenge sounds like a great idea." He gave her hand a little tug and she followed him up the barely defined dirt path. "Of course, you don't get to choose what it is. You'd just have to agree or not agree."

"Then that would be a dare." She wrinkled her nose as a layer of dust kicked up beneath their feet. "Not a challenge."

The rumble of cascading water grew louder, and the hair on the back of her neck prickled. What was he up to now?

A few more steps into the forest brought them up beside a small waterfall and a slow-moving creek where the crystal-clear water bounced and trickled over smooth rocks of different shapes, colors, and sizes. James dropped the bag at their feet but he held onto her hand and used it to draw her in closer. Her unsteady heartbeat shifted into a full run.

"Call it what you want. A dare. A challenge. A test." His large hands smoothed down her bare arms as his deep-brown gaze locked onto hers. Taunted her to refuse. "Are you willing to accept?"

"What is this, *Mission Impossible?*"

"Nothing's impossible." He leaned closer. Or maybe that was her doing the leaning. "Didn't anyone ever tell you that?"

"Not that I can remember."

"So what's it going to be? You in?" He smiled so wide his even, white teeth flashed. "Or are you too chicken?"

She swallowed her anxiety. She'd never been one to back away. Not from the murderous felons who threatened her at every turn. Not from associate lawyers who threatened to ruin her if she didn't play their game. Not from a guy who seemed to be having a good time at her expense.

She straightened to her full height, which happened to be a measly five-foot-three. "Bring it, Deputy."

He smiled. His eyes dipped down to her mouth and held like he had every intention of going there.

Kelly's stomach turned a flip.

She wanted him to go there.

She wanted him to kiss her.

Against her better judgment and the good sense God had given her, she found she wanted James Harley to wrap her in his big strong arms and kiss her really, really bad. She closed her eyes in anticipation and received her reward.

On her forehead.

"That's my girl."

Her eyes popped open.

Had she read him wrong?

Puzzled and a little embarrassed, she stepped back. His hands fell away from her arms. "So what's the challenge?"

He studied her for a breath then kneeled and unzipped

the huge duffel bag. He reached inside, came up with a small foldable shovel, and handed it to her. "You can start with this."

She looked at the pointy piece of steel in her hands. "What am I supposed to do with this?"

He looked up at her. "Dig a hole."

"A . . . *hole?*"

"Yep." He stood, turned a half circle, and pointed. "Right there by the water should be good. The ground should be softer."

"What are you going to do? Kill me and dump my body? Make me dig my own grave?"

A smile slid across his sensuous mouth. "Are you kidding? I can think of way more entertaining things to do with that sweet body of yours."

Ah. So *now* they were getting somewhere. "Then why dig a hole?"

He reached into the duffel again, pulled out a small cooler. From the cooler he pulled out a zip-locked bag of meat and held it up for her to see. "Need a fire to cook dinner."

Relief rippled over her. "Steak?"

"Porterhouse."

"Good. I'm starving." She unfolded the shovel, stuck it into the ground then looked up. "Hey. How come *I'm* the one who's digging the hole?"

"Because I already know how."

"Oh."

"Kidding." Laughing, James grabbed the small shovel from her hands and stuck the point into the ground. "You think I'd really make you dig a hole?"

She shrugged. "I don't know."

His hands stilled and he looked up. Sincerity darkened his eyes. "I'll take care of you, Kelly. I'd always take care of you. Never doubt that."

Though she didn't want them to be, his words were like a warm fuzzy blanket. Other than her father and her brother, she'd never had a man say he'd take care of her. And other than knowing James as the young boy who ran wild a mile long and the man she'd had the most intimate relations with—once—she knew zilch about him. Yet when he professed that he'd take care of her, she believed him.

"Thanks," she said quietly. "That's nice to know."

He gave her a smile that melted her heart, then he went about digging the fire pit. Kelly watched him, fascinated by the way he moved. The flex in the muscles beneath his cotton shirt. The confidence with which he knew this forest and his surroundings. He had her help him gather up wood for the fire, and once the flames licked the dry logs, James had her set the table.

While she spread the plaid blanket on the ground she looked up and watched him move about the area. Confident. Content. Looking like he belonged. She, on the other hand, felt like a sardine on land. She could set the plates on the blanket and place the silverware next to each plate, but other than that she was at odds. She could cook a mean steak—on a backyard grill. She could set a table—in a dining room. She had no idea how to play cavewoman, even though the idea was intriguing.

"Did you just assume I'd be up for this?" she asked him. "Or were you hoping I'd recoil at the idea and run home crying?"

He stopped fanning the fire and looked up at her. The firelight danced in his dark eyes and flickered like hot coals.

"Why would I want you to run away?" he asked quietly. "*This* is what I wanted to show you." His arms opened wide as if he was welcoming her to a golden palace. "*This* is what you missed all that time. It's beautiful, Kelly. Just like you."

His words washed over her, warmed her heart, and spread through her blood like a fine wine.

"Come sit down and enjoy." He held out his hand and gave her that smile that said he'd either protect her or devour her. She wasn't sure which. She wasn't sure it even mattered.

"Relax."

Easy for him to say.

Several hours later, with crickets chirping a symphony and the sound of water tumbling down the cascade of rock, James watched Kelly lean back on the big plaid blanket. "Dinner was delicious. I thought you said you couldn't cook."

He braced himself with one hand and drank his wine from a red Solo cup with the other. "I'm good with frozen pizza, grilling, or takeout. That's about it."

"Well, the steak and potatoes were amazing. I never imagined something so simply cooked could taste so good. Thank you."

He smiled down at her. "You're welcome."

A funny little flutter whispered around her heart as his gaze lowered to her mouth and held for several seconds before it traveled back up to her eyes.

"Look up." His voice came low and a bit husky.

"What?"

"Look. Up."

"Oh." She tilted her gaze up through the tunnel of tree-tops at the twinkling spray of lights. The sight was breathtaking. When a star shot across the sky, she gasped. "Does that happen all the time?"

"The shooting star?" He shrugged. "You see a lot up here. No city lights to dim the effect."

"I guess most people never think about things like that. What they might be missing."

"Most people don't care. They're too busy racing through life."

She laughed. "Is that a dig?"

"It wasn't intended to be." He lifted the red cup and drank, watching her over the rim. When he lowered the wine his bottom lip came up and pressed the moisture from his top lip. "It's just one of the things I've realized about life. Most people take it for granted."

The sincerity in those dark eyes made her realize something deep and profound had happened to him to bring about his insight.

"Big lesson in life?"

"Oh yeah." He nodded. Sat upright. Grabbed a dried pine needle off the ground and twirled it between his fingers.

"Care to share?"

"It's no big secret." He shrugged those big, strong shoulders. "I'm sure you remember that I was pretty wild back in the day. Pretty careless. Pretty pissed off at the world."

"Why?"

He looked at her like no one had ever asked that question before. "Just selfish, actually. Too young and stupid, and I wanted more than what I had."

"What? Like toys? TVs?"

"Like a mom who was actually home once in a while and paid attention to me. Like knowing if my father might be the old man who took up residence on the end barstool for twenty years down at the Timber Creek Saloon. Or Marvin Jennings at the Gas and Grub. Or hell, even Roger Cooper the butcher at Gridley's Market. Stupid shit like that."

He didn't know his father?

Her heart fluttered. "That's not stupid, James. It's—"

"Sad?"

"Yeah." She sipped her wine, noting the flashes of uncertainty in his eyes.

"Well, I realize now that my mom might not have been the smartest at choosing men, but I guess she did the best she could," he said defensively. "Which still didn't stop me back then from trying to destroy myself at full speed."

"Cryptic," she said. "Continue please."

He chuckled and flicked the pine needle into the fire. "You playing counselor with me?"

"This isn't a court of law. I just . . . care."

Those soulful eyes studied her face as if searching for something that said he could trust her. Then he gave her a tentative smile, which on the seemingly confident man spoke volumes.

He lay back on the blanket, locked his fingers beneath his head, and looked up at the velvet sky.

"I was the king of self-destruction. I drank. Smoked. Pot, not cigarettes. I broke almost every sin in the Bible willingly and happily. Then one night I took a challenge that almost killed me."

Her eyes widened at this surprise revelation. "*Seriously* almost killed you?"

"Seriously as in my heart stopped beating and they were close to pronouncing me dead."

"Holy crap. What happened?"

"I was selfish. And pissed off. Needed something to soothe the savage beast. So I stole a motorcycle from behind the Gas and Grub. Two guys challenged me to race against their cranked-up Chevy. I never turned down a challenge." A huge sigh pushed from his lungs. "Never."

"And?"

"I raced them. They lost control of their car. Flipped it. Three times. I couldn't avoid the wreck and went airborne. Came out the other side with every bone in my body broken." He gave her a small smile. "Except the big toe on my left foot."

"*Every* bone?"

"Okay, slight exaggeration. I didn't break my nose or any of the toes on my right foot."

Kelly's hand came up to cover her gasp. "Oh my god."

"Yeah. I'm thinking *He* must have been there because there is no reason I should be alive, let alone walking around."

"And you fully recovered after all that?"

"Oh, I'm pretty sure I'll pay hell when I get older and the arthritis sets in. But for now, I'm good thanks to all those who refused to let me die. Including Sheriff Washburn, that stubborn, wily old bastard."

"You say that with a smile on your face."

He nodded, and the firelight danced across his sandy

blond hair. "It took me eight months to get back on my feet. As soon as I did, there were charges to face."

"I can only imagine."

"Sheriff Washburn came to me, told me he'd convince the party from whom I'd stolen the motorcycle not to press charges *if* I'd clean up my life. Find a purpose. Give back to the community. When I agreed, he took me under his wing like I was his baby chick. He showed me the ropes around the station. Never lost faith in me. He told me if I wanted to be selfish, then I could get my kicks from the self-centered satisfaction of helping others."

"Sounds like Sheriff Washburn is a very wise man."

His head came up with a smile. "He's the best. Funny. At night when I'd lay there thinking about everything, I'd wish that he was my father. I guess in a way, he was."

"Then why didn't you run for his position when he retired?"

"Because your brother-in-law is my best friend. Matt Ryan was always meant to be a leader of this community. And I'm meant to back up his ass wherever and whenever he needs me."

Kelly realized there would be no point in trying to control the amazing sensations dancing around in her heart. Simply because there was nothing more sexy and alluring in a man than such honest, heartfelt loyalty.

James Harley would not only protect what was his, he would also protect what was everyone else's. Not because he owed *them*. Because he owed it to *himself*.

"Probably shouldn't have run my mouth off. Whenever I do I manage to get myself in trouble." He turned to his side and propped his gorgeous head up with his hand. "So what made you want to be a prosecutor?" he asked, obviously ready to redirect the conversation.

"I'm sure you've heard my nickname. Sister Serious?" She shrugged. Smoothed her fingers over a wrinkle in the blanket. "I think somewhere along the way I stopped fighting the image. Since I can't carry a tune to save my life, I knew I'd never be the next Madonna. Waiting tables at the Grizzle Claw Tavern didn't seem like a good career choice. So I started looking at other possibilities. I got hooked on *Law and Order*. And when I realized that practicing law was for serious people I got the fever pretty bad. So I studied hard. I gave up a lot of *play* time. And as soon as I earned my degree I began to intern for the state attorney's office. It took me a while to figure it all out, but I became very good at it. They hired me, and since the day they gave me an office, I've only lost one case."

"That's quite commendable."

"Is it?" She took a drink, and suddenly the wine didn't taste as sweet.

"Hell yes. How many criminals have you put behind bars? You can't let one take all that away. You should be proud of yourself."

"It was a murder trial. The Colson case."

"I read about that."

"I let everyone involved down." Her heart gave a hard thump against her ribs.

"How do you figure?"

"I pushed for the prosecution. The state attorney was sure we would never get a conviction, but I've never been one to back down when in my heart I knew it was right. This time I was wrong, and the loss devastated me."

"That's understandable."

She sipped the wine then shook her head. "I don't know how I could have been so wrong. My instincts have never let me down before, not even in high-profile cases. My intentions all along have been to help people. To stand up for someone who may not be able to stand up for themselves."

"So basically we're in the same business." He reached across the blanket and covered her hand with his. "Helping people."

"Yes. We have that in common."

He smiled. "Good to know."

"Only I think you have way more fun at it than I do," she said.

"I will admit . . ." His gaze searched her face. "There are some pretty cool tools of the trade. Handcuffs for instance."

Handcuffs?

Amazing how quickly he could move her thoughts away from being Sister Serious.

He stood, brushed off his hands, and held them over the crackling fire to warm them. She took that as a sign that their date had come to an end. She stood and joined him by the fire.

A smile whispered at the corners of his sensuous lips. "Which brings us to *you*, Counselor."

"Me?" She pointed to herself. "What have I got to do with anything?" *And were they still talking about handcuffs?*

"Your challenge."

"After hearing your story, I think challenges sound pretty dangerous."

"Not the one I have planned for you. His eyelids lowered to half-mast as he reached for her and drew her close. His palm came up and caressed her cheek as he looked deep into her eyes.

Her heart hit third gear, and all kinds of crazy heat bulleted down between her legs. "What if I don't want to participate?"

He leaned forward, his lips close and almost brushing against her own. "Are you afraid?"

"Hardly."

"Suspicious?"

"Very."

"Curious?"

She sighed. "Just tell me what it is."

He chuckled low and deep in his throat. "I think there's more to you than Sister Serious. I think deep down inside you may very well be the next Madonna. No, scratch that. Let's make it Katy Perry. She's cute in a flamboyant way. So your challenge is to . . ."

To what? Keep her hands to herself? Not grab him and kiss the pants off him? Not to push him down to the plaid blanket and have her wicked way with him? Yes. All that *was* a challenge. But judging from all the looks he'd been giving her with no action, James Harley seemed to be the king of tease. And she did not want to be the queen of rejection.

"Be flamboyant?"

He chuckled. "Your challenge is cliché but true. Life is too short."

"Meaning?"

He tucked a strand of hair behind her ear and trailed his

fingers down the side of her throat to her shoulder. A rush of warm tingles raced from her belly and spread across her chest.

"Find your hidden talent."

"I told you I can't sing."

"Not talking about singing. Look deeper. Find something to do that makes you *and* others smile."

Doing *him* would make her smile. "Like what?"

"That's for *you* to decide." His smile was as intoxicating as his warm male scent, and it coaxed the passionate woman inside her out of hiding.

"And if I decide to take on this *challenge*, Deputy Harley, what do I get?" She folded her arms across herself. "A trophy? A pony?"

One dark brow lifted. "I can think of something much better."

The problem was, so could she.

CHAPTER EIGHT

The grating whirr of a lawn mower exploded through Kelly's dream. She jerked upward and looked around the room through bleary eyes.

What in the . . . ?

The racket continued as she dropped back down to the mattress, grabbed the pillow, and jammed it over her head. Even goose feathers wouldn't stop the obnoxious buzz. She blew out an exasperated sigh. One of the benefits of living in a high-rise condo was you never had to hear yard work.

"How was the date, Cinderella?"

Kelly came up off the mattress again. "Jesus, Kate! You scared the crap out of me."

Her baby sister grinned. "Awesome."

"What are you doing here?"

Kate roamed the room, touched an old perfume bottle on the dresser. Resettled a stuffed dog on her old twin bed. Picked up the newest issue of *Vogue* from the nightstand, flipped it open, then tossed it back on the nightstand. "We promised Dad we'd help him go through Mom's stuff."

"Today?" Kelly rubbed her eyes, realizing she'd left her contacts in last night after her date with James. "What about the bakery?"

Kate plopped down on her old bed, drew her legs up, and crossed them. "Closed for the day."

"Can you do that?"

"Dad can pretty much do whatever he wants, since he owns the place. We cut back to every other Saturday a while ago."

"What about the revenue?"

"Oddly enough I don't think we're missing that much. Folks just know to come in the day before. We might have a delivery or two, but Dad has gotten it into his head that weekends should be spent with family."

"Wow. Really? After three decades of working six days a week in that place?"

"Something he feels strongly about." Kate shrugged. "I'm not going to complain. Because I get to wake up beside my husband and stay there for longer than a quickie."

"Ugh. TMI."

"So . . . how was your date?"

Kelly threw back the covers and got out of bed. She shoved her feet into her duck slippers and headed toward the kitchen. Kate followed like the pesky little sister she'd always been.

"Well?"

"I don't know how it went." She pulled two mugs from the cupboard while Kate filled the coffeemaker. "He's . . . odd."

Kate laughed. "James Harley is *not* odd. How can he be odd if he's so popular with the single women around here?"

Yeah. Well. There was *that*. "Maybe it's me then."

"Well, you are pretty serious about stuff."

"Apparently he thinks so, too."

"That doesn't sound promising."

While the coffee percolated, Kelly leaned back against the counter. "He issued me a challenge."

"Oooh. This is interesting. What kind of a challenge?"

"He wants me to find my hidden talent. Something to make me smile."

"Other than him and that hot body of his?"

"Yeah. I don't think he's interested in me that way."

"What? Are you blind? He totally takes your clothes off with his eyes."

Probably because he didn't want to take them off with his hands. Last night he'd had every opportunity to make a move. He didn't.

Kelly shrugged. "Doesn't matter anyway. I'm only going to be here for a short time. After Dean's wedding I have to head back."

"I got the impression you weren't in a big hurry to go back to the Windy City."

"I've got responsibilities. I can't just walk away."

"Why not?" Kate asked. "I did. And I don't miss it."

"Ever? Your job was like *Lifestyles of the Rich and Famous*."

"Have you seen my husband?" Kate grinned. "There's not a movie star, or Tiffany's Blue Box, or magnum of Dom Pérignon that can hold a candle to him."

"Good morning, girls." Their dad came into the kitchen in his old bathrobe and brown scuff house shoes. Beneath his robe he wore an old pair of sweatpants and a white T-shirt. What few gray hairs he had remaining stood up like he'd stuck his finger in a toaster.

"Morning, Daddy." Kelly gave him a kiss on the cheek, happy for the interruption of an awkward conversation. She poured steaming java into their mugs, and they all stood there looking at each other expectantly.

"Are you sure you want to do this today?" Kelly asked.

"We've got plenty of time," Kate added.

Their father sipped his coffee and shook his head. "One more day won't make it any easier."

Several reflective moments later they all walked into the bedroom he shared with their mother for three and a half decades.

The walls were a faded shade of mint, while the furniture was a Mediterranean set with the bulky design of the early seventies. A yellow chenille bedspread covered the queen-sized bed, and on the dresser sat a collection of frames with faded photos of the family in days gone by. Like the interior of the Buick, the room hinted of the scent of vanilla. Their mother had been no Martha Stewart, but she'd definitely given Betty Crocker a run for her money.

Kelly felt a lump lodge in her throat as her dad began to pull out drawers and opened the closet.

"You two sit down," he said, setting a drawer on top of the bedspread. "I want you to look through this together. Your mother never instructed me on what to give to who, so I want you to make the decision for her. And no fighting."

"Why would we fight?" Kate asked.

Their father's shoulders lifted beneath his robe. "Families

do weird things when someone dies. Kind of like in a divorce where people will fight over a single plate."

"No fighting." Kelly looked at Kate and held up her hand, little finger extended. "Pinky swear." She and her sister locked fingers and their father gave them a wistful smile.

Inside the drawer were boxes and boxes of costume jewelry. A string of simulated pearls. A butterfly pin with inlaid rhinestones of pink and green. A pair of chandelier earrings in the shape of a champagne glass.

"Gosh," Kelly said, admiring a Black Hills gold bracelet, "I remember when Mom used to let us play dress-up with this stuff. I can't believe she kept it all."

Their dad pulled down several shoe boxes from the shelf in the closet. "Remember, some of this needs to go to Dean, too. But mostly your mom wanted to keep it for the grand-daughters you kids would someday give us."

Granddaughters? Holy cow. Kelly could hardly get a date, and her mom had been thinking about grandkids? She looked up at Kate, who had gone all misty-eyed over a silver charm bracelet.

"Do you mind if I keep this?" Kate asked quietly, rubbing her finger over a charm in the shape of a baby carriage. "Mom once let me wear this to the Fourth of July dance. That was the night I knew I was in love with Matt."

"What do you mean you knew you were in love with him? You walked out of his life for ten years."

"Girls." Their dad used his warning tone.

"It's okay. Kel's right." Kate set the charm bracelet down with a sigh. "I *was* in love with him. But I was even more in love with this big idea I had running around in my head. That something better was out there. That someone needed me more. That he could never give me exactly what I wanted."

Their dad patted Kate on the back. "You just had some growing up to do, honey. And so did Matt. But look where it got you."

Kate laughed, and her smile was so genuine Kelly couldn't help but be just a little envious.

"Yeah."

"You look really happy, Kate," Kelly said.

"I am. I really am." She grabbed the charm bracelet. "I am so taking this."

Kelly wondered if she'd ever find that kind of contentment. "So much for being civilized about going through Mom's things."

"If you girls aren't ready to do this," Dad said, "We can put it off for another day."

"Oooh." Kate held up a pink crystal Victorian-style necklace. "This would go great with some of the gowns in Cindi's Attic," she said in reference to the charity-prom gown shop she'd created. "Can I have this, too?"

"Sure." Kelly didn't mind. She could always borrow. Besides, there were a few pieces she wanted, so she'd save all her bargaining power.

"We can get this done today, Dad," Kate continued. "Working so many hours at the Shack, it's hard to know when we'll get another chance to go through it all."

"I agree." Kelly placed her hand over the top of her father's when a sad expression fell over his weathered face. "What is it, Dad?"

"Just thinking about the Shack." He inhaled a large breath. "I've been meaning to talk to you both. For a while."

"Dad?" Horrible ideas flashed through Kelly's head. "Are you okay?"

He reached out, clasped both her and Kate's hands in his own and held them tight. "I think I've decided to retire. Or at least semi-retire, and I want to know your thoughts."

Kelly's gut tightened. Had it not been for the utter sadness and despair in her father's eyes, she might have panicked.

"What are you talking about?" Kate's brows shot up her forehead. "You can't retire. You're still young. You love that place."

"I *loved* it," he said. "When your mother was at my side. But every day when I walk in there, I look for her. And every day I realize she's never coming back. It's like going through that awful morning all over again."

Hot tears slid down Kelly's cheeks. She should *never* have gone back to Chicago after her mother's death and left her father alone. He was suffering. Heartbroken.

And then she wondered why her mother hadn't visited their father the way she'd visited her three children.

"I'm so sorry, Daddy." Kelly wrapped her arms around his warm neck. She pressed her face against his morning stubble.

His arms came up around both her and her sister, and soon they were all crying.

"I just can't bring myself to go on without her," he said, his voice clogged with tears. "Maybe if I don't have to go to the Shack every day, it will help me heal."

Kelly rubbed her hand across his strong back, admiring him for the passion in which he'd loved their mother. Even if their mother hadn't been perfect to her children, she'd been everything to him.

In that moment, Kelly recognized the one thing she'd been missing in her life. The one thing she'd tried to ignore. The one thing her brother and sister had both found.

She needed someone of her very own to love.

Saturday afternoon sunshine washed the fields of corn and alfalfa with warmth and beckoned James to stay outside and play. To discover a new hiking trail. Or take his ATV to his favorite swimming spot. But for him, weekends were filled with chores and obligations. After he completed his tasks, he'd often treat himself by going out to Matt and Kate's place and dropping a line in the lake. If he was lucky, he'd bring in dinner. If not, he'd just enjoy an ice-cold beer and some downtime. Today did not hold that promise. Today he had responsibilities.

He cruised through the old neighborhood, scrutinizing every rotting wood plank and layer of ill-repair in sight. Ancient oaks on either side of the road grew together like a cathedral ceiling above the pothole-marred street. Sun-dried lawns spread out like a patchwork quilt in various shades of green and gold.

The poor side of town.

That's what those in his community labeled this area. As he wound his way to his destination, a sense of longing knocked against his heart. Even with all the disrepair and obvious state of impoverishment, to him this was home.

He turned the truck into the gravel driveway of the white bungalow in which he'd grown up. He cut the engine and pulled the keys from the ignition as guilt swept over him.

Paint chipped off the house in huge flakes and lay like snow in the dried-up flower beds. A crack spread like a spiderweb in a side window. And several shingles were missing from the roof. The house needed some love. More than he'd been able to spare.

A long sigh blew from his lips as he stepped down from the truck and strolled past a patch of dandelions that bordered the walkway. He opened the front screen door and stepped inside the living room—a homey mishmash of white lace doilies, faded needlepoint, and outdated floral prints. Everything appeared worn, but neatly kept.

"Mom?" He trailed his fingers along the side table, and he swept up the mail as he walked through the room.

"We're in here, James," Mrs. Moore, his mother's caregiver called out.

The scent of warm bread hung in moist clouds above his head as he walked into the sunny yellow-and-white kitchen. His mother sat at the table with a cup of what smelled like orange spice tea in front of her.

"There you are." He tossed his ball cap on a nearby chair and bent toward his mother's wheelchair to give her a hug. Her arms were thin and shaky, but she managed to get them up to hug him back. "How are you ladies today?"

"Better . . . now," his mother said with her stilted pattern of speech. "Better."

"She's been waiting for you." Mrs. Moore set a bowl of apples and grapes in the center of the table. "Even got up early, had a shower, and let me do her hair."

"It looks beautiful." He brushed his mother's cheek with a kiss and placed on the table in front of her the bright bouquet of daisies and zinnias he'd brought. "These are for you." He gave his mother a smile. "Although they pale in comparison."

She gave him a small laugh and a jerky little pat on the arm. "You're a good . . . son."

"I'll bet you say that to all us boys."

The smile on the mobile side of her face fell. "How's . . . Alex?" she asked.

He pulled up a kitchen chair, reached forward, and brushed her wavy brown hair away from her face. Despite her severe health issues, his mother was still an attractive woman. And he knew her heart broke whenever she thought of her rebellious son and her lack of ability to be able to set him straight.

James had once been the hell-raising son. Until the day he'd learned his lesson the hard way. And no matter how horribly he'd treated her, his mother had been right there to help him heal—body and soul. He owed her everything. Since the stroke that had partially paralyzed her speech and movements, he'd made sure she was well taken care of. He paid for her private caregiver, and he paid for her to be able to stay in her own home. The only thing money couldn't buy was her good health. Some days it overwhelmed him, made him question his ability to take care of everybody, do the right thing. On the job he had all the answers. If he didn't, all he needed to do was look in the book. Real life didn't offer such a handy-dandy guide.

"Alex is doing better," he lied, giving her hand a little squeeze. "It's just going to take time."

Her brown eyes, so much like his own, filled with tears. "So . . . sorry."

James clasped her hands between his own and held them against her heart. "It's not your fault, Mom. He's going to be just fine. And when he pulls his head out of his . . . rear end, he's going to be right here, hugging you, and begging for your forgiveness."

She slipped a hand away and caressed her fingers down his cheek. "Like . . . you."

"Yeah, Mom. Like me." Hopefully without the near-death experience.

Several days passed before Kelly realized she'd barely left the house. Together with her dad and Kate they'd sorted out her mother's worldly possessions into piles for each of her children and items to be donated. Amazingly, she and Kate had hardly disagreed until they came to their mother's wedding band. They both wanted it. For several minutes each tried to convince the other why it would be better off in *their* possession. In the end, Kelly suggested it stay with the man who'd placed it on their mother's finger as he'd vowed to love and cherish her all the days of his life. So they threaded it onto a gold chain and gave it to their dad to wear around his neck. The circle hung right over his heart, and both she and Kate realized that if it couldn't be with its rightful owner, at least it had found the perfect home.

The thought did not evade Kelly that when you passed away, everything in your life resorted to being a yard-sale item. How depressing was that? She thought of all the nice furniture and artsy elements that decorated her Chicago condo and she realized that if anything was to happen to her, they'd probably all just be auctioned off for a buck or two.

The only thing that truly lasted was memories.

As she carried yet another box of her mother's worn overalls through the living room to the stack near the door, she took a look around. For years she, Kate, and Dean had tried to buy their parents a new house, or furniture. The pieces Kelly found scattered strategically around the room looked like museum pieces. Still, their parents had been content and repeatedly refused their offers of something bigger, better, newer. Nostalgia draped over her like a fuzzy blanket. There was nothing fancy about this home, but it had always been filled with warmth. And love. Kelly realized that now.

She wondered if all that warmth and all those memories haunted her dad each time he looked at something—a pillow her mother had crocheted. A silk floral piece she'd arranged. Maybe her father needed an escape from the memories at home, too. Kate had done that with the bakery. Last year when her father had gone hunting, she'd completely redecorated the Shack from floor to ceiling. She'd made the focal point of the bakery a large photo of their parents on their opening day.

Could too many memories be a bad thing?

Kelly decided to propose the idea to her father of redecorating the house, too. If he wanted no part of it, she'd leave it alone. If he wanted to move forward, she'd do everything in her power to give him what he needed. Paint. Furniture. Whatever it took. They only thing she couldn't do was take away his pain.

From the back pocket of her shorts, her phone chimed. She tapped the screen and saw a new text message from Daniel.

You ignoring me? Jury selection being moved up a week. Need you back asap.

Kelly hit delete and shoved the phone back into her pocket. She'd need to respond eventually. But not today. Today she was dedicated to life in Deer Lick. To helping her dad. And to finding her hidden talent.

She looked down at the box in her arms, opened the lid, and looked inside. Her mother's overalls. There were at least twenty pairs. She reached inside and touched the soft fabric. An idea sprang into her head. Instead of putting the box in the donate pile, she carried the heavy carton into her room and set it down by the closet. Maybe she could finally put her seventh-grade home-ec sewing skills to good use. She'd make quilts—for her dad, Kate, Dean, and herself using their mother's old overalls and the quilting fabric in the backseat of the Buick.

Now all she needed was a sewing machine.

That would make her smile.

She could be productive *and* meet James's challenge at the same time. Brilliant, if she did say so herself.

Before she lost the enthusiasm, she reached beside the bed and grabbed her purse off the floor. At the foot of the bed lay the Carhartt jacket James had lent her the night of their date. She thought of how openly he'd shared the most difficult moments in his life. She thought of his warmth. His sincerity.

The way he made her melt by just a smile or a touch. The way he challenged her to step outside her comfort zone and make life a little more adventurous.

Maybe she'd return the jacket to him on her way into town. Surely Kate would have his address. Kelly wouldn't think about how desperate she might look just popping up on his doorstep.

Nope.

Not going to think about that at all.

Before she changed her mind, she grabbed the jacket and headed toward the Buick. She pushed the keys in the ignition and was off toward We Heart Quilts, the little shop that sold anything quilt-related. Surely they'd have sewing machines.

By the time she rolled into town, the scent of the Sugar Shack wafted through the car window, and Kelly stopped by to sneak a warm sugar cookie. Then she dropped by to say hello to Mr. Crosby at the Once Again Bookstore and grab a new romance to read. A little further down the street she ducked inside We Heart Quilts. Marge Tucker, the owner of the quilt store, had been about to close up for the night. Lucky for Kelly she heard *cha-ching* and helped Kelly pick out a new machine.

With her new Singer, a romance novel, and James Harley's address in hand, Kelly finally headed out just as the sun dropped behind the mountaintops. She'd barely turned off Main Street before the radio station turned to static and Tom Jones began to sing.

"Oh, no." Kelly reached for the knob to turn off the radio. The glow in the backseat was quicker.

"Trying to get rid of me?" Her mother's tone possessed a twist of amusement.

Kelly glanced up at the rearview mirror, knowing the effort would be futile because her mother's reflection no longer existed. "Is that possible?"

"Weren't *you* always the obedient daughter?"

"Yes. And I'm trying to break that habit."

"Well, good for you." The glow brightened. "Going someplace special?"

"You writing a book?"

Her mother laughed. "By god, I like this sassy side. When did all this take place?"

Kelly turned the Buick onto Railroad Ave. "It's all a façade. I'm really just trying to talk myself out of thinking I'm completely insane for talking back to my dead mother who could do god-knows-what to me from beyond."

"I'm not going to do anything to you, honey. I'm here to help you."

"Help me what? Be fitted for a straightjacket?"

Her mother hooted a laugh. "You kids really do have a dry sense of humor in common. But you've got a lot more teeth to your edge. Maybe I should have visited you first."

"Why change now? Dean and Kate were always your priority."

"I beg your pardon?"

"Look, Mom. If you're going to come all the way back from the dead, we might as well talk straight about things, don't you think?" Kelly felt that old spark of resentment sneak up on her. She thought she'd left those days behind when she'd grown up and moved away. Apparently the old issues were new again. And the attorney inside of her, the one who loved a good cross-examination, raised her head.

"I treated all you kids the same," her mother said defensively.

"Wow." Kelly kept her foot steady on the gas. "Seriously? How's that river of denial working for you?"

Silence engulfed the interior of the car, and the glow dimmed until it became barely visible.

"Is that the way you really feel? That I ignored you? That I put Kate and Dean first?"

Kelly gripped the wheel. What was wrong with her? The woman was dead. Couldn't she just play along with whatever it was and let her mother rest in peace? She inhaled a sharp breath of air. "Sorry. Just having a bad day."

"You're an officer of the court, daughter. Sworn to tell the truth. And I hear what you're saying." Her mother's tone turned melancholy. "Obviously a lot of damage has been done. But I promise to fix that. If you'll just trust me."

Kelly turned, but the backseat was cold and empty. And her mother was gone.

CHAPTER NINE

Guilt, as heavy as the day her mother died, hung over Kelly like a soggy wool coat. She should have kept her big yap shut. Her mother had been distant enough while she was alive. No need to totally alienate her when she was dead.

Kelly wanted to call her back from wherever she had disappeared to, but how did one go about summoning the deceased? Angry with herself, she put the car into drive and headed toward the address on Railroad Avenue Kate had scribbled down on a pink sticky note.

The tree-lined street ran parallel to the train tracks, thus the name. Aside from being in a rather noisy location, the homes on the street appeared cozy and friendly. Front porches had swings or wicker chairs, and walkways were lined with petunias in vibrant summer colors. Although it held possibilities, one house on the street remained bare of a flower border and welcoming porch. Only one had a big black bad-boy truck in the driveway and a Harley Davidson parked on a lawn that barely clung to the color green.

Kelly parked the Buick at the curb and wasn't surprised to

hear Steven Tyler wailing about love in an elevator through the open windows of the small cottage-like house. Before she lost her courage, she grabbed James's jacket off the seat and opened the car door. She pushed her sunglasses to the top of her head and started up the walkway, kicking aside a football that looked faded from being out in the sun too long. She stepped up onto the doorstep, raised her fist to knock on the wooden screen door, and stopped cold at the sound of a male voice.

"Don't lick me there." The man's voice came out in a low groan, and Kelly dropped her raised knuckles back down to her side.

"Stop it." A long pause and then a deep chuckle. "Okay. Okay. As long as I can't keep you off me, have at it."

Looked like James had company. Of the female sort.

Kelly stepped back. He may have cheated death and he may be loyal to his friends, but when it came to women she should have known he'd be the same guy he'd been in high school. After all, he'd shown up at her brother's barbecue with bubble butt in tow, hadn't he? As far back as Kelly could remember, James had never been without a girl hanging all over him and at least two more waiting in the wings. Well, *she* wasn't the type to get in line.

Time to face the truth. Other than taking advantage of her inebriated state at Kate's wedding and a pretty nice date in the forest, he'd not shown any real sign of interest in her. Well, maybe he did seem to touch her a lot. And some of those long gazes with those deep-brown eyes did make it seem like he was intrigued by her. And he'd made that fifty-dollar bet with her about getting her into his bed again. But when he'd taken her on the date, he didn't even try to kiss her.

Talk about mixed signals.

Decision made, she dropped his jacket to a plastic patio chair near the door then turned on her heel to get the heck out of there before anyone saw her. Her tennis shoe squeaked against the wood porch, and in a flash the maniacal yapping of dogs hit the screen door with the force of a mini tornado. She jumped back, fearing the fur would fly right through the screen and sink razor teeth into her ankles.

"Knock it off, you two." The male voice growled from within the room, and Aerosmith abruptly ceased going down in the elevator.

Kelly turned to find two pint-sized fur balls jumping at the screen as though they were Dobermans and she was casing the place. Then the male voice from within the house appeared. Not James, but a younger version of the same. Same sandy-blond hair, just longer. Tall, lean, muscular, and cocky. Had to be related. Son maybe?

"Who are you?" he asked, scooping the two Yorkies up into his arms and studying her through deep-brown eyes.

"Who are *you*?" she fired back.

"Alex."

Well that told her plenty.

"You here for James?" He opened the screen door and held it, obviously expecting her to walk in. He gave her tank top and cutoffs a leisurely once-over. Obviously he'd been tutored by the expert in the house.

"I . . . uh . . ." She battled with Sister Serious all of two seconds. "Sure." She grabbed James's jacket off the chair and strode into the house to the simultaneous growls of the two pipsqueak pups in Alex's arms. Though the dogs looked identical, one wore a pink bandana around its neck, and the other wore yellow. At the moment, Kelly couldn't tell whether they were smiling or snarling. She pulled her gaze away from the dogs and took a quick look around the living room.

Someone had attempted to make the house a home with nice furniture and a few haphazardly placed pieces of artwork. But there was another element that screamed male domination. The walls were white. A flat-screen TV with a video game in stop-action took up half the wall. Surround-sound speakers were placed high in all four corners. And the leather sofa was in the perfect location to receive the full-throttle effect of it all.

Through a pass-through Kelly could see into the kitchen, where a few dishes were stacked lopsided in the sink. On the counter, pizza boxes had the same leaning-tower effect.

Alex flopped down onto the couch and let the dogs go. Both headed straight for her ankles. She backed up.

"They won't bite," Alex assured her while he grabbed the game controls, cranked up the volume, and dove into some kind of war game.

Kelly looked down. She'd never been afraid of dogs. Then again, she'd never been around little dogs, and these two looked like ankle-biting repeat offenders. The one with the pink bandana stood on its hind legs and did a little wave thing with its front paws, while the one with the yellow bandana sniffed her feet like Sherlock Hound. Kelly gave a fleeting look to the screen door and wondered how many steps it would take to make an escape. She shouldn't have come here. Obviously James wasn't around, and Alex had no interest in entertaining her. Or protecting her from the tiny-teeth team.

Heavy footsteps echoed down the hall. "Turn that shi— Oh. Hey."

Kelly turned toward the new voice.

Whoa. Apparently James *was* home, as he now stood in the living room, with a bath towel wrapped loosely around his lean hips. But the towel wasn't what Kelly noticed. Nope, she went right for the naked part. The perfectly etched tribal tattoo banding his right bicep. The hard muscles rippling down his stomach. Three droplets of water glistened on the tight, tanned skin of his broad chest and took a slow slide downward to the even more interesting parts hidden beneath that fluffy blue towel.

When she realized she was staring, she jerked her gaze upward and met his perceptive brown eyes. His firm sexy lips tilted with appreciation.

She wanted him.

He knew it.

Well, heck. There went all her bargaining power.

"Kelly." He forked the fingers of one large hand through his wet hair, while the other hand clutched the tucked-in section of the towel. "This is a surprise."

"I . . . brought back your jacket." Her eyes took another stroll down his body. "I thought you might need it."

He grinned and stepped forward. "In July?"

God, she was so busted. "Doesn't matter. Here." She thrust the coat at his chest and turned to get out of there. He grabbed her hand.

"No need to run off."

She glanced over at Alex. "Who is *that?*"

"My little brother."

Ah. Brother. Not son.

Clutching her hand, James called out, "Alex, don't you have some homework to do?"

"Summer vacation, dude."

"Then maybe somewhere to go?"

"Nope," Alex replied without even a glance toward his big brother.

"Yes. You do."

"He doesn't have to leave on my account," Kelly said.

Alex clicked the TV remote, tossed it on the sofa, and stood. The huge frown over his brown eyes verified he was an unhappy camper. "Can I at least take the bike?"

"When hell freezes over."

"That sucks." The teen stormed out the door, and the screen slammed behind him, which sent yellow-bandana dog and pink-bandana dog into a fit of scrambling feet and ear-piercing yips.

"Come on, girls. Be nice. We have a guest." Both dogs immediately quieted, trotted to James, and looked up at him with pure doggie adoration in their big eyes.

"Are they yours?" Kelly asked, doubtful that a man like James Harley would own anything less than a Rottweiler, German shepherd, or at least a Lab.

"Yeah. You don't remember them?"

Kelly looked down at the two pink tongues dangling between tiny sharp teeth. "Should I?"

"This isn't the first time you've been here."

"It's not?" Kelly looked around and found nothing familiar about the place. "It has to be. I'm sure I'd remember."

"It was dark. We were . . . busy." Then James looked

around, too, and shrugged those broad shoulders. "Sorry about the mess. I keep trying to teach Alex to pick up after himself, but he thinks we should live like bachelors."

We? Dear God, please tell her his little brother hadn't been in the next room while she and James were . . . "I wasn't judging."

"Sure you were." He gave a deep laugh. "Why don't you have a seat, and I'll go get dressed."

"That's not necessary." She began to back toward the door. "I just wanted to return your jacket."

"If that were true you could have dropped it by the station."

"Oh." She hadn't thought of that.

He caught her hand and tugged her close enough to inhale the fresh, clean scent of his man soap and shampoo. Every ounce of estrogen in her body went on *I-want-I-want-I-want* alert.

"You afraid?" he asked in a low, confident tone.

"Of?"

His gaze caressed her face and lingered on her mouth. "Me."

Why would she be afraid? Just because he was three-quarters naked and she hadn't had sex since December? "No."

"Then relax." The heat from his body seeped into her skin as he leaned in and took a deep breath. "Mmmm. You smell great."

"I've been at the bakery."

"Then you smell good enough to eat."

She ducked away, and he laughed again. "I knew it. You are afraid."

Before she could voice a protest, he tossed the jacket on the back of the sofa. "Stay here. I'll be right back."

He turned, and that's when she noticed the amazing tattoo that started at the base of his neck, spread across his shoulder blades like wings, then intertwined down the middle to the small of his back. The tribal design was simple and had the same elements as the band around his bicep. The tattoo had been designed to disguise a thin scar that dissected an otherwise perfectly muscular back.

Before James, she'd never been with a man who had tattoos. She'd always identified *those kinds* of men as dangerous. She might be thirty-two years old, but her experience on the romantic side of life had been semi-limited. She'd gone from home to a college dorm to an apartment in Chicago. Along the way she'd missed a few steps most women had taken into maturity. Instead of joining her college roommate at the local pub, she'd stay in her room to study. Once she graduated and moved into a place of her own, she'd gotten a job and had spent all her extra time trying to prove herself to those who'd taken a chance on her. Most of her romantic adventures had been limited to men who didn't mind taking her to a nice dinner but were never there in the morning when she woke up.

She'd spent two-thirds of her life trying to prove herself. To whom? Her mother? The state attorney who hesitated every time he spoke her name as if he couldn't remember? For what? A long string of lonely nights?

James was right. She really did need to find her hidden talent. Maybe she'd discover something really fun. And a bit risqué.

She exhaled a heavy sigh and glanced down at the dogs still looking up at her. "Mind if I sit down?" she asked them, wondering why she even contemplated staying. Pink-bandana dog sneezed, and Kelly took that as a *"Go ahead and sit, but don't be surprised if we sneak a bite out of your leg."*

She pushed aside a pillow that was meant to be decorative but looked as though it had been used as a TV tray. No sooner had she sat down than pink-bandana dog jumped up in her lap and began to lick her chin. "Oh." Kelly gave a startled laugh. "Okay then."

Yellow-bandana dog remained at her feet, glaring up at her.

"Princess. Get down."

Kelly looked up when James reentered the room. He'd dressed. Sort of. Worn jeans with a torn knee and nearly threadbare at the crotch. No shirt. No shoes. She didn't mind.

"Princess?"

He pointed to yellow-bandana dog on the floor. "And Poppy."

"You have dogs named *Princess* and *Poppy?*"

The dark slash of his brows lifted. "Obviously the name selections did not come from me."

"What happened? Old girlfriend sneak away in the middle of the night and leave them in your custody?"

"Nope." He grabbed an empty pizza box off the coffee table and tossed it through the pass-through into the kitchen. "Mother with a stroke who couldn't care for them anymore."

"Oh god." She clutched her hand to her chest. "I'm so sorry. I didn't know."

"It's okay." One very broad shoulder, now clad in a black T-shirt, lifted in a shrug. "It's just the way it is."

"Did you inherit Alex, too?"

"Yeah. And believe me, the dogs are much easier."

"He does seem a bit surly."

"He's seventeen and pissed at the world. Basically, he's me at that age." His large hand came up and he pointed at her. "You want something to drink?"

"No. Thank you. I really did just come by to return your jacket."

"I know. Doesn't mean you can't stay, though."

Her heart did a funky somersaulty flip thing. The invitation didn't come just from his words. Those dark-chocolate eyes of his were carrying on a conversation all their own.

From the time he'd been able to ride a two-wheeler, James had always been gorgeous. And he'd always known it. He'd always been enigmatic and sexy—even at the age of thirteen. Everything about him warned a sane girl to keep away, even though the mysteries of her body were telling her to forge ahead. Kelly had managed to do just that all through high school. Even when she'd caught him looking at her then the same way he looked at her now, like he wanted to pour pancake syrup all over her body and lick it off. Slowly. Somehow she'd managed to keep her wits intact.

Still, something about him didn't make sense. During her years in the courtroom, she'd been given varied signals from those on the witness stand, but she'd always been able to sniff them out and take appropriate measures. James had become a master magician at mixing his signals.

The night he'd taken her up into the mountains on his ATV he'd given her *that* look. The look that she'd misread as he wanted to kiss her. He hadn't even tried. So maybe that was just his look. Maybe he couldn't help the way his long eyelashes lowered just enough to spark some curiosity in a girl.

The problem? *She* knew James could deliver on those sparks. And had. Yet, since the night he'd apparently brought her home from her sister's wedding reception, he hadn't made a move. And he'd had plenty of opportunities.

"You want me to stay?" She decided to make light of it. If only to save herself the embarrassment when he revealed that he had no real interest in her. He'd had her once and apparently that had been enough. All his bets and challenges were just big talk. "Oh. I get it. You want me to help you clean your house. Is that it?"

"Hadn't even crossed my mind." He gave her a choirboy smile. "But it's not a bad idea."

She stood. "Sorry, Deputy. I've got a brand-new sewing machine and a box of fabric out in the car. And I've already got plans." Okay. Wow. She'd just painted herself to be the dullest person on the planet.

"For what?"

"I decided to make quilts from my mother's old overalls."

"That's a nice idea." He folded his muscular arms across that smooth, hard chest. "But it doesn't sound like much fun."

"It will be once I figure out how to actually use a sewing machine."

"Kelly?" His head tilted. "That's not your idea of meeting my challenge is it?"

"Maybe."

"No. Way." He shook his head, cupped his hands over her shoulders, and eased her back down to the sofa. His face was inches away from her own, and his sexy male scent caused the woman in her to jump to attention.

"You sit right here until I put some shoes on."

"And then what?" she asked, looking up into those dark, amazing eyes.

"And then I'm really going to make you smile."

If that was true, then why was he putting on his clothes?

James had never considered himself a smart man. But the fact that twice in one week he'd managed to put Kelly Silverthorne in the position to be hanging onto him for dear life and pressing her small but perfect breasts against his back was sheer genius.

Her fingers dug into his stomach as she leaned in and spoke close to his ear. "Did I happen to mention that I don't really ride on motorcycles?"

"You do now."

He hit the accelerator on the Softail and sped toward their destination, taking every back road possible to make the enjoyment last longer.

He may not be all that smart.

But he definitely wasn't stupid.

On a particularly sharp curve, Kelly leaned into him. "Where are we going?"

"You sure ask a lot of questions."

"Occupational hazard," she said over the roar of the engine.

"Then how about you just trust me?"

"I'm not sure that's a good idea at all."

"Yeah, well, try to do it anyway."

The wind felt great against his face as they whipped along the lake road and the headlight swept past dense stands of tall aspens and towering pines. Past enormous resort homes. Past private docks and colorful boats bobbing on the lake. Everything about the moment made him feel alive. Everything about the woman holding onto him made him want more than he had a right to desire.

But that wouldn't stop him.

He'd wanted Kelly almost from the moment he'd seen her way back when. Of course, in those days he'd been just a kid and hadn't understood the whole heart-pounding, electricity-snapping-through-your-body thing. He understood it now. And he wanted more. He'd go to hell with a smile on his face just to hold her as often as he could.

Several miles down the road James felt the tension leave Kelly's arms, and she began to relax. He wondered if she was smiling yet, because he certainly was.

"Okay," she shouted over his shoulder and above the roar of 1800 cc's of power.

"Okay what?"

"This is fun."

"Yeah?" He grinned. "Are you smiling?"

"Almost."

Pleasure danced in his veins. "Then prepare to let it all go . . . His hand tightened around the grip and he hit the throttle. "Now."

Behind him Kelly let out a squeak, then a giggle, then a full out "Yesssss!" as she grabbed onto him and held tight.

Man. He was getting smarter by the mile.

The bike followed the curves up to Lookout Point as smooth as aged whiskey. When they reached the top James found it gloriously vacant of the usual carload or two of teens who'd snuck away to make out and fog up the windows of their second-hand cars.

He rolled the bike to the edge and cut the engine, swung his leg over the seat, and held out his hand. Kelly grabbed hold and got off the bike a little wobbly. Fortunately for him that meant she practically fell into his arms. Every man's dream. A hot blonde fresh off a badass bike.

"Oops. Sorry." She caught herself, smiled, then used her hands to tidy up her windblown hair. "I must look a mess."

He captured her hands and stopped her from taking away that wild, fresh-out-of-bed look he loved so much. It made him think of her straddling him. Naked. Her mass of curls falling like a curtain over her breasts. Looking down at him like she had to decide where to lick him first.

"You look perfect." *Better than perfect.* "Come on." He took her by the hand and led her to the edge of the clearing that overlooked their town. Overhead the stars twinkled, and in the distance a campfire glowed in Founder's Park.

"Wow." She took a long look in both directions. "I've never seen the town from this angle before."

"Come on." James stepped back. With the glow of the moon highlighting her halo of ivory hair she looked as innocent as an angel. But nobody was *that* innocent. "This is the number one make-out spot in Deer Lick. You don't expect me to believe you've never been up here."

She held up her hand as if she was swearing in. "On my honor I have never been up here before."

"Then where did you go?"

"To make out?" She laughed. "Do you even remember me in high school?"

Did he ever. He could still picture her walking down the hall, her books clutched tightly to her chest, her snug jeans accenting every step she took. But his memories went far beyond the classroom fare. He'd become a master of conjuring up fantasies about her. "Of course I remember you."

She folded her arms and looked out over the town again. "Then how could you think I've ever been to any make-out spot?"

He cupped her shoulders and turned her to face him. He brushed her hair back, enjoying the softness against his skin. "Why do you sell yourself short all the time? I've always thought you were pretty amazing."

Her chin came up. "I wasn't fishing for a compliment."

"I know." His gaze touched her face, slid down her body, then came back up to her luscious mouth. God, he could almost taste her. "That would be totally unlike you."

Her sweet scent came up and tickled his nose, and he found himself drawing her slightly closer. "Did you enjoy the ride?"

She smiled. "Yes."

He smiled back. "That's what I was hoping to see. You should smile more often, Counselor. It looks good on you."

Without any direction from him, his hands drew her

closer until her breasts pressed against his chest and his insides caught fire. Her smoky-green eyes looked up at him, full of desire. Expectant. He wanted nothing more than to give her one more thing to smile about.

"Just so you know, I'm not seeing Brianna anymore," he said before he knew the words were even out of his mouth. "Or anyone else for that matter."

"It's really none of my business," she said, her lips just a whisper away from his.

He shouldn't kiss her. But since he was the king of talking himself into things he shouldn't do, he drew her closer, lowered his head, and then the phone in his back pocket rang.

Damn it.

Spell broken, she backed away from him and he had no choice but to yank the phone from his pocket and answer.

"This better be good," he growled into the speaker. But the news he heard from the other end of the line wasn't good.

It was bad.

Really bad.

Kelly followed James through the doors of Mercy Hospital, barely able to keep up with his long, urgent strides. He'd offered to take her home. But when he'd told her his brother had been talking with a girl at a kegger and her boyfriend had taken offense and beaten Alex until he was unconscious, there was no way she'd let James face the situation alone.

The admitting attendant, a woman who looked sweet and motherly, looked up as they entered the emergency-room lobby. "Room 104, Deputy Harley."

"Thanks, Alice." He pushed through the double doors into a sterile hallway cluttered with IV poles and rolling prep trays. His boots hit the tile floor hard, and Kelly couldn't help but notice that tension stiffened his broad shoulders.

James went straight to Room 104 as if he knew the way, had been there before. When he entered the room he stopped short, and Kelly almost plowed into his back. He stood motionless for a moment, pulling a deep breath into his lungs before he continued into the room. When Kelly could finally see around his big body, she had to cover a gasp.

"All this just for talking with a girl?" she whispered.

James nodded. "Guys can get pretty territorial."

That was just plain stupid. But Kelly wasn't about to voice that opinion. Right now the man in front of her needed her moral support. Or a tranquilizer.

On the gurney lay Alex, pale as a ghost, except for the purple bruises and swelling on his handsome young face. Some kind of maternal-instinct thing kicked in, and she immediately wanted to find the culprit who'd done this and take them down. The logical side of her recognized that teenage boys did not usually get their asses kicked without some kind of provocation. Just *talking* to a girl didn't seem like a fighting offense. The story would come out later. Now was the time to heal.

James went to the side of the gurney and gripped the steel rails with white-knuckled hands. For several long heartbeats he just stood there and looked down at the unconscious young man for whom he was responsible. Then he dropped down hard to the chair and buried his face in his hands. The gesture expressed his emotions as loudly as if he'd voiced them.

Failure.

Defeat.

Everything inside Kelly shifted. She knew that feeling. She knew it well. And when she'd had to face it, she'd been alone.

She moved further into the room. Went to James's side and laid her hand on his shoulder. "He's going to be fine."

"Is he?" James didn't look up. His shoulders lifted on a sigh. "This is my fault."

"How can it be your fault?"

"I pushed him out of the house tonight. If I hadn't done that . . ."

Kelly swallowed and decidedly shared the guilt in his decision to push Alex out the door. If she hadn't gone over to his house . . . "You're doing the best you can."

"I'm not, really." His voice was low and tight with emotion. "When he first came to live with me I probably didn't act all that happy to have him around. He was eleven. And needy. And I had just started to get my life together." His hands tightened on the bedrails. "Guess I never lost that selfish streak."

"It's never too late to change," she said, dropping down to a squat beside him. "You need to find what's missing inside of Alex. Maybe that will help heal a part of yourself as well."

James turned his head, his eyes as warm as his smile. "Anyone ever tell you you're a really nice person?"

She smiled back. "No. And don't tell the criminals I prosecute that either." She reached forward and covered his hand with hers. "I'm here for as long as you need me. Okay?"

"You sure?"

"Yeah. I'm sure." She pulled up a chair and sat beside him until the doctor came in and announced they were keeping Alex in the hospital overnight. He'd suffered some cracked ribs, and since he was still unconscious it was apparent he'd suffered some head trauma. They wouldn't release him until they were sure he'd be okay. And she wouldn't leave until either James or the doctors kicked her out.

Hours later, James finally convinced her to go home and get some sleep. She'd only agreed when he'd promised to call her with any updates on Alex's condition. When she'd realized that maybe James just needed to be alone with his thoughts, Kelly stood outside the hospital entrance and pulled her cell phone from her back pocket to call her dad and ask him to pick her up. She hated to wake him, but Deer Lick did not have the population to merit a taxi service. So one either drove by car, horse, or recreational vehicle to their destination. Behind her the automatic doors of the lobby whooshed open. Kelly turned to see who might be coming out and was surprised to find one of the clowns she'd observed at the Founder's Day parade.

"How are you?" The woman's cheerful voice made Kelly smile.

"I'm good, how about yourself?"

The woman stopped beside her. Growing up, Kelly had always thought clowns were a little creepy. Now, knowing the magic they created, she admired the clown's pink hair and jeweled eyebrows.

"I hate to admit it," the clown said, "but tonight I'm a little tired."

Beneath all that makeup, it was hard to tell the woman's age or whether she might look a little weary. She just looked ... happy.

"I'm Priscilla Stewart," she said, extending a fingerless yellow glove. "Aren't you Kelly Silverthorne?"

Surprised, Kelly shook the extended hand. "Have we met?"

"Yes, but I haven't seen you for years. I was friends with your mama. Served on the Ladies Auxiliary with her."

"Oh. Well, it's nice to meet you. Again." Kelly laughed. She just couldn't help herself. Priscilla's smile just urged a like response. "What are you doing here so late? Visiting someone?"

Priscilla nodded, and the mini-sized purple-and-orange top hat wiggled in response. "Almost every night. For over fifteen years."

"Seriously?"

The clown lady laughed then used her thumbs to smooth the frown lines on Kelly's forehead. "Don't stress, pretty girl. I like coming here."

"I don't mean to be nosy, but—"

"You're wondering why I would do that."

"Well, kind of."

"The answer is simple." She took Kelly's hand. "Sixteen years ago I lost my husband to cancer. It was a long, slow process. At the end, I came to this hospital every day, looking for some ray of happiness to break through the pain. When I needed a break from gazing down at the man I loved, knowing he'd be leaving me soon, I walked the halls. I chatted with families of other cancer patients. I grabbed onto what little comfort I could find before I went back to hold his hand again."

She took a breath and her smile lifted even higher, though it quivered a little at the corners. "After Martin passed away, I sat in my house for almost a full year, feeling sorry for myself. Drowning in my melancholy. My memories." She stroked Kelly's fingers and gave her hand a little squeeze. "Then one day, I was watching TV and the local news had on a group that perked me right up. That day I discovered the *Clowning Around* folks and I jumped in with both feet." She leaned forward and winked with her long purple eyelashes. "My clown name is Twinkie, by the way."

Kelly smiled. "Nice to meet you, Twinkie."

"Yep." Twinkie let go of Kelly's hand and hiked up her invisible suspenders. "After I learned how to be a clown, I came up with my persona, and I signed myself up to come read to the kids in this hospital. Each night, at the end of the story, when they smile, I smile. I can't change the world, but if I can make a difference for even one child who feels that need for comfort as I did sixteen years ago, well . . ." She gave a shrug of her wildly striped shoulders.

"It makes you happy," Kelly finished.

"Yes, it does." Twinkie gave Kelly a tweak on her chin. "You know . . . we're always looking for new blood."

"Oh. I'm not really the clown type."

"That's what we all say, darlin'. Until we put on the makeup and the big shoes. Then it's . . ." She did a little dance. "*Showtime!*" Priscilla/Twinkie headed to the parking lot. "Let me know if you change your mind. You take care now," she said with a wave of those fingerless yellow gloves.

"You, too." Kelly watched the woman's loudly striped overalls and big pink clown shoes head toward a compact car near the back of the lot.

When they smile, I smile.

Kelly thought of the big man inside that hospital, sitting by his brother's bed. Waiting with a heavy heart.

Find your hidden talent.

Find something to do that makes you and others smile.

Everything inside Kelly started twitching around like she had overindulged on jumping beans. Her fingers flexed and unflexed. And her heart picked up a rhythm that felt a whole lot like *Entry of the Gladiators.*

When the lone clown in the parking lot reached for the door handle of her car, Kelly's heart gave a leap. "Twinkie! Wait!"

Twinkie looked up, a smile already on her face. "Well, come on then."

Before Kelly knew it, her feet were flying toward the clown in the parking lot. Greasepaint appeared to be in her future.

CHAPTER TEN

As bridal showers went, the one Kate held for Emma had been tasteful and elegant. If Kelly didn't know her sister had spent ten years of her life styling celebrities for red carpet events, she would have pegged Kate as a party planner. There were white linen tablecloths, centerpieces with blue hydrangeas, delicate finger sandwiches, and a cupcake tower. Emma sweetly blushed through each naughty nightgown she opened, and admitted that Dean would love every one of them.

Of course he would.

As bachelorette parties went, Kate left tasteful and elegant off the menu.

The Naughty Irish, Deer Lick's most well-loved bar, owned by family friends Maggie and Ollie Barnett, offered everything from basic well drinks to Moose Drool and Guinness. Tonight, for the bachelorette and her posse, the Irish also offered sloe screws and sex on the beach. Kelly had been impressed that her sister had strayed from the gauche and over-used penis-cake design. Since Emma was marrying their brother, the thought of a penis cake was just wrong in so many ways. Instead Kate went for a sassy pink-and-black zebra cake. A little funky, but nothing that would embarrass the bride-to-be. Though god only knew how uber-nice Emma ended up with one of the biggest playboys in the universe.

Make that *ex*-playboy.

The minute Dean had met Emma, he tossed his partying days as precisely as he'd thrown a football into the end zone.

The décor of the Naughty Irish leaned toward a non-traditional blend of dark wainscoting, green walls, and deer antlers. Neon beer signs provided interior lighting, and for those who chose a game of billiards, the P in the Pepsi stained-glass light above the pool table had been knocked out.

A week had passed since the night Alex Harley had been beaten to within an inch of his life. Kelly had gone to the hospital the following day but found he'd been released. She'd called James, who informed her that his brother was currently being cared for by his mother's caretaker at her home and that the doctors thought he would be just fine. He thanked her for her concern. She offered her help if he needed it, and that was the last she'd seen of or heard from him. She knew he was busy, and she had no right to intrude on him when he already had his hands full. But she did miss that smile and all those innuendoes that seemed to flip every switch in her body like a nuclear meltdown.

Tonight, perched around a badly scarred table bursting with umbrella drinks, the party girls had to shout their conversation over the normal roar of bar noise as well as the cover band that had driven all the way down from Great Falls.

"You promise no strippers, right?" Emma asked.

Kate gave a slightly tipsy smile and a slow blink. "Where would I find strippers in Podunkville?"

"Good, because I can probably get the best show at home."

"Eeeew! God. Now I have to block that image from my mind."

Kelly laughed as Kate and Emma then engaged in a competition of *Who would you rather sleep with?* Some of the choices were ridiculous—Gilligan or the Skipper. Fred Flintstone or Barney Rubble. Some sounded delicious—Brad Pitt or George Clooney. Ryan Reynolds or Ryan Gosling. The game was interrupted when Kelly felt the cell phone vibrate in the purse at her feet. She pulled it out and swept her finger across the screen to find yet another text from Daniel.

What's with the silent treatment? Jury selection starts next week. You in or not?

Selfishly not wanting to re-engage in her regular life, she'd purposely ignored him. She'd come home to heal the wounds of losing that case, but the wounds were still raw. And she wasn't ready to go back. Still, it was ridiculous for her to think silence on her part would solve anything. So before she lost her party groove, she texted back.

Brother's wedding in 3 days. Housesitting for him. Extending my LOA another two weeks.

She hit send and pushed down the guilt as she shoved the phone back into her purse. Then she took a huge gulp of her drink, flinched at the brain freeze, and re-engaged in the festivities.

As the band on stage kicked into high gear with a gritty version of "Roadhouse Blues," Kate shouted, "Oh my god, I love this song." She grabbed the hands of those sitting closest to her and dragged them out onto the dance floor. Kelly, having enough buzz in her blood, joined in. Of course, it had taken two sloe screws to loosen up her freak flag enough for her to let it fly. She was now on her third.

"Dance with me, Emma." Maggie, an apple-cheeked, roly-poly, good-time girl and one of Kate's best friends, grabbed hold of the guest of honor and began a bump and grind. Emma was so busy giggling she almost fell on her butt while Kate did a suggestive solo. And then there was Edna Price, an ancient woman who smelled like mothballs and Listerine and didn't care that her elastic hose were sagging. She was getting her arthritic groove on.

Kelly sipped her orangey drink from a little red straw and was doing her own version of getting her sexy back when a man in a camo ball cap suddenly appeared.

"Want to dance?" He flashed a smile that dangled somewhere between "Yeah, I know you think I'm cute" and "Please don't say no."

She returned his smile because aside from the camo hat he *was* kind of cute.

He extended his hand. "I'm Jason."

"Nice to meet you. I'm Kelly."

Jason's pleasantries went bye-bye as his gaze took a leisurely ride down the front of her strapless cotton dress all the way to the toes of her blue-and-tan cowboy boots. His eyes came back up to meet hers.

"So, you want to dance?"

"I . . . um . . ."

A strong pair of hands from behind slid around her waist. She spun—ready to knock the offender on his aggressive ass—and came nose-to-deputy-badge with none other than the man who'd been saturating her dreams with all kinds of toe-tingling details. Jason and his wandering eyes disappeared from thought. And the dance floor.

"Hi." James gave her a slow, sensuous smile, and her slightly under-the-influence libido flew into overdrive. The pulsating lights above the dance floor glinted against his short, sandy hair and sparkled across the shiny surface of the star pinned above his shirt pocket.

"Hi." A warm flush spread across her chest. "What are you doing here?"

He shrugged those broad uniformed shoulders while his hands stayed on her waist. "Matt and I are both on duty, so we thought we'd come by to see if anyone needed a designated driver."

Kelly laughed and held up her sloe screw. "Pretty sure we're all going to need one."

"Affirmative." He glanced over the top of her head. "Edna's elastic hose are wilting."

Kelly leaned in. "Edna has been slamming back Harvey Wallbangers like an old pro."

A dark brow lifted over those amazing chocolate eyes. "You don't say."

"I think Edna's partied a time or two in her day."

"How about you?" His long fingers began to caress the small of her back. "Do you party often?"

"Me?" She laughed. "Obviously not. Have you heard what my brother and sister call me? *Sister Serious.* I mean, come on. Yes, I do have a serious job but . . ." *And why was her hand wandering up to touch his badge?* "I can be fun."

"I remember that about you."

"Yes. Well, I was drunk at the time."

"You're drinking now."

"Not drunk though."

"You sure? Your eyes aren't quite focused."

"Probably just my mascara."

"Right. Need a ride home?"

"Dance with me first." Yep. That was the alcohol talking.

"I'm on duty."

She glanced across the busy dance floor, where everyone was boogie-deep in the bluesy tune. She slid her hand up to his shoulder. "I don't think anyone will care."

While the band rolled into Luke Bryan's "I Don't Want This Night to End," James's dark eyes searched her face as though he was battling with inner demons. Then he plucked her drink from her hand, set it on a nearby table, and dragged her against him. His bulky utility belt made things a little awkward, and she didn't need to ask if that was a gun in his pocket because it was. Or at least it was in the holster strapped to his side. Heaven help her, but there was something just a little exciting about being held by a man wearing a weapon. A man who knew how to use that weapon to serve and protect.

With his thigh pressed between hers, they swayed together to the melodic tune. For Kelly, their height difference made for some really interesting friction. Or maybe she'd just been turned on by the man holding her from the moment he put his hands on her waist.

The warm male scent of him filled her head as he held her close. The heat from his hard, strong body radiated through his deputy uniform and her cotton dress to warm her skin. Before she did something over-the-top crazy like drag his mouth down to hers for a kiss, she struck up a safe conversation. "How's your brother?"

He leaned his head back. "Better. Thanks for asking."

"How did your mother handle his . . . accident?"

"It's been stressful for her."

"I can imagine. I—"

"You wanted to dance." He tightened their embrace until her breasts were pressed against the buttons on his shirt. "How about we just do that?"

Even in her state of tipsiness, she recognized his avoidance of the matter. She did care about it, but if he didn't want to talk, she wouldn't push.

"Sorry if I interrupted something with Jason." His hand tightened possessively at the small of her back.

She tilted her head and looked up at the smirk on his face. "No, you're not."

"Yeah. You're probably right." He tucked her against him a little tighter, and for a moment they just swayed together. "Are you heading back to Chicago after the wedding?"

"Not right away. I'm housesitting while they go on their honeymoon. They didn't want to take Lucky to the kennel. He's a pretty spoiled kitten."

"I know." His chuckle rumbled against her heart. "And your brother hates cats."

"But he loves Emma."

"That he does. It was pretty fun watching those two come together."

"Or painful, depending whose point-of-view you watched from." Kelly looked up to find a wistful look on his face. She couldn't help wonder what put it there. James Harley seemed like a man who'd taken life by the horns and was in full control. That confidence was just one of the things that made him so attractive. She glanced around the dance floor and the single women who watched him. Waiting to pounce. Obviously *she* wasn't the only one who found him irresistible.

The song ended on a long note, and he slipped from her arms. Her hands fell to her sides, and a chill rushed over her from head to toe.

Odd.

He never missed an opportunity to throw a few zingers in her direction. Tonight he seemed unusually reserved. Maybe he was just worried about Alex.

"Think I'll check to see if anyone's ready for a ride home yet," he said, backing off the dance floor.

"Sure." She watched him walk toward the bachelorette party table where the other attendees were laughing and twirling the umbrellas in their drinks. Matt stood close to Kate, no doubt wanting to get her home and take advantage while the happy buzz still tickled her system. Ah, newlyweds. Kelly wondered if she'd ever know that feeling. That someone was there for you no matter what. That they would have your back in any situation. And that you could put your hands all over them any danged time you wanted.

She shuffled off the dance floor. As she got to the table, both Edna and Emma stood.

"It's getting pretty late," Emma said. "James offered to take us home. You want a ride?"

"Maybe we can even catch a 9–1–1 call on the way," ancient Edna pitched in, her weathered cheeks rosy from the Wallbangers she'd consumed.

"I'll do what I can, Mrs. Price," James said with a chuckle.

"Hell. Just throw on the lights and siren," Edna added as she lifted her monstrous purse onto her stooped shoulder. "That'd be more action than I've seen in years."

James turned to Kelly, his sensuous lips curling into a smile. "You interested?"

Oh yeah. "Sure." She leaned down and lifted the Coach demi bag from where she'd left it near her chair. James's eyes tracked her every move, and she realized she'd probably given him an eyeful of her cleavage when she'd bent over. Now *there* was the interest she was used to seeing. The sloe gin warmed in her blood, and she smiled. "Ready?"

James pulled his eyes back into his head. "Always." He placed his hand behind Edna's back. "Right this way, ladies."

Kelly happily followed. Because the only thing better than watching James Harley enter a room was watching James Harley leave a room.

Kelly never knew being in a car full of intoxicated females and one very straight and sober male could be so much fun.

While Edna and Emma tittered from the backseat, Kelly watched James maneuver all the bells and whistles of the patrol car. She had to admit he was quite impressive. Nothing like a man in uniform.

As an ever-dutiful representative of law enforcement, James assisted the wobbly-kneed Edna Price safely into her house while dodging an ankle-biting Pomeranian named Skipper. He got Emma safely home to her little bungalow and promptly called in the reinforcements. Namely Dean, who seemed only too happy to assist his fiancé in her moment of alcohol-induced giddiness.

Now, with the clear night sky above them, James rolled the patrol car to a stop in front of her father's house. He put the SUV in park, stretched his arm along the back of the seat, and looked at her. The red, yellow, and blue lights from all the gizmos on the dashboard lit up the side of his face.

"Home safe."

She smiled, trying to ignore the snaps and sizzles popping through her bloodstream. "Thank you. I really do appreciate the ride."

"My pleasure."

And if that phrase didn't set off ideas in her head, nothing ever would.

"So what are your duties for Dean and Emma's wedding?" he asked.

"I'm strictly an observer this time." She gathered her purse up off the seat next to her. "No maid-of-honor duties."

His gaze dropped to her mouth. "That's too bad."

Her gaze dropped to his mouth, too, and she wished he'd stop with all the looks and innuendo and just kiss her. She was paid to read people in the courtroom. To have her facts, read the signals, and push for the truth. There was no way she was misreading James.

So why didn't he kiss her?

"Well, you know, I pretty much sucked at it last time, so . . ." She reached for the door handle.

"I'll get that for you." He moved fast. Literally was out of the car and opening her door before she could take a deep breath. He held out his hand.

As he helped her from the car, the heat and electricity that zapped between their palms ricocheted through her heart and down between her thighs. Breathless, she came up out of the car and into his arms. "Thank you."

"I'm sure Kate thought you were a wonderful maid of honor." His big hands slid up her bare arms, and the tingles made an encore. "If you were amiss in your duties, she can always blame me."

"You?" Kelly tilted her head and looked up at him, the unusual crinkling at the corners of his eyes, the tightness in those tasty lips. "Why would she want to blame you?"

"If you remember," he gave a hesitant smile and tucked a strand of her hair behind her ear, "I distracted your attention and ended up stealing you away altogether."

He could steal her away right now.

All he had to do was ask.

Before she could breathe.

Before she could blink.

Before she could talk herself out of it, she leaned into him, wrapped her arms around his neck, and kissed him.

James's initial reaction was surprise. And for a foolish moment he just stood there letting her kiss him. When everything came together in his mind, he wrapped his arms around her and pulled her tight against him. His pleasure groaned deep within him as her soft lips brushed his mouth, and he met her slick tongue with his own. Her fingers caressed the short hair at his nape. Pressed against him, she smelled sweet and powdery. Her nipples hardened against the cotton fabric of her simple sundress and pressed into his chest.

He got hard in half a blink.

All he could think of was sliding that dress off her body and paying careful attention to all her sexy curves before he buried himself deep inside of her.

This was what he'd wanted from the moment she'd come back to Deer Lick. To hold her in his arms. To kiss her. Make love to her until the sun came up and then make love to her until the sun went down again.

She tasted delicious, and passionate, and like everything he'd ever wanted.

When a little moan bubbled from her throat, common sense gave him a good hard slap.

She was everything he'd ever wanted.

But he didn't want her like this.

Kelly opened her eyes when she realized something was wrong. She was no longer holding James, and he wasn't holding her. In fact, he'd moved completely out of arm's reach. It took her a moment to realize what had happened. When she lifted her gaze, the look on his face sent a clear message.

All the warm tingles in her body went on shutdown mode, and her brain went on red alert.

She'd just thrown herself at a man who *had* been sending her mixed signals. He hadn't kissed her because he didn't want to kiss her. Not because he just hadn't gotten the job done yet. She'd made it all up in her head.

He didn't want her.

Maybe he never had.

Maybe at Kate's wedding *she'd* been the one pursuing *him*.

Maybe he was too nice of a guy to tell her to back off.

"Oh, my god." She clapped her hand over her mouth and backed away. She turned and jogged up the pathway to the front door.

"Kelly!"

While she grappled with her purse trying to get the key out, he started up the path.

"Kelly, wait."

She would not force him to explain. It was her error, not his. She'd misread all the nice things James had said and done. She'd misread the facts on the Colson case. She'd misread the pain and sadness that had eaten away at her father's happiness. The only thing she couldn't misread was the bitter taste of humiliation and regret rising up in her throat.

"I am so sorry," she told James as her fingers found the keys at the bottom of her bag. She shoved them into the lock and disappeared into the house. Too bad she couldn't hide as easily from the shame.

She went into her room, tossed her bag on Kate's old bed,

and sat down on her own. She toed off her boots and flopped back on the mattress. The ceiling began to spin, and she squeezed her eyes shut. Tomorrow she'd have to open them and face the way the real world operated—not the one she'd fooled herself into believing.

Hot tears slipped from her eyes and slid down her temples.

Once upon a time she'd thought of herself as smart. Intuitive. Even edgy.

Everything had changed.

She didn't know who she was anymore.

Chapter Eleven

Three days later, on a gorgeous Saturday afternoon, Kelly placed an overnight bag and the carefully wrapped wedding gift for Dean and Emma—a denim quilt fashioned from her mother's old overalls—on the front seat of her mother's Buick. She couldn't believe she'd finished. Then again, she'd had plenty of time. What else could she have done with all those empty hours?

The task had given her plenty of time to reflect. Somehow while keeping her fingers from beneath the needle of the sewing machine, she'd come up with a wonky plan to move forward with her life. What she hadn't yet resolved in her mind, she'd have plenty of time to finalize while she house-sat for her brother while he was off on his honeymoon.

She'd always been a person of dogged precision in her methods. True, lately she'd gotten a little sloppy—and stupid—but she remained a believer that once you put your mind to it, you could accomplish anything.

Today she planned to put her mind to the task of keeping as far away from James Harley as possible.

No sense embarrassing him or herself any further.

She slid into the driver's seat, using her hands to straighten out the fitted summer dress she'd borrowed from Kate's charity gown shop Cindi Rella's attic. It wasn't often one had the opportunity to wear a dress previously owned by a movie or music star, but that's what her sister's shop was all about. Kate had started the place so young girls who couldn't afford to buy prom dresses could feel like princesses for a night—at the low cost of only a ten-dollar rental fee plus dry cleaning.

Kelly didn't exactly want to feel like a princess. If she could just not feel so crappy, it would be a good start.

The dress she'd chosen had once been worn by dancer/actress Julianne Hough and should help to pick up her spirits. If not, the dreamy Valentino wedges definitely would.

She hoped.

She put the Buick into reverse, backed out of the driveway, and headed toward the Clear River Lodge, where this day her big brother would marry the love of his life.

Would she ever capture that in her own life? Or would she just end up the crazy old maid aunt to her sibling's kids? The inevitable response burned like acid in her stomach.

As she made a left on the main highway and headed toward the lake, the afternoon sunshine cut a glare across the rusty brown hood of the Buick. Kelly pushed her Coach sunglasses up on her nose. The air was hot, and the air conditioner had taken a dive years ago. She had two choices, roll down the window and let the breeze blow all the curl from her hair, or sweat it out. Whoever said women didn't sweat, they perspired, was full of it. She reached for the crank window opener. She turned on the radio as she drove out of town.

While Tim McGraw liked it, loved it, and wanted more of it, she glanced up at the rearview mirror.

Would her mother show up today?

They hadn't parted on the nicest terms the last time. Then again, when had they ever? She'd tried to be the good daughter. Instead she'd become the invisible one. Not that she could really blame her mother for focusing on the youngest and oldest children. They were both far more interesting than Kelly the bookworm. Kelly the mouse. Kelly the serious one. She'd been tempted a time or two to go out and break the rules. Explode like a Fourth of July firecracker and deal with the repercussions later.

Had that been what she'd done with James the night of Kate's wedding? Just given up pretense and let go?

Man, when she screwed up, she screwed up big.

"Whatever you're thinking is a bunch of crap."

Kelly slammed her foot on the brake. "Mom! You scared the bejeebers out of me!"

"Yeah. I get that a lot."

"No warning song today?"

"Eh, I'm giving old Tom a rest. Pull the car over, will ya? We got some talking to do."

"I can't. I've got—"

"I know where you're heading. I'm going there with you."

"You are?"

"Pffft. Yes. Do you think I'm going to come back and then miss my children's weddings? I don't think so."

"You were at Kate's wedding?"

"You bet I was. Her dress was lovely although a little subdued for a woman who styled celebrities for a living, dontcha think?"

"I think she married a man who leads a more modest life, and gobs of glitter were a bit much for him. Simple elegance. Always the right choice." Kelly glanced in the mirror, even knowing she'd see nothing there. "Were you at the reception, too?"

Her mother hooted a laugh. "If you're asking if I saw you tipping the champagne a bit too much and sneaking out the door with James Harley? Nope. Didn't see a thing."

Great.

"I'm not judging you, Kelly Grace. I quit doing that when they dumped a pile of dirt on top of me. Which, by the way, thank you for the beautiful sunflowers you brought to the cemetery the other day."

"You're welcome. So . . . how does this . . ."—Kelly waved her hand through the air—"death/coming back to earth thing work?"

"Well, it's complicated."

"I can imagine."

"And as much as I would like to explain it all, that's not why I'm here."

"I know. You're here for Dean and Emma's wedding."

"Other than that."

A whisper of cool air brushed the side of Kelly's neck, and she shivered.

"I told you I'm here to help *you*."

Kelly wanted to say she didn't need any help. But any outsider could take one look at her life in the past few months and they would say differently. She'd been on the fast track to disaster.

"You've always been so careful. So diligent. So smart," her

mother said with a sigh. "You're right, I did overlook a lot. You never gave me any trouble. Not like Dean or Kate. You were the one I thought I didn't have to worry about. And look at you. You're a mess."

"I know. And if you're trying to make me cry, you're heading in the right direction."

"I'm sorry, honey."

A tissue from the box on the seat next to her flew up and landed on her lap. She clutched it between her fingers.

"The last time we talked, you showed me a different side of you," her mother said, a little closer to her ear now. "And I liked that girl. She was sassy."

"Just a façade." Kelly dabbed the moisture in the corners of her eyes.

"I don't believe that, and neither do you. You've just trained yourself to be—"

"Sister Serious?" Kelly said.

"Yeah, honey. *Sister Serious*. You want some advice?"

"I'm not sure."

"Kick that girl to the curb."

"Mom!"

"You take it from me, honey, you only get one chance at life. Do *not* screw it up."

"But, Mom, I—" The chill in the car dissipated. "Mom?" When she received no response, Kelly knew her mother had disappeared.

Must be nice to just pop in and out of places.

She put the car into drive. If *she* had the ability to do that, she could certainly have saved herself a lot of heartache.

James set the wedding gift he'd brought on the table with the others and headed toward the meadow at the Clear River Lodge. The place looked postcard-perfect. Tall pine tops contrasted with a background of bright blue sky and craggy mountain peaks. Dotted with wildflowers, the meadow spread out in a carpet of brilliant green. In the center stood the new rustic lakeside gazebo that Dean, as promised, had built for his bride. In front of that were perfect rows of white wooden chairs. Even James had to admit it was an ideal stage for a wedding.

A long table, covered by a white linen tablecloth, held flutes of champagne and pitchers of lemonade. James tugged at the knot of the tie pressing into his throat. He wasn't exactly thirsty, but he needed something to do while he searched for Kelly. They needed to talk. For three days she'd managed to avoid him like he had a terminal case of the cooties.

He accepted a glass of champagne from the server and walked out onto the newly mown lawn. He wasn't surprised to be surrounded by some elite football players, as Dean had been the star quarterback for the Houston Stallions. But even standing among the greats he watched on TV during football season took a backseat to the energy gathered inside him to see Kelly again.

He'd screwed up. And he had to set things right.

"Hey, buddy." Dean came up, grinning like an extremely happy man, and gave James the one-armed guy hug-shoulder bump thing.

"You nervous?" James asked.

"Me?" Dean waved at an elderly couple passing by. "Naw.

Not a bit. I'd have hauled Em off to Vegas the minute she said yes if I'd had my way. I'm ready to spend the rest of my life with her."

James smiled. "You two sure took the rocky road to getting here today."

Dean let out a huge laugh. "And it isn't over yet. That's one of the things I love best about Emma. She won't put up with my shit. Most of the time I'm smart enough to remember that. But I'm also smart enough to know that that kissing and making up thing is pretty fucking great."

Speaking of . . . "Where's your sister?"

"Which one? The complete lunatic? Or the one who just thinks she's crazy?"

"Kelly."

"Ah." Dean turned and looked back at the house. "Both of them are upstairs helping Em get ready. They'll be down in a few."

"Thanks."

Dean gave him the once-over with a raised brow. "Any particular reason you're asking?"

"Probably."

"Do I want to know why?"

"Nope."

Dean leaned in. "Do I need to kick your ass?"

"No need. Been doing enough of that myself."

"I feel your pain, buddy. And as long as you don't make my little sister cry I'll let you live to see another day." Dean clamped his throwing hand over James's shoulder. "Now come on over here and let me introduce you to two of the nicest guys you'll ever meet. Unless it's in the red zone."

James realized they were heading right toward two Super Bowl champs. Yet even while he shook the superstar quarterbacks' hands, he remained on alert for the evasive blonde who'd invaded his dreams and made him wish for things that could never be.

There was no doubt in his mind that he wanted Kelly Silverthorne. But there was also the truth that no woman in her right mind would ever want to tie her pony to his wagon. He was a man with way too much baggage and too many responsibilities to ever be able to give her what she needed or deserved.

And that was just a damned shame.

Kelly waited until the last possible moment to take her seat next to Edna Price in the front row. As she'd scooted down the aisle just before the wedding party, she'd caught a glimpse of James seated in the fourth row. Not that it mattered, but since he was between two men who looked like they tackled people for a living, it appeared he hadn't brought a date. Unless her name was Bubba.

He'd been easy to pick out in the crowd with his sandy-colored hair looking like he'd given it a little more consideration than his usual finger-combed style. The toffee-colored sports coat he wore blended well with his light hair and golden tan.

Kelly sighed. He looked amazing.

As soon as she realized she was staring, she jerked her gaze to the flower-adorned gazebo and made her way to her seat. No sense torturing herself over something she couldn't have.

Scratch that.

Some*one* who didn't want *her*.

Moments after she sat down, Dean made his way to the steps of the gazebo and waited for his bride. The string quartet began to play, and Kate, the maid of honor, came down the aisle on the arm of her handsome husband, who today was not the sheriff but the best man. They were a beautiful couple, and, as anyone could judge by the smiles they wore, they were also a happy couple.

A little twinge tweaked Kelly's heart.

It had taken Kate and Matt a decade to find each other again. But that didn't mean anything was possible.

The urge to turn and look at James again was a living, breathing thing inside Kelly. She fought it and lost. As she turned, the quartet began the wedding march, and everyone stood for the bride, who came down the aisle on the arm of Robert Silverthorne. Kelly smiled with pride at her father, who'd offered to escort Emma because she had no one to do the honors.

Emma beamed with radiance in the strapless A-line princess-style gown. The chiffon floated like a cloud, and the iris bouquet brought out the blue in her eyes. The adoring look on Dean's face as he watched the woman he loved come up the aisle caused everything inside Kelly to tumble and twirl.

Someday she wanted a man to look at her that way. Like he couldn't live a day without her. Like she was life and breath to him and nothing else mattered.

Dean and Emma had written special vows themselves, which interjected a sense of humor into the ceremony, and everyone laughed when Emma promised not to sack the one-time NFL superstar quarterback—unless he asked her nicely. Then laughter turned to happy tears while they smiled lovingly at each other and recited traditional vows. "Dean James Silverthorne, do you take this woman . . ."

Kelly clasped her hands together. Her big brother—the one-time *Sexiest Man Alive*—had found the woman of his dreams. Who'd have ever imagined?

What seemed like mere moments later, the joyful couple sealed their vows with a kiss. Kelly had to dab at her eyes with the tissue she'd been wise enough to tuck into her clutch.

She glanced out over the gorgeous meadow and wondered exactly from where her mother had watched the ceremony. At that moment a whisper of cool air brushed past her cheek and she knew.

With the ceremony completed, the reception began with a celebratory toast. After that, Kelly managed to make herself scarce. Not that she missed any of the activities, just that she became quite proficient at ducking and weaving whenever she saw James headed in any specific direction. She did not make eye contact if at all possible, because the single time she did those eyes of his grew dark with question. They drew her in, and she felt herself weaken until she realized that it was that same dark gaze that had misled her. Lured her to the point where she'd thrown herself at a man who wasn't interested in her in the same way that made her heart race and her blood flow through her veins like warm honey.

Once the afternoon sun dipped behind the craggy mountaintops, the dance floor came alive with twinkling white lights and tiki torches. Dean had brought in a band far more crowd-pleasing than the locals who haunted the Naughty Irish. After the bride and groom's first dance, which was just too cute for words, Kelly danced on the arm of her father to Vince Gill's *When Love Finds You*.

With his strong arms surrounding her, she felt safe. And when a cool breeze rose from nowhere and ruffled her hair, Kelly knew they were not alone.

"Daddy? Do you believe in life after death?"

He pulled his head back and looked down on her with a tentative smile. "That's an odd question, honey. What's on your mind?"

She let go a long sigh. "I don't know. Sometimes I think . . . sometimes I think I can feel Mom. You know." She lifted her shoulders and shook her head. "I know it sounds crazy, but every once in a while, I feel like if I turn around she'd be standing there."

Her father drew her in a little closer and rested his chin at the top of her head. "I feel that too."

"You do?" Kelly looked up into her father's sweet, aging face.

He nodded slowly. "Sometimes I think it's just because we don't want to let her go. Then other times, I swear I can almost smell the vanilla that lingered in her hair long after we'd left the bakery. And sometimes when I'm dozing off, I'd swear I can feel the softness of her lips press against my forehead."

"Oh, Dad."

"Do you believe, honey?" His forehead wrinkled, and the creases at the corners of his eyes deepened.

"I didn't used to. I mean, in my job I deal with so many awful situations, I've always hated to think that some of those poor people who'd lost their lives . . ." She shook her head and looked away toward the twinkling lights outlining the gazebo. Even now she didn't want to believe that life went on in another dimension and that those people, who had suffered at the hands of others, could remember every detail of how they died. But since she'd come back home and a certain somebody had hitched a ride in her old Buick, Kelly had no choice but to believe. "Yeah, Dad. I believe."

"Excuse me, sir. May I cut in?"

The deep voice coming from behind her father sent chills up Kelly's spine. She looked for an escape, but the task would be impossible without making a scene. The last thing she wanted to do was to take away from the happiness of the day. So she pulled up her big girl panties and prepared herself for a sensory overload of renewed humiliation.

James stepped from behind her father, his sport jacket and tie now gone. The long sleeves of his creamy shirt had been rolled up to his elbows. His hands were buried in his pants pockets. As her father bowed and backed away, James gave her a smile and held out his arms. "Shall we?"

She gave a quick glance around the dance floor looking for one last escape route. Nope. Outta luck. "Sure. Why not."

His arms came around her in a too-familiar way, like he'd been holding her against him all his life. Like she belonged there. She tried to put some distance between them, but someone bumped her from behind and James held on tight. She wished she didn't like being held in his arms. She really did. Just went to prove that you could have all the college degrees in the world and still not be smart enough to know what was bad for you.

James Harley?

Seriously bad.

"Nice song," he said with a tilt of his head, looking down into her eyes.

"I suppose." Beneath her hand his shoulder felt hard and strong. His chest, warm and wide, pressed into hers.

"Relax, Counselor. I'm not going to bite."

"Not worried about you biting, Deputy. Otherwise I'd have gotten a rabies shot."

He chuckled. "Have you enjoyed your brother's wedding?"

A slow sigh pushed from her lungs. "After the other night are we really going to make small talk?"

"We could start with that and work our way up."

"Or not," she said. "There's really not much to say, is there?"

"I beg to differ. There's a lot to say." Small lines creased the corners of his eyes. "In fact, how about we go over to the gazebo since there's no one there right now. We could have a nice little chat."

"Not interested." Kelly stepped from his embrace. "My line of work has made me a believer that actions speak louder than words, Deputy Harley. And I believe your actions have made your point very clear. Case closed."

Though everything inside her rebelled, she turned on her heel and calmly walked away with her head held high. Even while everything inside told her to tuck her tail and run.

Chapter Twelve

Kelly woke in a huge bed in one of the guest rooms at the Clear River Lodge to a pair of very blue eyes and twitching whiskers.

"Good morning, Lucky." She stroked her fingers across the top of his head and laughed as he turned on his motor. "How long have you been sitting on my chest waiting for me to wake up?"

"Meeeerrow."

"And you're hungry, too?" She ruffled the fur between his pointy ears. "Well, let's not keep that tummy waiting any longer." She tossed back the covers and padded to the big French doors overlooking the meadow and lake, where a fisherman in a small trawler had just cast his line. The whip of the filament glittered in the sun. What a wonderful view.

She turned to grab her silk kimono and found Lucky rolled up on the bed like a big puff of gray fur. Somehow he'd twisted himself up so he was looking at her upside down. "Untangle yourself, young man, and let's go get some chow."

The kitten sprang from the bed and trotted down the

stairs and into the kitchen. While he walked a figure-eight around her ankles, she reached for the container of cat food, then poured a splash of it into his bowl. His purr motor sputtered between bites and Kelly laughed. "You are one content little dude."

While Lucky munched his meow chow, Kelly filled the coffeemaker, tried not to think about James, and sat down with her to-do list. She'd always been a great multi-tasker, but even she had to admit she had a lot to accomplish. The first call went to the painters she, Dean, and Kate had hired to paint the inside of their father's home. Once she verified they would arrive at their scheduled time, she planned to meet them and let them into the house. Next came the call to the decorator Dean had contacted—the same person he'd previously used at the lodge house to make the masculine master bedroom more Emma-friendly. Kelly was glad their father had allowed his children to give him the makeover as a gift. It was about time. Of course, talking him out of his favorite recliner might be a colossal feat.

Though their parents had never allowed any of their children to upgrade anything they owned, when their mother had died, Kate had taken the stubborn bull by the horns and completely reinvented the Sugar Shack. Their dad had been so happy he'd cried. Kelly thought the day would never come when he'd be willing to let go of the houseful of memories he'd been surrounded with. Maybe the loneliness had finally won. Whatever the reason, once he'd announced he was ready to retire and take on some new challenges, all his children jumped at the chance to help.

The jury was still out, however, on whether Kelly would

actually take him up on his request for her and Kate to completely take over the bakery. While Kate adored her new life making cupcakes and cookies, Kelly wasn't so sure where she'd fit in or what she could add to the already successful and booming business. She truly enjoyed getting to know her hometown again, and she loved not being tied to an office or a desk. Or a courtroom. All she'd known since college was law. It was all she'd ever worked for and she wasn't sure she could be successful at anything else. However, if she could think of a way to make a difference at the bakery then she'd have her answer on whether it was the right thing to do.

Once she showered and got dressed, she gave Lucky a kiss on his soft little head and she jumped in the Buick. Today, she began clown class. As odd as that sounded to Sister Serious, she found herself far more excited than she had ever been the day she began classes at Northwestern.

On the long winding drive from the lake into Deer Lick, she didn't think about James Harley once.

Twice, yes.

James smoothed his hand down the front of his uniform shirt before he walked into his mother's house. He pasted on a smile and grabbed hold of whatever optimism he could find. He'd never been very good at juggling emotional situations. Cop business? Piece of cake. Anything that fell north of hook 'em and book 'em, he definitely needed more practice. Since he'd screwed his head on right a few years back, he'd used the slow and steady approach. But the situation with Kelly and the trouble just beyond his mother's innocent-looking front door were full-tilt, no-holds-barred gotta-be-handled-right-freaking-now.

Whether he liked it or not.

He opened the door and stepped into the living room, which registered only slightly cooler than the heat wave outside. He found his mother in her wheelchair in front of the TV, watching some afternoon talk show and worrying a tissue between her stiff fingers. When she looked up with tears in her eyes James nearly buckled at the knees. Understandably she'd made some poor choices in men. However, life had not been fair to his mother, and he'd vowed to do everything he could to make things right. Sadly, he couldn't control others, and sometimes that's exactly what he needed to do to provide her some peace of mind.

"Hey, beautiful." He knelt before her wheelchair, leaned in, and kissed her cheek. He covered her hands with his own. "How are you feeling?"

"Sad." A tear slid down her cheek. "Helpless. Angry."

"I know. And I'm going to take care of this. Okay?"

Her hands clenched, and she gave a silent nod. His heart broke in so many pieces he didn't think he'd ever find them all to put it back together again. He gave her another kiss on the cheek, stood, and headed for the bedroom at the back of the house.

Mrs. Moore, his mother's caregiver, clasped her hand over his arm as he passed. "Thank you, James. She's just been so upset. He's fine one minute, then the next he's just . . . hostile."

"I shouldn't have brought him here in the first place. I just didn't—"

"Don't blame yourself. You did the only thing you could think of, and I certainly didn't mind trying to help."

James nodded, patted her hand, and continued down the hall. He pushed open the bedroom door.

"You can't fucking knock?" Sprawled out on the bed, Alex growled without even looking to see who had entered the room.

It hadn't taken long for Alex's belligerence to reappear after his *accident*. Of course, James and anyone who knew Alex realized there had been nothing accidental about what had happened. No one would be foolish enough to believe the bullshit story Alex told. And as grateful as James had been that Alex was still alive—this time—he couldn't let him reign chaos over their mother's house like a thankless tormenter.

"Get up."

"Fuck you." His little brother's lip curled in a snarl, and James wished he could just slap it off his face. Even with his chosen profession, he'd never been a believer in violence. Not even if someone was begging for it. He'd been given a second chance, and he believed everyone else deserved one, too. Alex, unfortunately, was on number ten.

"I said get up," James repeated. "Now."

Alex glared at James then turned his attention back to the small TV on the dresser. "And if I don't? What are you going to do, kick my ass? I've got three broken ribs. Think you can add more before I take you down?"

"I've taken down bigger blow-hard know-it-alls than you'll ever be." James leaned in, letting his size—and maybe the gun strapped to his waist—do the talking. "You are no longer welcome in this house. At least not until you pull your head out of your ass and realize how much that woman in there loves you. She doesn't deserve the way you treat her."

"She doesn't give a shit about me."

Rage, hot and sharp, exploded in James's veins. He'd never wanted to smack someone so badly in his life. But that wouldn't help the situation. So he used whatever he could pull out of his hat. He'd deal with the repercussions later.

"You selfish little prick," James said in a calm voice that belied the disgust clenching his fists. "That *woman*—our *mother*—is paralyzed. She can barely speak to tell you she cares or lift her hands to hug you, but she loves you with all her heart. She took you in to give you a place to heal, but you're so ungrateful and selfish you can't even see that."

"I don't—"

"Shut up, Alex. And get your sorry selfish ass out of that bed before I yank you out. I don't give a shit if your ribs hurt. I don't give a shit if you pass out from the pain. You brought this on yourself. I don't understand why you have all this rage bottled up inside, but until I figure it out I am *not* going to let you make that woman in there miserable one second longer."

James sucked in a deep breath of air to slow the pounding in his blood. He grabbed Alex's shirt off the chair next to the bed and threw it at him.

"Fine." Alex grabbed the shirt and held it up in his fist. "But as soon as you leave, I'm gone."

"Yeah?" James leaned down and shoved his face right into his obstinate sibling's face. "Try it."

"You've got to work." Alex snarled. "How are you going to stop me?"

James gave him an evil grin. "Easy, baby brother. I got you a babysitter."

"A babysitter!" Ten shades of outrage flashed on Alex's face. "You think I can't push past some little old lady?"

James grabbed hold of Alex's arm and pulled him up and out of bed. The flinch Alex tried to hide didn't deter James from doing what he had to do. Though it didn't make the job any easier.

Tough love sucked.

"Your babysitter weighs two hundred and sixty pounds and goes by the name of *The Executioner*. Any questions?"

Mouth agape, eyes wide, Alex stood silent.

"Didn't think so. Now get your ass in the car."

The following day James ended his night shift and headed home. Life had been anything but pleasant in the Harley household since Alex had come back. But that didn't mean James would give up. Even if guilt swept over him like the breath of the devil for not staying home and dealing with the situation.

There had been no way he could have called in sick. With Stan Bradshaw on vacation and Jeremy Reinbolt off after knee surgery, the station was short-handed. And though Matt was his best friend and would most likely understand his current situation and insist he take the time off, James would never impose. Not to mention he'd need the money. Because sure as shit, Alex's hospital bill would be big enough to choke an elephant.

As a last resort, James had called in a favor from his old friend Rocky Hamilton, who just happened to be a UFC fighter. The man struck an imposing image, though he was a big pussycat with his wife and two little girls. Rocky had agreed to help, stating he could use the extra cash because both his daughters wanted a Barbie Dream House for their birthday. And they didn't want to share. According to Rocky, Barbie didn't come cheap.

Personally, James had never been into big boobs—real or fake. He liked a woman to look like a real woman, not a plastic doll. If the Hamilton girls wanted expensive toys, it only worked in his favor. There had been no way he could have left Alex alone today. At least not until he convinced the hardheaded little fool that *he* wasn't the enemy.

He parked the truck in the driveway, took a deep breath, and went into the house. As the door shut behind him, Rocky stood up from the couch and gave him a fist bump.

"You've got your work cut out for you," Rocky said with a shake of his gleaming bald head.

"What did he do?"

"Not really what he did and not what he said. But that kid has a bigger chip on his shoulder than anyone I've ever met. What the hell happened to him?"

James shrugged. "Life."

"You want some advice?"

"I'll take all I can get."

Rocky lifted a dark brow. "Talk to him."

"As you can see he's not much of a communicator."

"Hey, I've got two girls who offer conversation in the form of squeals and snarls. I get what you mean. But if you want to keep your sanity, I'd try to find out what's pushing his buttons."

"You mean other than me?"

Rocky barked out a laugh and clapped him on the shoulder. "Yep. And good luck with that."

James watched his friend stroll down the path toward his car, then he turned toward the empty living room. "Guess there's no time better than the present."

As he made his way down the hall, no sound came from Alex's room. Either the kid had snuck out the window or he was asleep. One would lead James to a wild chase. He prayed for the other. He eased open the door and found Alex lying on the bed with a book in his hands and the dogs stretched out across his lap. Even more amazing—the room was clean. Spotless. Not a single T-shirt or pair of boxers was on the floor. Looked like little bro had been busy. It was a good sign. A small one, but James would take what he could get.

"What are you reading?" he asked, surprised, because he'd never seen Alex pick up a book before.

"A book some chick gave to me."

James tilted his head and noticed a pair of hands cupping an apple on the cover. "Isn't that the vampire book?"

Alex looked up. "Yeah. I thought it would be dorky, but it's actually kind of good."

"Reading is a good use of time." James entered the room and stood beside the bed. "You got a few minutes?"

Dark brows pulled together over dark eyes. "You gonna yell at me?"

"Nope." He folded his arms across his chest. "I just thought we could have a talk."

Alex closed the book, stroked the dogs' heads then sat up with a wince.

"How are your ribs feeling?"

"Busted."

"You're young. They should heal pretty fast. Although next time you might want to choose to talk to an unattached female instead of one who has a boyfriend with a good right hook."

A staggered breath lifted Alex's shoulders. "You know that's not what happened, right?"

"I figured. You want to tell me the truth?"

"Nothing really to tell. I went looking for a fight."

"Why?"

Alex leaned back against the headboard. "Stupid, I guess."

"Stupid—which you are not—doesn't usually lead someone to pick a fight."

"Guess I'm just a problem child then."

James pulled air into his lungs. That's what he'd thought about himself years ago. "Maybe you're a child with a problem. How about we talk about that? And don't worry. You probably aren't going to shed light on anything I haven't already seen, said, or done."

With the exception of Poppy releasing a long sigh, silence hung heavy between them.

"Promise you won't laugh," Alex said, lowering his gaze to the blue plaid comforter.

James sat down on the edge of the bed. "Promise."

A long pause stretched out between them before Alex opened up. "I'm afraid. And that makes me mad. Only pussies are supposed to be afraid."

James's heart jumped, and he respected the admission for what it was. Honesty. "Are you calling me a pussy?"

"You're *never* afraid," Alex said.

"Are you kidding? There have been times in my life when I was so scared I cried like a little girl."

Alex gave a brief chuckle that died out on a long sigh.

"What are you afraid of?"

Brown eyes stared into his own, and James felt their desperation to his core.

"I'm afraid that no one wants me," Alex confided. "My father never wanted me. Mom didn't want me. And I know you didn't want me when I moved in here after mom got sick."

"That's not true, Alex. I can't answer for your father . . ." *Who was a total scumbag.* "But I can tell you that it wasn't that mom didn't want you. She loves you. But she can't even care for herself."

"I would have helped her."

"You were eleven."

"I still could have helped."

James's heart did a funny sidestep in his chest that stole his breath. Alex had never been given that option. Everyone who thought they knew what had been best for him had made the decisions for him. Alex had never been brought in on the conversation.

"You're right. We should have talked to you before we made arrangements that would affect your life," James admitted.

Alex shrugged. "Just would have been nice, you know?"

James understood. There were many situations in his past where he'd not been allowed to have a say. Not when his mother brought home a new daddy who'd hated James on sight. Not when she'd brought home a new baby brother who'd taken over his room and his life. Not when she'd put fifteen-year-old James in charge of an infant while she went looking for husband number three.

Seems he'd always been responsible for Alex. And he'd done a piss-poor job. "I'm sorry I've been such a bad brother," James said. "And I'm sorry you hate living here."

"It's not that bad. You just . . . yell all the time. That's how I know you don't want me here."

"It's not that I don't want you here, Alex. It's just . . ."

Why couldn't he just open up and say what he felt? That yes, sometimes he didn't want Alex there, but that other times he was ecstatic to have him around. That sometimes Alex could be a total pain-in-the-butt, and that his behavior brought back a slew of bad memories James would rather forget. Like the night he'd been put in charge of his colicky baby brother who wouldn't stop crying. After hours of trying to calm him down, James had lost his mind and walked out. He'd left his baby brother alone, stolen a motorcycle, and almost died.

He'd deserved to die.

He was lucky nothing had happened to Alex that night.

James knew he'd been selfish, and irresponsible, and irrational. And even though he'd been only a kid at the time, he'd never been able to forgive himself. Not even now, which is only one of the reasons it was so hard to explain things to his baby brother.

After the accident it had taken him a long time to look into Alex's young insightful eyes. Because when he looked deep enough, James saw the reflection of his own failures.

James's chest tightened and his eyes blurred. He looked away. "It's just complicated."

Nervous and questioning her sanity, Kelly opened the heavy steel door of the Grange—the epicenter of important events in beautiful downtown Deer Lick. She stepped within the century-old cinder block wall structure that exhibited Jack Wagoner's award-winning moose antlers and boasted community events—from wedding receptions to the Beefy Bros. arm-wrestling competitions and the flower-arranging contest held during the county fair.

Behind her the steel door closed with a bang, and the three women near the kitchen area turned in her direction.

"Tramp," said Elvira Schlodemer, a large woman with shocking red hair.

"Decidedly not," said Priscilla, aka Twinkie. "I say grotesque."

Well, Kelly thought, there went any chance for her to keep a speck of confidence.

The third woman, whom Kelly did not know, exclaimed, "She's a character. I'll put money on it."

Why did everyone want to bet on her? James had done the same thing, indicating he'd get her back in his bed when he knew he really had no interest. Were these women trying to scare her off as well?

"I'm sorry." Kelly backed toward the door. "I don't think I belong here."

Priscilla caught up to her and took her arm before she

could bail. "Not so fast, young lady. We weren't insulting you."

"You weren't?"

"Don't be silly. Until later." Priscilla led her to the other women, who looked quite comfortable in their spandex pants, flip-flops, and floral muumuus.

Kelly would never say it out loud, but there were some women who should never put on a pair of spandex. Present company included.

"We're talking clown types. Whenever we get new blood we always try to guess which personality type they're going to choose."

"There are different types?" Kelly asked.

"You just sit yourself down, and we'll give you a brief history and rundown. Then we can get to figuring out just who your alter ego might be.

Kelly swallowed. She'd been a lot more confident before she'd walked into the room. Now with three pairs of eyes on her, she felt like she was about to step out onto the stage again. Only this version was much different from her customary courtroom.

A cup of coffee appeared in front of her, and for several hours she listened while her new friends gave her a condensed version of Clowning 101. She learned that clowns, of a sort, existed five thousand years ago in ancient Egypt, and that the word clown did not come into use until the sixteenth century. She learned the types of clowns and the specific jobs and personalities that went together. They showed her several routines, and by the time they had taken a bow, Kelly knew exactly what type of clown she wanted to be.

The quitting time siren was about to go off as Kelly strolled through the back door of the Sugar Shack and caught Kate closing up shop.

"Hey, big sister." Kate pulled the icing-stained pink apron over her head and dumped it into the nearby laundry bin. "What's up?"

Kelly dropped the keys to the Buick and her purse onto the desk in the office and joined Kate near the display case. "Oh, nothing much. Just thought I'd drop by and see if you've given any more thought to Dad's announcement about retiring."

Kate adjusted the frilly paper doily beneath a plate of sugared lemon cookies. "Why? Have you?"

"Actually, I have."

"And?"

Kelly plopped her butt on a stool and braced the heels of her cowboy boots on the foot rest. Her cotton sundress slid up her legs, and she pushed it back down into place. "When Dad first told us, I'll admit I kind of panicked."

"Because you don't really know what you want to do with your life?"

"I thought I knew." She reached inside the display case, grabbed a cookie, and bit into it. The lemon and sugar rolled across her tongue and made her pucker.

"Hey." Kate cut her a dark glare and slid her hands to her hips.

"Put it on my tab."

"You don't have a tab."

"I do now."

Kate shook her head. "Finish what you were saying before you eat up all my profits."

"I've been practicing law since the moment I graduated from college. I followed all the rules. Got all the degrees. Passed all the tests." She bit off an edge of the cookie and chewed. "With all that schooling, all that training, how could I be such a royal screw-up?"

"Just because you lost a case doesn't mean you're a screw-up, Kel. Shit happens. Didn't anyone ever tell you that? Jesus. Our mother is dead. Yet she's still floating around in the backseat of her car because she can't bear to move on until we're all happy in our lives." Kate tossed up her hands. "Who knew that was even possible? Shit happens. Sometimes it's good shit. Sometimes it's shitty shit."

Kelly laughed and took another bite of cookie. "When did you get so brainy?"

Kate laughed, too. "Since our mother decided to freaking appear in the backseat of her piece-of-crap car. As much as it pains me to admit it, that woman is right-on with everything she says. Too bad I didn't listen years ago."

Kelly lifted a brow in surprise.

"Seriously," Kate said. "If it hadn't been for her, I would never have come back home. I would never have run into Matt again. And I would never have thought there was anything in life for me to do other than dress celebrities in expensive clothes for their frivolous affairs."

"So, you're saying if Mom speaks I should listen?"

"Mom—post funeral—convinced me to take a deep breath of life. I fought it. All I could think of was getting back to my life in L.A." She tucked a strand of hair behind her ear. "Look at me, Kel. I thought I never wanted to be in this Podunk town or this bakery again. But here I am, and I love every minute of it. I never thought I'd find the man of my dreams. Yet he was always right there, just waiting for me to come home."

"Yeah, but that's—"

"If you don't believe me, look at Dean. That man lived and breathed football from the first moment he stuck a stupid helmet on his thick skull. He loved what he did. Loved the life he lived. Mom—again, post funeral—convinced him that he was more than football and that he should take a closer look at his life. Look at him now. Have you ever seen him happier?"

Kelly shook her head and finished off the cookie. "Do you know what Mom told me?"

"I can only imagine."

"She told me to kick Sister Serious to the curb. I'm taking her up on it."

Kate sang a choir note and raised her hands. "Amen and hallelujah. Praise be to Mom."

When Kate finished laughing, Kelly said, "I want in."

"In?"

"Whoopie pies or fudge?"

Kate plopped down on a stool. "I'm not sure I follow."

"Right now I don't know if I'll be here a week, a month, or a year. I don't want to get in your way, Kate. I know how much this bakery has come to mean to you. It shows in everything you do. Even the way you redecorated it. I don't really know what the future holds for me or if you even want me here. But as long as I am here I'd like to contribute something. You've got Kate's Red Carpet Cake designs. I wanted to be able to bring something new to the table, too."

"Well good, let's talk about that. What about Chicago? What about that really important job you have putting bad guys behind bars?"

Kelly exhaled long and hard. "The truth?"

"Of course."

"I'm not sure I can go back." Kelly let go a sigh of defeat. "I'm not sure I have it in me anymore."

"It was just one case, Kel. Everybody loses once in a while."

"I don't."

"Wow." Kate's brows shot up her forehead. "Ever?"

Kelly shook her head. "Until the Colson case. Whatever I missed or didn't define or didn't state clearly . . . it was all on me. I don't know *how* Alicia Colson died, but I do know she's dead. And the man responsible is free to go on about his business, feeling bolder because he got away with it."

"Maybe he'll slip up."

"I can only hope. In the meantime, I've done some thinking." Kelly folded her hands together and squeezed until her fingers burned. "I think I've lost my drive—the desire—and what it takes to put myself back in the game. I don't know if I'm ready to go back right now. I may go back next week. I may never go back. But I do want to be right here. Right now. If you want me."

"Are you kidding? Of course I want you here." Kate stood and hugged her. "And if I had my way, you'd never go back to Chicago. I hated being halfway across the country from you and Dean. When I have kids I want them to know their aunt and uncle."

"Kids?"

"Not yet. We're still practicing." Kate smiled. "A lot."

Kelly laughed. "Okay then. So what's it going to be? Whoopie pies or fudge?"

"Duh. Fudge. What's your plan?"

"New menu items beneath the heading *I Got Fudged . . . at the Sugar Shack*. We could even make bumper stickers."

"Slightly on the racy side." Kate grinned. "I like it so far. Go on."

"Seasonal fudge like . . ." Kelly's heart pounded in anticipation. "Cookies-and-cream for summer. Ghost fudge for Halloween. Pumpkin-pie fudge for Thanksgiving. Moose-drool fudge for hunting season. I've got an entire list going."

"Kelly, that's an awesome idea. Dad will love it."

"And Dad will be able to either retire or work as much or as little as he wants because I'll be here to pick up the slack. I just have one condition."

"Now you're scaring me."

"I want a portion of the proceeds of the fudge and anything related to the fudge to go toward building a playroom at the hospital."

"That's kind of out of the blue."

"Not really. When I was with James at the hospital after Alex's accident I realized it might be a really nice thing for the kids who are there to have a special room they can go to and escape their illness for a few minutes. You know, someplace that's painted bright and cheerful with colorful things to do to take their mind off of shots and medicine and poking and prodding."

Kate wiped the moisture from beneath her eyes. "I think that's a wonderful idea. Dad will be thrilled too."

The warmth that surrounded Kelly's heart signified that

she might not know exactly where she was headed in life, but she was on the right track. "Thanks, Kate."

They shared a hug. "Just one favor. If you do decide to go back to Chicago, please give me adequate notice. I'm already up to my ears in alligators."

"Absolutely. I'll let you know." Unlike what she was doing to the prosecutor's office right now. Them she was letting hang forgotten like a burned-out string of Christmas lights. What did that say about her? Nothing she should be proud of. But it was a definite indicator that she had started to move her life in another direction. And at the end of the day, that's why she had really come home.

"When can you start?" Kate asked.

"How about tomorrow?"

"Even more perfect."

Kelly looked around the clean kitchen area. "Mind if I hang around for a while tonight and try out a couple of recipes?"

Kate went into the office, grabbed her purse, then came back in the kitchen and gave Kelly a hug. "Have at it. But don't make me come in tomorrow and clean up after you."

"Yes, mother."

Halfway out the door, keys in hand, Kate turned and laughed. "Oh, no. We've got one mother already. And believe me, having you kick Sister Serious to the curb is just the first among many things she will trick you into. But no worries. She's going to be right no matter how much you protest." The door closed with a bang behind Kate.

Kelly had a feeling her sister was dead-on, but tonight she wasn't going to think about that. Tonight she would enjoy herself. Celebrate the progress she'd made with her clown persona. She would not think about Chicago, or the Colson case. And she absolutely would *not* think about James Harley.

All her thoughts were going to be immersed in chocolate, and caramel, and cream, and all the things that made her go "Mmmmmmm."

CHAPTER THIRTEEN

It had been a hell of a day. The clock had seemed to be stuck on 9 p.m. for hours until finally his shift ended.

Hot and tired, James tossed his utility belt and semi-automatic on the passenger seat. Then he unbuttoned and un-tucked his uniform shirt, climbed up into the truck, and headed toward home.

He checked in with Rocky, who'd agreed to stay with Alex until James got home. With Rocky on the job, James decided to take the leisurely route to clear his head before he walked through the door and into adolescent-with-an-attitude territory. He and Alex had talked things over a little, but there was still so much unsaid. Mostly because James had never been good with words. He wished to God he had the gift of intellectual conversation, but there was just something wrong in his DNA that prevented him from finding the proper words for the proper situation.

He punched the buttons on the radio until he found a Blake Shelton tune to calm him down.

On top of all his normal chaos there was Kelly, who'd

managed to avoid him since the wedding. She confused the hell out of him, and she wouldn't leave his thoughts for a moment. Frustration made him grip the steering wheel like he could squeeze out all his troubles, which seemed to be mounting with every breath he inhaled.

He eyed the Naughty Irish as he passed by, wishing he could stop for a cold beer. Farther down the road he could almost hear the sizzle on the steaks cooking at the Grizzly Claw Tavern, and his stomach growled. As the nose of his truck pointed toward the center of town, he anticipated the lingering scents from the Sugar Shack's daily barrage of sweets. The bakery would have been closed for hours, but the fragrance of the breads, and muffins, and cupcakes baked there every day would float in the air above Main Street like a cloud of goodness.

He expected tonight to be no different, and he rolled down his window to capture the scent. As he cruised past the front window, he noticed lights on in the back of the shop. Since his job was to serve and protect, he swung around to the back alley to make sure nothing was amiss.

As he rolled the truck to a stop in the alley behind the bakery, the only car there was Letty Silverthorne's rusty Buick—the car Kelly had been driving around town. Perfect, now maybe he could set things straight between the two of them. Maybe then he'd be able to get some sleep tonight.

He closed the truck door, stuck his handgun in the back of his waistband, checked the back door of the bakery, and found it unlocked. He stepped just inside the building and stopped at the blast of music blaring from the radio.

Looked like the entertainment committee had already arrived.

At the front of the prep area and with her back turned, Kelly rocked out at the top of her lungs to Carrie Underwood's "Undo It."

She was a little off-key, but he couldn't care less.

His eyes traveled slowly from the heels of her worn cowboy boots, up her bare, shapely legs, to the short yellow sundress with straps as thin as spaghetti over her smooth bare shoulders.

Her skin looked tan and smooth and beneath that floaty little dress her hips swayed to the music. Right or wrong, James leaned back against the stainless sink to watch. While he watched he couldn't wipe the smile from his face. He'd never seen Kelly quite so animated. It looked good on her.

Really good.

Lust twisted in his gut, and everything inside him shifted, heated up, and expanded.

He'd never wanted a woman more in his life. Not just any woman. He wanted *her*. She was like a fantasy that wouldn't fade whether it was day or night. He might not be obsessed, but he was damned close.

The song ended way too soon, and as the music rolled into Brad Paisley's "Mud on the Tires," she did a cute little two-step then turned to grab a big bowl from the counter and froze. She gasped like she'd been caught naked. Too bad for him she hadn't been. While she squeaked with indignation, James took his time examining all the little buttons dancing down the front of her dress and wondered if later she might need a little help unbuttoning them.

He might have been heading home, but she was one hell of a good detour.

"**W**hat are you doing here?" Kelly started at James's sudden appearance.

He leaned back against the counter with one booted foot propped against the cabinet behind him. His uniform shirt was unbuttoned and hung open to reveal his taut, tanned skin and rippled stomach muscles. He was hard, and strong, and gorgeous, and she wanted to lick him up like a cherry flavored Slurpee.

"I saw the lights on," he drawled. "Thought there might be a problem."

"Well now you've seen that everything's fine." She sucked in a big gulp of air to chase away the flash of desire humming through her veins. Not so easy to do even when she knew for a fact that the man just wasn't interested in her. "So feel free to leave."

"What is your problem, Kelly?" He pushed away from the counter and came toward her, his stride slow and deliberate. "Is it my imagination that just last week *you* were kissing *me*?"

"I do *not* want to talk about that." She held onto her bowl of melted chocolate like it was some kind of protection. Although truth be told, he probably needed protection from *her*. Not vice-versa.

"Well too bad." He stopped directly in front of her, and at once she was dizzy with the warm, blatantly sexual scent that rose from his body like a welcome mat. "Sometimes we just don't get everything we want."

"No kidding."

His head tilted and he looked down at her, eyes dark with frustration. "What the hell does that mean?"

"Like it isn't obvious?" She lifted her chin in a show of pure stubbornness to camouflage her humiliation. "I threw myself at you. You pushed me away. You're not interested. You don't want me. I get it."

"I don't want you?" His dark brows shot up his forehead. "Are you out of your mind?"

"I have been a time or two, but not about this. You stopped kissing me. You pushed me away. End of story."

"So that's what you meant at Dean's wedding? That actions speak louder than words?"

"Yes."

He shoved a hand through his hair. "Jesus, Kelly. Do you even know why I pushed you away?"

"I don't think I need to know. Actions—"

"Yeah. Yeah. I got it. For your information, it wasn't because I didn't want you, Kelly. It was because I wanted you to remember."

"What are you talking about?"

He dropped his chin and shook his head. When his head came back up and his eyes met hers, something in their depths—something undefinable—changed.

"When we were together at Kate's wedding," he said, "you were drunk. But you were funny and flirty, and I've wanted you practically my whole life. When you offered yourself I took advantage and we had a hell of a great time that you seemed to forget. Then you ran and never looked back. I swore if that opportunity ever came again, I wanted you sober. I wanted you to remember who made love to you. I didn't want to be just a shadow in your memory or someone you tried to avoid. I wanted *you* to remember *me*. Is that too much to ask?"

"No, but—"

"The night I took you home from the bachelorette party you'd been drinking."

"I wasn't drunk. I think . . . you're just using that as an excuse."

"An *excuse?* Are you kidding me?" His voice raised a level. "I've lost sleep over you, Kelly. I think about you all the damned time. Even when I do sleep I'm thinking about you. I can't get you out of my head for one minute. And you think I'm making up excuses not to kiss you?" He reached for her.

His words didn't make sense. Then again, maybe she had been looking too hard to find an excuse herself. To find a reason why a man like him would ever be interested in Sister Serious.

"Wait—" She flattened her palm against his bare chest, but not before the bowl of warm chocolate flipped upside down and fell to the floor. He looked down to where the handful of chocolate she'd grabbed now dripped from her fingers and onto his bare chest. "Oops."

Sparking with disbelief, those dark eyes shot back up to her face. She let go a nervous laugh and backed away. "Sorry, I—"

"You want to play dirty, Counselor?" A corner of his sensual mouth lifted in amusement. "Count me in."

He grabbed her by the spaghetti straps and yanked her against him. He kissed her long and hard, slow and soft. His tongue caressed and attacked. He tasted wild like unrestrained passion and hungry male. When he pulled back, his breathing was unsteady. He glanced down at the chocolate that had now spread from his chest to hers, and he smiled as if he approved.

"How do *those* actions speak?" he asked.

"I—"

"Shhhh. Rhetorical question." His tongue gave a slow lick up the side of her throat. "Kiss me again," he murmured in her ear.

She didn't have time to decide. He was on her, kissing her with the taste of chocolate on his tongue, touching her everywhere with gentle, greedy hands. For several seconds she'd been stunned. When the initial surprise evaporated, she gave into the hot ache spreading through her belly. The beat of desire pulsing through her blood. She leaned into him, and the kiss became feverish. A hot tingle shot from between her legs up into her breasts. Her hands slid up through the chocolate on his chest and wrapped around his neck as he pulled her even closer. Then his big palms slid down the small of her back and cupped her bottom. He pressed his long, thick erection against her pelvis and a sound of pure need groaned deep in his chest.

"I want you, Kelly." He lifted his head and he looked down at her through eyes dark with desire. He kissed her cheeks, her ear, her mouth. "For months I've waited for you to want me back. Tell me you want me."

Her skin was flushed with need, and she became mindless to anything but wanting him deep inside her. "I do want you, James," she whispered.

"Thank god." His mouth crushed against hers as he kissed her, teased her, and drew sensation to focal points in her breasts and between her legs. Slowly, step by step, with his leg between her thighs he moved her backward until her back hit the wall. He leaned into her as his hands came up to her face, held it, and tilted it for better access while his tongue plundered and withdrew. Caressed and stroked. Teased and taunted. Then his big hands brushed the straps from her shoulders and pushed the bodice of her dress down. The fabric fell to the floor.

His tongue did a slow slide from the side of her throat down her chest to her breast. "I've waited a long time to have you like this," he said, his breath a warm whisper across her aching nipple. He flattened his tongue across the puckered flesh and gently sucked her into his mouth.

Kelly wound her fingers into his hair and held him there, sure that if he stayed for any length of time she could orgasm without him even touching her below the waist.

But he wasn't satisfied with that. He gently sucked at her nipple while his big hands slid down her body in a sensuous caress then touched her through the tiny panties.

"Mmmm." He smiled against her skin. "You're wet. I like that."

With a long moan, Kelly dropped her head back against the wall as his long fingers slipped beneath the silky fabric and he found her slick, hot flesh. He explored, stroked, and circled. Everything about him sent her into overdrive. His scent. His warmth. His heart.

She may have had alcohol in her blood when she'd made love with him before, but she remembered what James Harley felt like. And she wanted to feel. All of him. She pushed the chocolate-streaked uniform from his shoulders, and it sailed to the floor. Her hand clasped onto the tattoo circling his bicep. His head came up, his eyes dilated with passion. "Tell me what you want, Angelface."

"You. Inside me," she panted. "Now." Her hands went to his belt buckle.

"Hold on a sec." He reached behind him, pulled the semiautomatic from his waistband, and set it on the counter beside them. "Wrong kind of fireworks."

Kelly looked at the weapon, and her hands stilled. For some reason, knowing the man carried a weapon to serve and protect turned her on even more. She looked back up at him and smiled. "That puts a whole different spin on *going off*." She lowered her hand and wrapped her fingers around his erection through the khaki pants. "This is the kind I'm interested in."

He reached into his wallet and pulled out a condom. "At your service, ma'am."

No further words were necessary. No questions needed to be asked. They were going *there*, and she was in a hurry to get to their destination. While she unfastened his pants and pushed them and his boxer-briefs down his muscular thighs, he slid her panties down her legs. His long, thick penis jutted free into her palm, hard and smooth, and she rolled on the condom. The latex stretched tight as she stroked him from base to tip. He pushed himself into her grasp and she felt him grow even larger.

"I need you, Kelly." He lowered his forehead to hers. "I have to have you right now."

"Then I'm all yours."

His hands smoothed down her bottom and lifted her. She wrapped her legs around his waist, her arms around his neck. The hot head of his cock nudged her slick opening. Their flesh met and melded as he tilted his hips and thrust up inside of her. The penetration was powerful and complete, and it pushed the air from her lungs in an erotic sigh. He paused a millisecond as her body stretched and welcomed the invasion.

His fingers gripped her bottom as he slightly withdrew then plunged deeper with a slow roll of his hips. She tightened her legs and hooked the toes of her boots around him as she moved with him on each thrust and retreat. Her breasts and hardened nipples pressed into his chest, and the added friction drove her mad as his thrusts grew faster. His breathing grew harsh, and her heartbeat pounded in her head while he pushed her closer and closer to orgasm. He shifted his hips and dove in even harder. There was nothing smooth or refined in the way the intense pleasure grabbed hold and twisted her from inside out. As the tremors shook her, the fire spread in a flash across her skin and stole her breath.

His arms crushed her to him, and he swallowed her scream into his mouth. Her muscles contracted, pulled, and gripped him tight. His heart pounded against her breast. As her spasms took hold, a deep groan rumbled in his chest and beneath her hands his muscles tensed.

"Remember me." Her name rushed from his lips as he pushed into her one last time. Her arms and legs tightened around him as he let go of her with his hands and braced them against the wall beside her head. He held her against the wall with his body as it shuddered, and his knees nearly buckled. Kelly clung to him, too immersed in the hot tingles dancing through her body to worry about him dropping her.

When the sensations eased, he rested his forehead against the tattoo on his bicep until his breathing slowed. Then, still pulsating deep within her body, he pulled back to look at her. "You okay?"

Her body buzzed with the after-effects of the powerful orgasm. "I'm great."

"Me too." He slid out of her, kissed her deeply, then headed toward the bathroom. She grabbed her dress and her panties off the floor in an attempt to put herself back together. In a dress smeared with chocolate? Not so easy.

James reappeared, shirtless with pants fastened. A sudden wariness came over her. Funny how when the heat of the moment was spent, everything went back to the way things were. A little awkward. When he picked his shirt up off the floor, she expected him to give her a quick exit speech.

"Well this is a mess," he said with a chuckle, holding up the chocolate-smeared uniform shirt. Then he looked at her. "That dress isn't in much better condition.

"No. I don't suppose it is."

"Guess there's only one thing to do."

"What's that?"

He grabbed her hand and started hauling her toward the back door.

"Where are we going?"

"To bathe."

"But . . . I can't leave. Kate will kill me if she sees this mess. She warned me."

He tugged her into his arms. "If you only knew half of what your sister has done in this bakery, you wouldn't worry."

"I'm not sure I want to know."

"Then come with me now. I promise to show you some amazing things."

"What kind of amazing things?" He kissed her, and with the smile he'd just given her, Kelly knew she'd follow him anywhere. Even straight into hell. Although she may have already done that.

"By the way." He grinned. "You owe me fifty bucks."

A gasp stuck in her throat. Had that been the point of all this? To prove he could have her one more time? She opened her mouth to retaliate, and he had the perfect come back—a hot, wet kiss that knocked her silly thoughts right out of the ballpark.

He lifted his head and smoothed a strand of her hair behind her ear. "But don't worry if you don't have the cash. I've decided to take it out in trade."

Then he lowered his head again, and she realized she'd pay him more just to keep his kisses coming.

"No way." Kelly backed away from him. "You are *not* going to get me to do that. Not even with *that* smile."

The night air was warm and scented with pine. A full moon floated in the sky accompanied by a blanket of glittering stars. James stood beside the calm waters of the lake and sank his toes in the sand watching the woman he'd fantasized about for years back away from him. He didn't know how far he could push her *fun meter*. The fact remained that he wanted her to *want* to break out of that serious shell she'd locked herself behind. Still, he thought he'd try another approach to see. And since she apparently wasn't beyond making a bet . . . "You said you wanted to see my favorite swimming hole." He waved his hand toward the lake, where the moon reflected off the water like a spotlight. "This is it."

"No. *You* said you wanted me to see your favorite swimming hole. You mentioned nothing about climbing up into a tree, swinging out over the water, and letting go. That's just crazy."

"Kids do it all the time. It's fun." He folded his arms and grinned. "I think you're just chicken."

"Me?" She pointed at those pretty little buttons dancing up her dress. "Chicken? I've already gotten on your ATV *and* your motorcycle. I think that proves I'm not chicken."

"Fifty bucks says you won't do it."

She wrinkled her nose. "I already owe you fifty."

"Sweet. And since I already said I'd take it out in trade, let's make it a hundred."

She glanced behind her at the huge cottonwood and the long limb that dangled over the water with a knotted rope attached.

"All right." She exhaled a huge sigh. "You're on. I'll do it." Her sundress clung to her thighs as she started to walk toward the tree.

"Naked."

She spun around. "What?"

"That's part of the deal, Angelface. You jump naked."

She laughed. "You're crazy."

About her, maybe. "Come on. It's late. There's not a soul around for miles. Who's going to see?"

"You are."

"I'll close my eyes until I hear the splash."

"You are such a liar."

He held up two fingers. "Scouts honor."

"Were you ever actually a boy scout?"

"Not that I can recall." Again she laughed. The sound rippled through his heart and danced across his skin.

"Then it doesn't count."

"Will you do it if I jump first?"

She gave him a playful smile. "Naked?"

"I thought you'd never ask." Never one to be shy about his body, he grabbed her hand and tugged her toward the tree. When they reached the shade of the canopy, he stripped off his pants. She giggled as he stepped up onto the low overhanging branch and held out his hand. "Your turn."

"Oh, my god. I cannot believe I am doing this." The moonlight danced in her eyes as she began to undo the buttons down the front of her dress. His fingers itched to give her some help, but watching her slow, steady movements was more exciting than watching a strip tease. When her fingers reached the buttons below her small waist, she pushed the soft cotton away. His breath caught in his chest when she reached for her tiny panties and did a little hip wiggle until the strip of fabric fell to the sand.

Much to his surprise—and pleasure—she did not try to cover herself. Her body was firm. Her curves luscious. She made his mouth water.

The moonlight played over her shoulders, the peaks of her breasts, and her shapely thighs, and cast shadows on her narrow waist. If he could capture that picture in his mind forever, he'd die a happy man.

Eyes bright with trust, she looked up at him. His heart shifted into a higher gear. He'd never had a woman affect him the way she did. He wanted to hold her close and never let her go.

"Happy now?" She reached for his hand, and he pulled her up beside him.

He wrapped her in his arms and knew at that moment nothing had ever felt as amazing as holding her bare flesh against his own. Feeling her heart beating wildly against his chest.

"Now I am." He kissed her quietly. Softly. Just a gentle meeting of lips. "You ready?" he leaned his head back and asked, sensing no trepidation from her now.

In response she slid her hands up his chest and around his neck. The hardened peaks of her small, perfect breasts pressed into his flesh. Her hips pushed into his and between them his penis came to life. She gave him a bold smile. "Hmmm. Looks like *you* are."

He lowered his head and took her mouth again—more urgent this time. He reached behind her and cupped her bottom, then pressed his erection against her to relieve the ache. She lifted onto her toes so he hit just the right spot. And while her amazing mouth responded wildly to his kiss, and she clung to his neck, he grabbed hold of the rope, and together they swung out over the water like Indiana Jones and his damsel in distress.

He let go. Kelly shrieked. And they both landed feet first with a splash.

"Oh my god." Kelly came up laughing and wiping the water from her eyes. "That was amazing."

As he swam over to her, the smile on her face lifted his heart. "You want to do it again?"

While he treaded water, she wrapped her arm around his neck then reached below the water with her other hand

and cupped his testicles. "I'm ready if you are," she whispered against his mouth.

The sudden shock of the cold water may have momentarily diminished his ardor, but it was back with vehemence and he moaned. "Wrap your legs around me." She did and he maneuvered them to where he could touch the sand and not drown them both. He liked that she felt comfortable enough to at least let him know what she wanted, and when she wanted it. Because god knew he was ready for her all the time.

When he finally touched ground he wrapped her in his arms and pulled her closer. Not shy, she fed him hot, wet kisses that made everything below his waist rise up and pay attention. His blood boiled in his veins. If he had a million years he could not make love to this woman enough.

He started moving them closer to shore and the blanket he'd laid there. With his arms wrapped around her, he couldn't think. But by the desperate, reaching little moans coming from her he knew she needed more than what he could give her standing up. *He* needed more, too.

"Hold on," he moaned as they came up out of the water and made it to the edge of the blanket. Gently he laid her down and followed.

Her wet hair spread out like a fan, and chill bumps pebbled on her skin. He warmed her with his hands, his mouth, and as he moved lower down her body, he heated her with his tongue. When he finally allowed himself to sink into her, she rewarded him with a soft sigh and a long moan. He made love to her slowly and gently until he joined her in that free-fall over the edge. When their heartbeats eased he lifted his head and looked down into her amazing eyes.

Her soft fingers caressed his cheek. "How about after another swim . . . we do that again?"

James knew he needed to get home, but for the moment Alex was in good hands. And though he knew it was selfish, he'd waited so long to feel Kelly in his arms again he hated to let her go. He usually got into trouble when he let his selfish side take control, but tonight he would gladly pay the devil for just a few more minutes with this woman who made him feel like all was right with the world.

"Sounds perfect," he said. "I have plenty more amazing things I can show you."

Beneath him, with her breasts pressed against his chest and her heart beating in time with his own, she smiled. "I can hardly wait."

Neither could he.

CHAPTER FOURTEEN

In the early morning, James came back to pick up Kelly on his way to work and drop her off at the Sugar Shack, where she'd left her car. While she had wanted him to stay in the big lodge house with her, he'd explained that he needed to get home and keep an eye on Alex. Though what they had shared the night before had been new and exciting and wonderful, and she'd wanted to keep him all to herself, she admired his dedication to his little brother. Some would tag Alex Harley as a lost cause, but she knew James never would. And if she was in his size-thirteen shoes, neither would she.

She had imagined things might be awkward between them this morning, but they'd flowed as naturally as if they saw each other every morning and had scream-out-loud sex every night. He'd been sweet and attentive. He'd carried her duffel bag down the stairs and had questioned what was inside. She could only tell him it was the first step into finding her hidden talent. She couldn't reveal her plans to anyone until she was ready. Until she'd made someone smile. She was close, and she'd come far, but it wasn't time yet for everyone to know what she'd done on her summer vacation.

James had dropped her off at the Buick, kissed her once, twice, okay, maybe six times and then gone off to serve and protect the good people of Deer Lick. Kelly dumped her bags into the backseat and then went inside the Shack to snag a breakfast muffin.

When the back door closed behind her, applause erupted. Kelly looked at Kate, her dad, and Edna Price all gathered around the coffee pot.

"Bravo." Kate applauded loudly.

"What's going on?"

Edna Price's wrinkly face broke into a broad grin. "You'd have a better answer than us," she said with a wink of a rheumy hazel eye.

Kate walked over to the wall and did her best Vanna White in front of the two very large chocolate handprints at about head level. Kelly groaned. So much for keeping her private life private.

"No sense calling 9–1–1 to fingerprint the culprit."

"Oh, you are so funny, Kate."

"You're just in time." Edna filled a cup of coffee for Kelly. "We were about to celebrate."

"I'm afraid to ask what for."

They all simultaneously lifted their cups in a toast. "To the death of Sister Serious."

"May she rest in peace," her father chimed in.

"Dad!"

"Sorry, sweetheart. It's your sister's fault. I've been hanging around her too much."

Edna whooped. "Oh, come on, hon. Your sister got outed in front of the whole town when Buddy Hutchins announced her and Matt had been doin' the dirty on the floor of the bakery."

"Eew. Buddy Hutchins was watching you?"

"Could have been worse." Kate shrugged. "Could have been doing it in the back of the Buick. Know what I mean?"

"That's it." Kelly tossed her hands up. "All I came in for was a breakfast muffin. Unless you want me to autograph those chocolate handprints."

"They aren't yours to autograph, sister dear. I'll wait until James comes in for his tuna sandwich. Dad? We have a Sharpie around here somewhere, don't we?"

"Yep. Got a whole pack of them in the office next to those you-know-what shaped cake pans of yours."

Kelly shook her head. "I am so out of here." She marched to the display case and removed a cinnamon apple muffin.

Kate came up beside her. "Sorry. I know we shouldn't be making fun at your expense. I know how you feel about . . . are you laughing?"

"No." Kelly took a bite of muffin to conceal her smile.

"You are too." Kate folded her arms across her pink apron. "What's so funny? You need to spill right now, Kel, or I'm taking that muffin away."

She shoved another bite into her mouth and washed it down with a drink of coffee.

"Come on," Kate whined. "Sisters share."

"I'm not sharing."

"You have to. It's in the rules."

"What rules?"

"The *sisters tell all* rules. I told you everything about Matt."

Kelly lifted an eyebrow and sipped her coffee, enjoying every second of making Kate squirm.

"Okay, *almost* everything. Just tell me this . . . did you have fun?"

"I had fun."

"Is he as good as he looks?" The gold flecks in Kate's green eyes flashed like coins in the sun.

"Well . . . ." If Kate truly wanted her to kill off Sister Serious, there was no time like the present to bust a move. "You know how much I don't like talking about this kind of stuff."

"I know."

"But if you swear you'll keep it to yourself."

Kate drew an imaginary X across her apron. "I swear I won't tell a soul."

Kelly took a small bite of muffin and chewed to make her sister jitter with anticipation. "Promise?"

"Yes! I promise."

"Okay." Kelly leaned closer to Kate's ear. "He has a really huge— Oh, wow. Look at the time. Gotta go." She spun on the heel of her cowboy boot. "Bye, Daddy. Bye, Mrs. Price."

"Paybacks are a bitch, Kel," Kate threatened with a laugh.

Kelly gave her a little wave and pushed open the back door. For perhaps the first time in her life she didn't feel like the joke was on her. She made the joke. She owned up to the joke. She liked the joke. A lot. And there was a lot more to come.

Two hours later Kelly stood inside Twinkie the Clown's bathroom and inspected herself in the tall mirror hooked to the back of the door.

"Okay, *Sprinkles*, when you come out I want Kelly to step aside," Twinkie said from the other side of the door. "Show me the fun!"

Kelly smiled at the sound of her alter ego's name. *Sprinkles.* She liked the sound and the fact that it loosely tied into the Sugar Shack. She stood back and did a little curtsy, then she made several faces and laughed out loud at how her brightly painted eyes and dotted pink nose reacted. At Twinkie's suggestion, she'd created the flesh-tone-based look all on her own. First on paper, until the design spoke to her inner goofball, then by trial and error. Still a little creeped-out by a full clown make-up job, she'd kept hers to a minimum. More Patch Adams than Stephen King's clown from *It*. The process had taken her four tries to get perfected. Now the rainbow of accent colors came to life.

She'd taken an old pair of jeans and shredded them at the knees. Then she'd added a pair of pink cowboy boots and a red-and-white dress. The dress barely came to the tops of her thighs and was fitted at the bodice then flared out in the skirt with layers of crinoline to keep it floaty. Around her neck she'd fashioned several necklaces with carnival-colored rhinestones and jingle bells. And on top of her hair, which she'd washed, let dry into its own naturally curly style and then tucked up in a waterfall of curls, she wore a tall lavender top hat adorned with a purple ostrich feather and a big red cabbage rose.

She looked silly. And she wondered what the associates in the prosecutor's office would say if they could see her now. More importantly, she wondered what the children in the hospital she was about to visit would think.

She took a deep breath, pushed her old self aside, and let *Sprinkles* come out to play. She opened the bathroom door and jumped into the world of make-believe. Minutes later she'd received the applause and approval from her brightly costumed peers. After a little rundown on the order of things—because even as goofy as clowns appeared, they did keep things in a somewhat orderly jumble—they all jumped into Twinkie's Volkswagen and headed for Mercy Hospital.

They'd just turned onto Main Street when who should drive by in his very serious patrol car?

James looked their way and gave them a smile that melted Kelly's heart into a big lump of bubbly goo. Since she was in clown mode, he'd have no idea it was her. Playing the part of *Sprinkles* she leaned out the passenger window and melo-dramatically blew him kisses. Much to Kelly's surprise he blew one back. She captured it in the air, and as they drove away, she clutched it to her heart in a silly ba-boom-ba-boom gesture. He laughed, and she figured that was a good sign of things to come.

On the way to the hospital they practiced their routine, and Kelly hoped with all her might that James Harley's heart was just the first of many she would win over that day.

Days later James stirred the spaghetti sauce on the stove and prayed to the pasta gods for the meal to turn out edible.

He'd never attempted more than heating up a jar of Ragu in the past, so putting together a sauce from scratch was quite the accomplishment. Hopefully he wouldn't poison anyone. Sure, he could have taken the easy way out by opening a jar and saying he'd made it, but anyone with a taste bud would be able to tell it wasn't homemade.

He didn't want to disappoint Kelly.

He'd never made dinner for a woman before. He'd never been the type to go overboard to impress women or share much of his personal life with them. He'd kept them at a distance, appreciating whatever they chose to share with him, and then either he or they would move on. It wasn't that he never thought about finding the right woman and settling down. He figured that would happen at some point in his life when he'd grown bored with being alone. Being with Kelly was different. When he wasn't with her, he wanted to be. When he was with her, he wanted her to stay. He thought about her all the time.

So what was he doing?

He had a boatload of obligations, and she was in Deer Lick on a temporary basis.

He wanted more.

Was he getting too old for just a summer fling? Better yet, why would a woman like her ever choose to be with a man whose life was so cramped with responsibilities that he could barely make time for her? Or them? Or even himself?

She deserved better.

He wanted more.

Suddenly he'd become a greedy son-of-a-bitch.

For two days Rocky had been unable to watch Alex in the

evenings and James had needed to stay home. Though it was wrong for him to feel as he did, James felt like a fly trapped behind a curtain. He could see what was going on outside in the world but he couldn't taste it. And that was beyond selfish. He shouldn't be thinking so much about what *he* wanted, he should be thinking about Alex. The kid needed so damned much. He deserved more than he'd gotten. He had his whole life ahead of him. But in the same sense, James realized, so did he. Since the day he'd been laid out on that hot pavement taking his last breath, he'd come far. He'd made huge improvements on his life. But there had always been something missing.

He thought of Kelly and how she made him want to be a better person. She was an amazing woman. In fact, she had been the one to suggest she come to his house tonight. Though the night would be anything but romantic with his surly little brother wandering from room to room, James missed her. So he'd agreed—albeit a little hesitantly about throwing her to the teen wolf. She'd laughed and pointed out some of Dean and Kate's antics. She'd told him his family's quirks couldn't be any worse than her own.

He hoped she was right.

She'd even come up with an idea to both help and entertain that James had to admit was outside the box and intriguing. Unfortunately it had nothing to do with kissing or touching her.

At his feet Poppy and Princess sat like perfect little angels, waiting for him to drop just one meager tidbit. He'd already *accidentally* dropped several bites of sweet Italian sausage for them. How could he resist the look of adoration in those big brown eyes?

"That's a helluva lot of work to do for a girl," Alex grumbled.

"She's a woman, bro, not a girl."

"Yeah, well they're all trouble if you ask me."

The wooden spoon in James's hand came to a stop in the middle of the pot. He looked up at the long, lanky teen lounging on the sofa and hitting a new level on the Xbox game. "You know, I used to think like you."

"Yeah, what? Like two weeks ago?"

James heard the rumble of a car engine die in front of the house. "Did you shower today?" He turned the burner off from beneath the sauce and turned up the heat under the pot of water. The dogs gave up begging and went in the living room to perch their tiny paws on Alex's lap.

"Why?" Alex gently stroked the dogs' silky ears.

"Kelly's bringing a guest. I thought you might like to make a good impression."

"Yeah? Who's she bringing? Her grandma?"

"Actually, someone you might know. Chelsea Winkle? She's an honors student at the high school. Helps out at the Sugar Shack and Kate Ryan's prom-gown shop? Nice girl."

"I know who Chelsea is." Alex popped up off the sofa. "But why is she coming here?"

"Dinner." *And to tutor you so you can graduate high school.*

Alex glanced down at himself in a panic, then he disappeared into the hallway as a knock came at the door. The dogs scrambled and dove into their frantic yips and yaps.

"Where are you going?" James shouted.

"To take a shower."

James smiled as he wiped his hands on a towel. Nothing like a woman to light a fire under a man's ass.

The dogs continued to bark as James did one last glance around the room to make sure it still looked clean. "All right, girls, calm down." He scooted the dogs aside with his foot, held open the screen door, and smiled at the little pink sundress Kelly wore. She looked great in those flimsy little things. She looked even better in nothing. "Welcome, ladies."

Kelly came into the room and her green eyes lit up. "Wow. You cleaned up."

"Trying to make a good impression. Is it working?"

Her eyes dropped to his mouth then came back up. "Yes. And it smells great in here, too." She held up a large bowl and smiled with that luscious mouth he wanted to kiss more than he wanted to take his next breath. "I made a salad."

Trailing behind, Chelsea held up a basket of bread. "I brought French bread."

The dogs maintained their frantic barking while they simultaneously danced on their hind legs as if they couldn't figure out whether they wanted to act tough or give in to the excitement of having guests. Since their entire behinds were wagging, James estimated the latter to be winning. "Come on, girls. Give our company a break." Both dogs looked up like he was the world's biggest party pooper.

"They're fine." Kelly said. "They're just curious."

"I love dogs," Chelsea added, as she bent down to pet their heads. "I love their bandanas."

"It's the only way I can remember which one is which," James said.

"The one in pink is Princess," Kelly told her. "And the one in yellow is Poppy." She looked up at James. "Did I get it right?"

He nodded, thinking there was little she *didn't* get right.

"They're so cute." Chelsea gave them both another head rub. "I always picture guys having big bad dogs."

"Are you calling my dogs girly?"

Chelsea laughed. "Totally."

"I can live with that." James led them both into the kitchen. "I guess spaghetti really isn't summertime fare, but I don't own a grill."

"I love spaghetti." Kelly set the salad down on the kitchen table. "Even cold the day after."

"Me too," Chelsea added with a long glance around the room. "Where's Alex?"

"Taking a shower. He should be out in a minute if you want to have a seat in the living room."

"You sure you don't need any help in here?" she asked.

"I think we're good."

Kelly turned to him. "A shower?" Her delicate brows lifted. "Sounds promising."

"I can guarantee it isn't for you or me. The second I mentioned Chelsea was coming here, he jumped up and ran into the bathroom." James leaned in close and inhaled the sweet scent of her hair. "Mmmm. You smell great."

"Thanks. I showered, too."

And didn't that just put all kinds of naked thoughts through his head? James looked down to where the dogs sat at attention at Kelly's feet. "They usually don't take to newcomers that quick."

"It's my secret weapon."

His gaze dipped to the front of her sundress. He smoothed his hands down her arms and smiled. "And I give that dress my full approval."

"The secret weapon isn't my dress. And it isn't for you."

"Because I'm kind of easy, right?"

She laughed. "Kind of?"

He met her smile.

"I had to win over . . ." she pointed toward the floor and whispered, "Them. Last time I was here they wanted to bite me."

"Only because you're so tasty. What do you have hidden in that straw bag? A roast?"

"Beggin' bits. Is it okay if I give them one?"

"They may nibble off your arm if you don't."

James watched as Kelly reached into her purse and pulled out the bag of treats. Both the dog's tailless rear-ends wiggled. As Kelly knelt down, James did the total guy thing and glanced down her top.

Yeah, men were pigs. So what.

Then she began to baby talk to the normally ornery pooches and make kissy sounds and everything inside of him that was male wanted to grab hold of her, throw her down on the kitchen table, and take her. She broke off tiny bites for each dog and made them do tricks he didn't realize they even knew.

Imagine that.

He wasn't the only one she could conquer with just her hands. At that moment he became a little envious of all the attention his dogs were getting from her.

He wanted her.

Alone and naked.

Alex chose that moment to come into the room with wet hair and an unusual air of reticence. Chelsea looked up at him from the sofa and smiled. James couldn't help be amazed at the genuine smile Alex gave her just before his shoulders went back and his chin came up like he was some total badass.

James sighed. Suddenly the night ahead of them seemed like a long stretch of desert road.

Kelly sat next to James at the dinner table. She watched him study his little brother with his brows pulled together. She'd seen that look before and not just on him. It was either the wide-eyed disbelief of *"I can't believe you were dumb enough to say that"* or the *"Are you purposely trying to embarrass the crap out of me?"* grimace. Her own brother had perfected those distinct facial expressions back in the day, when he'd brought home a date and had been forced to sit at the dinner table with her and Kate. As Dean's pesky little sisters, they had felt it their duty to humiliate him as much and as often as possible. The same as Alex was doing to James now. It made Kelly feel right at home.

No question the younger Harley was a handful. But Kelly thought she saw something different in him than James perceived. While on duty, James made his arrests based on the available evidence or action. He locked them up, wrote up his report, then handed them over to the courts. On the other hand, she'd had the opportunity to sit across the table from those men and women who'd chosen crime as a profession. Who'd chosen to steal or kill or destroy their lives in numerous ways. Without conscience.

Alex Harley did not fit into that quotient.

Beyond the stubborn set of his chin, or the narrowed eyes,

or the cocky grin, he had moments of humor and even a flash or two of sweetness. He cried out for attention—for someone to see past the wall he'd erected around his emotions. Though Kelly knew James meant well, she wasn't sure he was adequately equipped to handle someone who was so much like himself. When he and Alex butted heads, it was like two alpha males battling for dominance.

Maybe she could help by adding that third and subtler point-of-view.

Maybe Chelsea Winkle tutoring Alex would help. Not just to give Alex someone to help with his school work, but to be a sounding board for his troubles. Chelsea was a good girl with a strong sense of who she was and who she wanted to be. She reminded Kelly a little of herself at that age. But Kelly honestly hoped Chelsea wouldn't take it to the extremes that she had. No one deserved to close themselves off from life that much.

Still, she didn't think Chelsea should be alone with Alex giving those tutoring lessons he now seemed so eager about. Chelsea was an adorable girl-next-door with blond hair and bright blue eyes. Alex obviously had logged many more miles on his experience meter. Not to mention he could be a smooth talker just like his big brother when he wanted to be. A chaperone would definitely be in order.

With the dinner plates cleared and Chelsea describing the volunteer work she did at the Sunny Bridge Nursing Home where Emma's grandmother lived, beneath the table James reached for Kelly's hand. His calloused thumb softly stroked her palm, and her body responded with a flush of tingles across her breasts. She watched him as he listened intently to

Chelsea speak. His eyes may have been focused on the kids across the table, but the electricity humming through his touch told Kelly where his thoughts were *really* fixated.

As his dark brows pulled together over those understanding eyes and a smile tugged at the corners of his sensuous mouth, Kelly studied him. There was a side of him that thrived on a sense of danger and adventure, and a whole other side of him that seemed weighted down with seriousness and responsibility. When he made love, he brought both sides together in an explosion of sensuality.

He tickled her palm, and she hummed a small laugh.

He turned his head, his dark eyes smiling. "What's so funny?"

"Nothing. I—"

"Can you excuse us for just a minute," he said to Chelsea and Alex as he stood and pushed away his chair with the backs of his legs. Then he pointed to Alex. "*You*, do *not* move until I come back."

Alex grinned. "Yeah, whatever."

James held his hand out to Kelly then led her to the front porch. They'd barely cleared the door when he pulled her into his arms and kissed her. She went willingly with a sigh. The kiss began with an edge of desperation then slowly changed to something soft and sweet. Within a heartbeat, she found herself wishing for things that may never be. But that didn't mean she wouldn't wish for them anyway.

James lifted his mouth from hers and looked down into her eyes with the smile that never failed to send a surge of anticipation fluttering through her stomach.

"I've been wanting to do that for two days," he said, tucking a strand of her hair behind her ear with his long fingers.

"Mmmm. I've been wanting you to do that for two days."

He glanced toward the front door. "I wish things were different. That I didn't have so many—"

"Responsibilities?"

"Yeah."

She laid her hand against the side of his face, trailed her fingers down his cheek. "No one understands that more than I do. You know in your heart you're doing the right thing."

"Sometimes the right thing isn't always easy to recognize."

Though he wasn't speaking about her, she felt the impact of his words just the same. She'd always tried to do the right thing. For everybody else. So much so that she had lost what was the right thing for herself. "And sometimes doing the right thing can be very complicated."

His gaze swept over her face. "Are you talking about Chicago?"

She nodded.

"Are you going back?" His words sounded constricted.

"I don't know." She shrugged. "I recused myself from the case I was working on before I left. They needed me back to start the jury selection, and I . . . just wasn't ready to go back. My dad wants to retire, and I promised Kate I'd help her out at the bakery until she could figure out what to do. That's what I was doing the other night when you came in. I came up with something new for the menu, and I was trying it out before—"

"It ended up all over us?" His smile brought back tingly memories.

"I'm making seasonal fudge. We're calling it *I Got Fudged . . . at the Sugar Shack.*"

"How appropriate."

She laughed.

The smile slipped from his lips, and he studied her face as though branding it in his mind.

She lifted her hand and lightly touched the lock of hair dipping over his forehead. "What?"

"Stay."

"I don't think we would be setting a good example for Alex."

"I don't mean the night. Although I want that more than just about anything." He leaned his forehead against hers and his arms surrounded her with warmth. "I mean stay here. In Deer Lick. Don't go back to Chicago."

Kelly inhaled a surprised breath.

He lowered his head and pressed his lips to hers. Once. Twice. "Stay," he said. Then he drew her in close to his heart and whispered, "With me."

With James's request still pounding in her heart, Kelly pulled the Buick into Chelsea's driveway and waited while the teen gathered up her belongings. Chelsea paused with one foot out the door and gazed through the windshield with her blond brows tipped together.

"What is it?" Kelly asked, turning down the radio.

Chelsea shifted in her seat and looked at Kelly across the darkened interior of the car. "Can I ask you something?"

"Of course."

"What do you think of Alex?"

"Alex?" Kelly inhaled a slow breath, something she'd taught herself to do to clear her mind before she approached the witness stand. "I'm probably not the most experienced person with guy stuff. You know? I've pretty much been stuck behind a desk or in a courtroom for the past—"

"But you're a lawyer. So that makes you a good judge of character. Right?"

The sincerity in Chelsea's blue eyes made Kelly realize she needed to treat the teen as an equal, not as a child. And she needed to do it with honesty. "Not necessarily."

Chelsea blew out a sigh that ruffled her blond bangs. "Woman to woman, then. What are your thoughts?"

"All right." Kelly pitied any man who thought he could pull one over on this young woman who was quickly coming into her own. "I think Alex is a complex person. I think the world sees exactly what he wants them to see." *Just like his big brother.* "I think he pushes the envelope because he needs attention. But I think deep down inside that churlish devil-may-care exterior lays the heart and soul of a really good guy. I just think it may take a pickax to find him."

Chelsea scooted to the edge of the seat. "I kissed him."

"What?"

"When you and James went outside. I leaned over and just . . . kissed him."

"On the cheek?" *Please say yes.*

"His mouth."

"Oh." Kelly's stomach tumbled. She and James were outside only a few minutes. Still . . . "What did he do?"

"Well, he didn't kiss me back, I can tell you that."

"He didn't?"

Chelsea shook her head. "He smiled though. He smiled the whole time he was telling me what a nice girl I am and that he wouldn't ever want to do anything to get me into trouble."

Wow. Go Alex. "He did?" Kelly gave Chelsea a sympathetic pat on the shoulder. "Do you understand what he was saying?"

"That he's not interested."

"I'd say he's very interested."

Chelsea's eyes grew as big as MoonPies. "Really?"

"Really."

"Then why wouldn't he kiss me back?"

"Because he obviously respects you. And I think he knows that if you had anything to do with him people might not look at you in such a favorable way."

"I don't care about that."

"This is a really small town." Kelly reached out and took Chelsea's hand. "Everybody knows everything about everyone. And they all have an opinion. My sister Kate had a lot to live down because of the way she left here ten years ago. So maybe Alex is right."

"But I really like him."

"Then give him a chance to figure out who he really is. I think once he does, he's going to be exactly the kind of man you want."

A broad smile filled Chelsea's All-American face. "I can wait for that."

"Good." Kelly wrinkled her nose. "Then how about you go on about your life? Your plans. If things are meant to be, it will happen. Look at Matt and Kate. They found each other after ten long years apart."

"Yeah." Chelsea laughed. "Those two are crazy about each other."

"They were meant to be."

With an exuberant hug, Chelsea said, "Thank you. You're a really good friend."

Kelly hugged her back. She waved as Chelsea shut the car door and ran up onto her front porch. She waited until the girl was safely inside the house before she put the Buick in reverse and backed out of the driveway. Then she turned the radio back up and sang along with Taylor Swift's "Our Song."

Half a mile down the road, Tom Jones took over the airwaves and a nuclear glow and blast of cold air radiated from the backseat.

"Bravo, daughter."

"Hey, Mom." Wow. How oddly casual did that sound for someone talking to a ghost? "Where've you been?"

"In the doghouse."

"Why?"

"Apparently you're not supposed to just come and go as you please. They've got *rules*."

Kelly looked up into the rearview mirror. "Seriously?"

"I just got out of trouble and now I'm back in again."

"Mom. That is so unlike you."

"Right." Her mother chuckled. "But I took a risk that I wouldn't get the feathers plucked from my wings to come see you."

"You've got wings?" Kelly pulled to the curb, slammed on the brakes, and turned around. "Where?"

"Figure of speech." A smile tilted her mother's lips.

"Oh." Darn it. Kelly really wanted to see some wings.

"I heard the advice you were giving our young Chelsea. Such a nice girl. And I just wanted to tell you how impressed I am."

"What was I supposed to tell her? That Alex Harley could be the next *Night Stalker* so she better keep her distance?"

"It wasn't necessarily what you told her, darling daughter. It was your insight on young Alex Harley."

Kelly sighed. "I don't think he's misunderstood. I just think—"

"He's a lost boy?"

"Yeah."

"Just like James."

"James is hardly a boy, Mom."

"Indeed. He's grown to be quite the man. But he's lost all the same." Her mother's sigh whispered through the interior of the car. "Kind of like you."

Though Kelly hated to admit it, lost was exactly how she'd felt for a long time. The only time she didn't feel lost was when she was wrapped in James's arms.

"Maybe you two can find each other," her mother said. "Maybe you were meant to be just like Kate and Matt or Dean and Emma."

Meant to be. Kelly's heart gave a hard thump against her ribs. He'd said he wanted her to stay. With him. That certainly changed things, didn't it?

"Sometimes," her mother continued, "when you dole out the advice, you've got to be willing to heed it as well. And sometimes you might just think that if you have an understanding heart and a willing ear, you may be in the wrong business."

"Gee, that's hardly cryptic at all."

Her mother hooted a laugh. "Well, if I just sat you down like I did when you were a kid, you probably wouldn't listen to me. Being that I ignored you and all."

"I'm sorry I said that."

"You were just being honest. And that's okay. But think about what I said, would you? And by the way, congratulations on kicking Sister Serious to the curb."

Whoa. "Mom! How much do you follow us around?"

"I was talking about your alter ego, *Sprinkles.*"

Whew! "Oh. Thanks. It was pretty fun entertaining the children the other day."

"You did good. Love the purple hat." Her mother's gaze rolled skyward. "Oops. Gotta go."

"When will you be back?"

"Don't know with the doghouse thing and all. In the meantime . . . clean those chocolate handprints off the bakery wall, will ya?" In an instant her glow fizzled to a spark and Kelly found herself staring at an empty seat.

Crap.

Kelly turned around and shoved the gearshift into Drive. It was hell living in a small town where secrets weren't safe. Even from the dead.

CHAPTER FIFTEEN

A loud noise jarred Kelly awake. She sat up and shifted the clock radio on the nightstand by the bed.

Two o'clock.

A surge of panic raced through her heart. Had something happened to someone? She grabbed her cell phone and looked to see if she'd missed a call or a text, but there were no messages.

At her feet, Lucky, her brother's kitten, opened one blue eye as if to say, *"Lie down and go back to sleep, dummy."* When the noise happened again, Kelly recognized it as a knock on the front door. Apologizing to the cat, she rolled out of bed and threw on a silk kimono over her sleep shorts and tank top. She ran down the stairs and reached the door just as another knock echoed through the large house. On tip-toe she peeked through the peephole and was surprised to see a shiny deputy's badge winking back.

She unlatched the deadbolt and opened the door. "James. What are—"

Her words ended as he dragged her into his arms and

claimed her with a hot, urgent kiss. He tasted sweet like peppermint, intoxicating like wine. Their breaths mingled as he slid his hands through her hair and cupped her head. The kiss turned into a wild feeding of need and greed. Their tongues mated and danced. The rhythm of the kiss flowed into their bodies. Her pulse throbbed in her throat as she melted into his body and wrapped her arms around his neck.

Breathless, he murmured, "I missed you," and a thrill shot up her spine.

He kicked the door closed behind them and backed her into the living room. The backs of her thighs met with the arm of the leather sofa. Then his eager hands were everywhere, touching her, feeling her, exciting her. He pushed the kimono from her shoulders while her fingers fumbled to unbutton his uniform shirt. She pushed the khaki off his broad shoulders and spread her hands across the light golden hair on his chest. God, she wanted to lick him all over, taste the saltiness of his skin. But he was on a mission, and she was happily along for the tour.

His tongue swept her mouth as he caught his thumbs in the elastic of her sleep shorts and yanked them down her legs. She kicked them free. The tension and anticipation inside her pulled in every direction until she was mindless with need. Oblivious to anything except him, his warm scent and tight, hard body.

He eased the pressure on their mouths and lowered his head to her breast. Through the thin cotton he gently sucked her nipple into his mouth. Her body reacted with an intense flash of need. She speared her fingers through his hair and tightened her hold when the suction of his mouth on her breast became almost too stimulating to bear. His hand moved between their bodies, and he touched her between her legs. Slid his fingers into her slickened flesh and gently stroked her. A moan rumbled from her throat.

He lifted his head as his fingers propelled her toward utter madness. "I've been thinking about touching you all night. Wanting you," he whispered, his voice husky with desire. His tongue swept across her bottom lip and a hot shudder rippled from her heart to her core. "Do you want me?"

"Yes," she said on a long sigh. "I want you." She reached for his belt, unbuckled it, and unzipped his pants. She pushed them down his long powerful legs, then she reached inside his boxer briefs and wrapped her hand around his thick erection. In her palm he throbbed and the breath pushed from his lungs. A deep groan rumbled from his chest, and his long fingers swept down to hold her hair back away from her face.

For a few moments, she was the master of his sighs, and moans, and shivers. But then he slid the little tank top from her body, and laid her back on the sofa. The leather was cool on her spine as she watched him roll on the condom he'd removed from his pocket. She wanted that ridge of male heat inside her so badly she could barely think. He smiled as if he could read her mind, and he followed her down. His warm skin pressed against the length of her. She wrapped him in her arms and legs, and he entered her with slow, sweet possession until he completely filled her.

Urgency aside, he took his time making love to her. Between each controlled push of his hips, his unhurried, deliberate kisses seduced. His hot mouth and tongue teased her breasts. She arched against him. He held himself in check until she felt the slow, steady pressure build inside her and the tingles start up from her toes. She moaned and his thrusts became faster. Harder. Pushing her. Absorbing her.

"Take me with you, Angelface," he whispered against her hair. "You're everything to me."

Her fingers slid down his back and bit into the flesh of his tight buttocks. He slid his hands beneath her butt and lifted her. He thrust hard and her breath left her body as intense white-hot pleasure washed over her skin, grabbed her, and turned her inside out. Wave after wave of decadent release rolled through her. Her muscles contracted and gripped him tight in her heat. He gave one final stroke, and a long, deep groan rumbled from his chest. Beneath her fingers, his body shuddered and turned hard as granite. His heartbeat pounded against her ribs. As she floated back down to earth, she held him in her arms.

He shifted his weight, and she turned her head slightly to look at the shining object on the floor that caught her eye. His deputy star.

Something deep in her heart reached out and grabbed hold of that which she had always imagined impossible.

Love.

Like a foolish girl, she looked at that star and wished she could stay right there in his arms forever.

James woke to a room full of bright sunlight and the sensation of soft kisses trailing down his spine. He rolled to his back, pulled Kelly into his arms, and tucked her head against his shoulder. He liked having her there, soft and warm against him. He knew eventually she'd go back to Chicago. When she did, he would miss her. The loss of her would steal his breath. He'd never felt this way about a woman before—one moment fierce with longing and desperation, the next content and optimistic. If he wasn't careful he'd very likely fall in love with her.

And that would be a mistake.

For both of them.

"I like your tattoo," she said, smiling up at him.

He chuckled. "It helps cover the scar. And I figured since I almost died, I deserved a pair of wings."

"Mmmm, and nice wings they are." She laid her hand on his chest and ran her fingers through the fine hair in a slow, hypnotic motion. "And as much as I love that you showed up at my door last night, I have to ask why you were out in uniform? You didn't tell me you had to work."

"Mac Gibbons's wife went into labor. He called and asked if I could cover the end of his shift for him."

"Well, that was nice of you."

"Nah." He glided his hand down her smooth back. "He would have done it for me."

"What about Alex?"

"Got him a babysitter."

"He's almost eighteen. Isn't he old enough to stay by himself?"

"Yeah. And he was sound asleep when I left. But these days I just . . ." *Don't trust him.*

"You don't owe me an explanation," she said.

"I know." He covered her hand with his own. "And believe me, I'd love to share but . . ."

"You do know its okay to lean on someone else once in a while, right? You don't have to do it all alone."

That would be nice. But he'd been handling things by himself for so long he wouldn't even know how to lean.

She kissed him. Just a soft press of her lips that meant everything to him. *She* meant everything.

"Lean on me," she said.

He knew she meant it. He just didn't know if it was possible. He trusted her, but Alex wasn't her problem. She had enough going on in her life. She didn't need his pile of shit, too.

"Thank you," he told her. "It's just that everything with Alex is so complicated, it's hard to explain."

"I get what you mean. Some things are just difficult." She nodded and her silky hair slid lusciously against his skin. "Like the deal with my mom popping up all over the place."

"Your *mom?*" He lifted his head. "What do you mean?"

Her eyes widened as if she'd spilled a big secret and gotten caught.

"I meant to say the *memories* of my mom."

Her explanation was believable, but the hitch in her voice said there was more. "Is there something you want to tell me?"

She blinked. "No."

"You sure?"

"Of course."

"Because I'd understand."

Blink. "Nothing to understand."

"You sure?"

"You already said that."

"I know. It's just that Matt says once in a while he catches Kate talking to your mom."

Blink. Blink. "He does?"

And why didn't she sound surprised at that? He had a feeling all the blinking she was doing was a cover up for when she fibbed. He'd have to make a note of that.

"Mmm hmmm. He said before they got married she'd go out and sit in the Buick and he'd see her talking like she was having a conversation."

"Well, Kate's kind of odd like that."

He laughed. "Kate is a lot of things, but I'm not sure odd is one of them." He smoothed his hand over her shoulder. Matt hadn't been the only one to mention seeing their better half sitting in the Buick talking to *no one*. Emma had mentioned it about Dean as well. So either their family had taken a stroll down Cuckoo Lane or something *otherworldly* was going on.

He'd never mentioned his beliefs regarding life-after-death to anyone before, but he had some strong opinions. When he'd been laid out on that pavement more dead than alive, he'd had an experience that pretty much made him a believer. One he was sure he could sell to the *National Enquirer* if he felt the need to become Fruitcake of the Year.

"You know you can talk to me if you need to."

"No." She looked up at him while her top teeth worried her bottom lip. Blink. "I'm okay."

A wave of protectiveness washed over him, and he kissed the top of her head. He'd protect her. Just as he'd protect Alex, or his mom, or even those silly little dogs he'd come to love so much. After all, he'd been brought back to life for a reason. Watching over those he loved must be it.

Loved?

His gaze swept over the woman in his arms, and his heart

went all crazy in his chest. He knew it was too much to ask, but was it so wrong to just want someone really special in his life? Someone who knew his past and didn't care? Someone who knew all his burdens and was willing to share the load? Someone who would just love him for who he was? Faults and all?

"I'm here if you need me," he said.

Kelly looked up at him with her big green eyes and settled her warm hand over his heart. Then, as if she'd read his mind, she said, "And *I'm* here if you need *me*."

Darned if his heart didn't start going all crazy again.

Scrambled eggs had never tasted so good. It didn't matter that they were a bit overcooked because her attention had been deliciously distracted while she stirred the mix in the pan, or that she'd over-salted them. Kelly had this amazing hum vibrating through her body as she sat at her brother's kitchen table across from James, sharing breakfast and coffee as if it was the most normal thing in the world. She was sure he'd shared many a morning-after meal with his *dates*. But it was new for her. In fact, it was a first.

She could imagine sitting across the table from him every morning. Sharing in the every day events that made up couples' lives. Snuggling together at night and holding each other until another day rolled around. She could picture holidays and picnics and such simple pleasures as cozying up on the sofa to watch a movie.

She could picture just being with him. Period.

She sipped her coffee and gazed out the window to the spectacular view of the vibrant meadow and the glimmering lake. The sky was a cloudless blue. Typical for a Montana summer. He was right, it was easy to forget the beauty of nature. Especially when you were knee-deep in concrete and chaos.

The touch of a warm hand on her cheek broke her thoughts.

"I'd offer you a penny, but those look like more expensive thoughts."

Kelly shifted her gaze to James, an equally amazing sight with his hair tousled from making love, and his chest bare and tan. Her gaze slipped down his broad shoulder to his muscled bicep. Mmmm. She did love that tattoo. It said something about the man he was—a bit wild, yet steeped in tradition.

"I was just thinking how amazing it would be to wake up and look at this beautiful view every morning."

"Definitely beautiful." He was looking at her when he said it.

"I'm talking about the scenery."

"I am, too." He chuckled as he speared his eggs with the fork. "Oh. *That* scenery. Don't forget all that will turn into snow and ice."

She rested her chin on her fist. "I know. But there's a beauty in that, too. And hey, aren't you the one who's been selling how beautiful this area is?"

"Absolutely." He stretched his long arm across the table and covered her hand with his, stroking his thumb over the top. "I'd love to show you the area from a snowmobile."

She shuddered. "Sounds cold."

He gave her a slow, sexy smile. "I know a great way to warm up."

She laughed, then stood and reached for his empty plate. He caught her wrist, and she ended up on his lap. He slid his hand into her hair and brought her mouth down to his for a kiss.

"Don't you have to go to work?" she murmured against his lips.

"I've got time." He kissed her again. "I've always got time. For *you*."

True to his word, he gave her time. And a lot more.

Mid-day, the parking lot at Mercy Hospital bustled with cars. Whether they belonged to staff or those visiting patients, Kelly didn't know. She only thought of the smiles she and the clown group had brought the other day to those inside. This morning after James had gone to work she was filled with energy. She thought of going for a run. Or going in to the bakery. But something bigger called to her, and she'd ended up here.

She parked the Buick in the last row and looked in the rearview mirror to check her makeup. She raised her accented eyebrows. Wiggled her pink dotted nose. Grinned with her kewpie-doll smile. She gave a tap to the brim of her purple top hat and checked the position of the big red rose perched near the orange satin band. She gave her bell necklace a jingle and laughed.

Everything looked in place.

All she needed now was for Sprinkles to appear.

Kelly inhaled a slow, steady breath. She closed her eyes and channeled her alter ego—her hidden talent. Since she'd made love in a bakery and jumped into a lake naked, conjuring up her silly side wasn't as difficult now as the first time she'd tried.

Laughter was the name of the game. And if she couldn't laugh at herself, no one else could either.

Inside the hospital, she was greeted enthusiastically by the staff and those in the waiting room, where she paused to give a toddler a tweak on the nose and a balloon dog. Okay, so maybe thus far she'd only become proficient at balloon canines, but by the end of summer she intended to graduate to giraffes and mice, too. A happy goal that, at the moment, seemed far superior to sticking her nose back into stacks of folders and files and dealing with mean people. She liked who she'd become in the past weeks, and she was excited to discover even more about herself.

Today the possibilities seemed endless.

With a little hop and a skip, she made her way toward the second floor, where the younger patients were clustered. She paid a visit to Andrea, an eight year old with an antibiotic-resistant skin infection. Then she discovered a little boy named Donovan, who had a nasty upper-respiratory infection. While she made her rounds, she even took time to read get well cards to a few in the senior citizen crowd. Finally she came upon the little girl with golden curls and a bright smile she'd met the other night.

Charity was her name. And Kelly's heart broke when she found out just how sick this angel of a girl really was. Today Charity was awake and ready for company. So Kelly, sans the rest of the clown clan, knew she had to put on a really big show all by herself. Her first solo act.

She gave the parents sitting bedside a smile as she danced her way into the room, did a few simple tricks with scarves and a big yellow daisy. Her reward? A big two-front-teeth-missing smile. As Kelly wrapped up her rookie routine, Charity crooked her tiny finger. Kelly went to the bedside.

Charity crooked her finger again. "Closer," she whispered.

Kelly leaned down close, as if Charity wanted to tell her a secret.

"I love you, Sprinkles." Charity placed a sweet little kiss on Kelly's cheek. At the same time Kelly fought back tears, her heart burst with a mix of happy and sad. In that ripple of emotion, Kelly realized things about herself she'd never paid attention to before. Somehow she always managed to find strength when she seemed at her weakest moments. She found love and forgiveness in a heart she thought had grown dark and cold. She found a hidden talent that she'd never have known she possessed if one man hadn't suggested she look for it. And she found that giving someone hope was perhaps the most powerful gift she could share.

She'd never have found any of these things had she not come back home.

"Will you read me a story?" Charity asked, giving the mattress a pat with her small hand.

Kelly glanced at the parents, who gave her a nod. Then she looked down at the numerous tubes and IVs, worrying about where she could sit without dislodging something vital.

"It's okay, Sprinkles. They don't hurt." Charity handed her a book. "This is my favorite."

"*Where the Wild Things Are*," Kelly said in her Sprinkles voice. "It's my favorite, too." She proceeded to read about

King Max, while Charity listened intently. Kelly imagined she'd heard this story many times, but judging by her rapt attention, it was indeed a very special story. When she finished the very last page, she closed the book and noticed that Charity's big blue eyes were looking rather sleepy. Best she make an exit so the little girl could get some rest. But when she moved to rise from her place on the mattress, Charity touched her hand.

"Do you know why I like that story?"

Kelly shook her head. "Tell me."

"Because Max tames the wild things, and then he gets to go home. That's what I want to do, Sprinkles. I want to go home."

Kelly looked to the parents, who seemed to be fighting for the courage not to cry. The father gave Kelly an almost invisible shrug.

They didn't know if their beautiful little girl would ever come home.

Kelly inhaled a steadying breath, and she fought for courage much harder than she'd ever fought in any courtroom. She needed to find the strength not to break down and cry for this tiny little girl who wanted something so simple.

To go home.

"Soon, little one." She gently brushed the curls away from Charity's forehead. "Soon."

"Will you hold my hand until I fall asleep?"

Kelly took Charity's small hand in her own and lightly stroked her chilled little fingers. "Absotively."

Charity smiled and closed her eyes. "Come back tomorrow?"

Kelly kissed the tiny fingers. "Absotively."

She didn't move until she was certain that Charity was asleep, then she gently untwined their fingers.

The mother, an attractive woman not much older than Kelly herself, followed her out into the hallway. She reached for Kelly's hand and held it. Her hand trembled. "I don't know how to thank you for coming here today."

"I hope I helped brighten her day just a little."

The mother nodded. "Six months ago, she was happy and healthy. Today, we don't know . . ."

Kelly couldn't help herself; she gathered Charity's mother in a hug. "If there's ever anything I can do, just call the Sugar Shack and I'll be right here."

As they parted and Kelly walked down the hall toward the elevator, her steps were a little slower and a lot less silly. This would take some getting used to, if that was even possible. At the end of the day, she knew she was exactly where she was supposed to be at exactly the right time.

All it had taken was the simple request from one gorgeous man with a huge heart to challenge her to make others smile.

Without even trying, James Harley had made her a better person than she could have ever imagined. She knew he struggled with demons of his own. She just hoped somehow she could return the favor.

A hot breeze blew off the mountaintops as Kelly strolled toward the Buick at the back of the parking lot. If anyone saw a clown driving her mother's car she'd have some explaining to do, and she wasn't quite ready to let the world in on her little secret. She was just discovering who she was deep inside, beyond the Brooks Brothers suit and the thick lawyer's skin. And maybe, just maybe beyond the exterior that had taken years to form, she was really just a big soft marshmallow.

She opened the door and slid onto the seat. Instead of shoving the keys in the ignition, she sat there for a moment and gathered her thoughts. So much had come to light in such a short time. She felt things she'd never felt before. Things that made her smile. Things that made her heart hurt. And things that made her hopeful beyond reason.

She fanned herself with her jingle beads then leaned forward and turned the key in the ignition. She cranked up the air conditioner that no longer worked, just so she could try to imagine herself in cool air, and reached for the volume knob on the radio.

"*It's not unusual . . .*"

"Oh, Tom, don't you have somewhere else to sing?"

"He does, but he likes it here with you."

Kelly laughed. "Mom? I could really use a little of that cold air you bring with you."

"Oh. Sorry. Here you go."

Though Kelly couldn't see her mother, she totally felt the rush of icy air lift from the backseat and swirl through the interior of the car. "Ahhhhhh." She leaned her head back on the headrest. "Thanks."

"You really did do a tremendous job on that outfit."

"Kate would probably say I need silver platform Louboutins instead of the pink boots."

"Nonsense. Kate doesn't know what she's talking about

anymore. Have you seen what she wears now? Tennis shoes and jeans. Every day."

Kelly chuckled. "I've even seen her in a pair of stretch pants and a stained T-shirt."

"Better alert the media."

They both chuckled.

"She's going to be all right, just so you know."

"Kate? Yeah. She's really happy. That's all that matters."

"Not Kate, honey. Though she's going to be just fine, too. I meant the little girl you just visited."

Kelly swung around in her seat. "Charity?"

"The one with all those golden curls."

"Yes. That's her. How do you know?" She couldn't see her mother, but she could feel her energy, and that's where Kelly focused her gaze.

"I may get into the doghouse once in a while, but I know who to sweeten up when I need something."

"Isn't that against the rules?"

"Of course." Her mother tsked. "You'd think they'd cut you some slack after . . . you know. But noooooo."

"So really? Charity is going to be okay?"

"She's got a bit of a rough road ahead, but she's going to make it."

Kelly felt a rush of relief push from her lungs. "Oh. I am so glad to hear that."

"You did a great job in there, daughter."

"Thanks. I really don't know what I'm doing yet. I probably should have waited for the rest of the clowns, but I just had this energy racing around inside me, and I needed to come here."

"As long as you follow your heart, you're going to do just fine."

"I haven't done such a good job so far."

"You've done an amazing job. Sometimes when your path in life takes a different direction, the best thing you can do is just hang on for the ride."

Kelly felt a whisper of cool air brush past her cheek.

"Your daddy and I have always been very proud of you."

"You have?"

"Always. But we would have been just as proud if you'd decided to push the cash register keys at the Gas and Grub. You're our daughter."

Kelly felt a little hum in her heart. "It's really nice, you know? To be able to talk with you like this."

"Now that I think on it," her mother said, "We really never did do much talking when you were younger."

"I tried." Kelly sighed. "And I gave up."

"I'm sorry about that. I really didn't know. I was—"

"Too busy," Kelly said.

"Yeah."

"I'm going to vow that if I ever have kids I'm going to treat them all equal."

"No, you won't," her mother said. "But you will love them all equal. Everyone is different, honey. You can't treat one child the same as another, anymore than you could have prepared for one court case against another. Everyone is unique. Kate? She was a handful from the moment she took her first bawling breath. She was always getting into something. Always pushing my buttons farther than they needed to go. I could control it when she was little, but then she grew up and got her own opinion. We were too much alike, I think."

"Seriously?" Kelly laughed. "You *think?*"

"Now your brother, he caused us even more worry. But he was so darned charming he could talk his way out of a one-way trip to trouble."

"He still can."

"Yeah, but Emma's on to him. She's a smart cookie. I think his BS-ing days are over." Her mother sighed. "And you . . ."

Kelly didn't know if she wanted to hear what her parents had thought about her.

"You were quiet. You never got into any trouble. Straight A's and no backtalk. Unfortunately, you were so easy to raise we often took that for granted."

"So you're saying I should have been more of a rebel?"

"Oh, honey, no. You are perfect just the way you are."

Kelly's throat tightened. "I'm far from it."

"If you're still talking about that murder case, let it go. They don't come up with phrases like *What goes around comes around* for nothing."

"Does that mean Andrew Colson will get what he deserves?"

"Well, I can't tell you the details. But I do believe when Karma bites him in the ass, she's going to have the teeth of a piranha. Now . . ."

A cool gust of air spun around the front seat of the car.

"Put this jalopy in gear," her mother said, "and go have yourself some fun."

Kelly had never been one to wish ill-will on anyone, but sometimes things changed. Right now she didn't have time to focus on anything except meeting James at the lodge house after he got off work.

Maybe she'd meet him at the door in something skimpy.

Or maybe nothing at all.

"I'm really sorry about this." James shoved his hands in the pockets of his uniform pants as he stood in the entryway of Dean Silverthorne's grandiose home apologizing to the woman who'd stolen his heart. He'd known better than to let it happen, but he hadn't been able to stop it. Situations like the one that had popped up in the past half-hour were the perfect reason he needed to stay unattached. His life was just too fucked-up. What woman in her right mind would want to be a part of constant chaos?

The tiny little shorts and midriff top she wore weren't making it any easier. All he really wanted to do was touch every part of her luscious body and make love to her until they were both blind. Not go run all over town and hunt down his missing little brother.

"Don't apologize," Kelly said through those full lips that always tasted as sweet as honey. "I completely understand."

Her hand came up and stroked his cheek, and he could tell by the look in those amazing eyes of hers that she really did understand. But that still didn't make it any better.

"When did he go missing?" she asked.

"Rocky called me about half an hour ago."

"You shouldn't have come all the way out here just to tell me."

"Maybe." His chest tightened. "I just needed to see you."

She smiled. Rose up to her toes and gave him a quick kiss. "I know you're in a hurry, but can you wait here for just a minute?"

"Sure."

"I'll be right back." She turned and jogged up the stairs.

In his mind—which seemed to be focused on her day and night—Kelly Silverthorne was breathtaking to watch coming toward him. Watching her walk away completely stole his breath.

He heard her shuffling around upstairs in the guest room she'd been using while housesitting, and then he heard a door close. Before he could catch his breath, she was back, in a pair of jeans and a simple cotton shirt.

"Okay, let's go," she said, tucking the strap of her shiny pink purse over her shoulder.

"Where are you going?"

"With you."

"Why?"

One small hand slid to her curvy hip. "You know why."

"Uh-uh." Even while his heart flipped upside down he slowly shook his head. "Tell me."

For a moment she hesitated. Then she stepped forward and wrapped her arms around his neck. She smelled sweet and clean like wildflowers after a cool rain.

"Because I care about you. And I think you've been going through all this alone for long enough." She gave him a slow kiss. "Now if you really don't want me—"

"I want you." And there lay his entire problem.

He wanted her.

So much so that he'd gotten to the point at which he

couldn't think about anything except her. He'd been ignoring his responsibilities, pushing everything else aside because he wanted to spend every waking—and sleeping—moment with her. It wasn't about the sex, although that was amazing. It was more. The way she made him feel. The calm she brought to his troubled soul. The warmth. The laughter.

Before her, he'd been content with some superficial one-on-one with a pretty girl. But it wouldn't take long before they'd grow bored with his lack of commitment and they'd move on. So would he.

With Kelly it was different.

He didn't want to go anywhere without her. He wanted to touch her silky skin. Breathe her sweet scent. Kiss her when she laughed. Hold her when she cried.

She'd become as important to him as air.

And because of that, his brother was now missing.

He needed to focus. To pull his head out of his ass and pay attention.

Without another word or thought, he took Kelly by the hand and led her out to his truck. He opened the driver's door, and when she began to slide over to the passenger seat he clamped his hand over her thigh. "You stay right here." He kissed her sweet mouth. "Beside me."

He didn't know how long he'd be able to hold onto her, or if he should just let her go altogether. After the family mess she would most likely see today, there would be no doubt she'd leave.

They all did.

After two hours and four rounds of checking Alex's favorite hangouts, James looked exhausted and worried. Mile by mile the creases in his forehead had deepened. His beautiful lips had flattened and thinned until they were almost indiscernible. With each location and no sign of Alex, she'd heard more creative profanity and self-recrimination than she thought possible from one man. She couldn't stand it anymore.

"Stop."

He slammed on the brakes in the middle of Mule Deer Road. "What is it?" James peered through the windshield. "Do you see him?"

"Pull the truck over," she said. "Please."

Through the dark interior of the truck, he looked at her like he thought she might be crazy. But after two beats, he pulled to the curb. Kelly shifted in the seat to look at him. She reached up and cupped his face in her hands. Smoothed her fingers over the worry lines marring his forehead. Leaned forward and pressed her lips against his.

"I know the panic that's burning inside you right now, James. But you aren't going to do yourself or Alex any good if you're tied up in a knot. Take a deep breath."

"Kelly. I—"

"Please. If you won't do it for yourself, do it for me."

His chest and shoulders lifted on a deep intake of air.

"Again."

He complied, and she smiled. "That wasn't so bad, was it?"

"I don't know what to do," he admitted. "I've looked everywhere I can think of. I'm a cop for god's sake. I should be able to find him."

"We'll find him."

A harsh breath pushed from his lungs. "I suck at this."

"What?"

He glanced out the side window. "Being a brother."

"Well, the job certainly doesn't come with an instruction manual, does it?" she said, trying to make light of it. When he turned to look at her and she saw the despair in his eyes, the laughter died on her lips.

"Tell me what happened, James."

His shoulders lifted in a shrug. "He took off."

"I don't mean tonight," she said. "Tell me what happened with him that twists you up in a knot."

His mouth opened, then closed. He looked at her as though he had much to say but the debate at war in his head prevented him from doing so. Then the chains that held him broke.

"Do you remember when I told you about the time I nearly died? And how things with Alex were complicated?"

"Vividly."

"There's more. I've never admitted it to anyone." His brows lowered. "I'd like to tell you. If you don't mind."

If that didn't verify trust, nothing did. "Of course."

He shifted his gaze out the windshield and quietly told her the story of a fifteen-year-old boy who'd been put in charge of a colicky infant while his mother went out every night in search of a new husband. He told her of the night that infant had cried and cried and that nothing could be done to make him stop. He told her of his fear of losing his temper so he walked out and left that crying infant alone. He told her of the inner rage and guilt that had consumed him that night.

Consumed him enough to take a dare, steal a motorcycle, and proceed to nearly kill himself.

The tale stole her breath and made her heart ache. The dark expression on his face convinced her that nothing in his mind would absolve him of his reckless actions—not the harm he'd done to himself, but that he'd abandoned Alex.

Now she understood.

The enormous responsibility of raising Alex—doing right by him—paralyzed James with fear. How could she convince him to forgive himself? That he'd been only a boy himself that day?

"If anything happens to him I'll—"

"We're going to find him." She curved her fingers over his hand. Kept her tone quiet and even, just as she would while trying to soothe a victim who was about to take the stand and face their attacker. But this was so much more personal. "I promise you."

His eyes searched her face, and he nodded. And then he kissed her. On his tongue, Kelly could taste his fear, his regret, and his guilt. No matter how badly she wanted to kiss all of his troubles away, it was something he had to work out for himself. All she could do was offer support.

"Let me take you home," he said. "You look tired."

"Are you tired of me?"

"No." His eyes widened like she'd just made the stupidest statement in the world. "I just thought—"

"Well save all that thinking for when you really need it. I'm no Tinker Bell," she reminded him. "Now put this truck in gear and let's go find Alex."

Relief eased the furrows in his forehead and at the corners of his eyes. "Thank you."

All she could do now was hold his hand. And pray.

As he took his foot off the brake and eased the truck back out onto the road, Kelly reached for his hand and did just that.

They had two deputy units keeping an eye out for Alex. She and James had exhausted all avenues and were heading back to the little house on Railroad Avenue to come up with some other angles. Two blocks from home, they spotted him.

"Son of a bitch."

Kelly heard the huge sigh of relief push from James's lungs at the sight of his six-foot-tall baby brother ambling down the sidewalk as if he didn't have a care in the world.

The truck rolled up alongside Alex, and James rolled down the window. "Nice evening."

Alex looked up. "Yep."

"Get in."

"I'm good." Alex turned his head and looked back down the sidewalk.

"Get. In." James's deep, demanding tone left no room for quarrel.

Within seconds, Kelly was sandwiched between the brothers while anger and resentment rolled off them in waves. Two alpha males battling for leadership. No question who would win, but that didn't necessarily mean he would best the other. Too much of the past continued to serve as a wedge between the two of them.

She looked up at James's profile caught in the shadows and highlights from the dashboard lights. Jaw clenched, muscles twitching. Then she turned her gaze to Alex, slouched in the seat like he didn't care. Yet every muscle in his long, lanky body was tight and on alert.

James turned the truck into the driveway, and before the tires came to a stop Alex was out the door and heading toward the house. James threw the gearshift into park and was out the door right after him. Forgotten, Kelly sat in the center of the truck debating whether to stay put or follow them into the house. When the battle within those four walls began with a vengeance, she chose a third option. The front porch. Just in case there was blood drawn.

As soon as she sat down in the old wicker chair, Poppy and Princess scratched at the screen door, looking for an escape from the turmoil swirling though the living room. Without making any abrupt moves, Kelly eased open the door and the little dogs ran out. She lifted them both into her arms and eased down into the chair. Princess quivered beneath her silky fur while Poppy looked up at her with worry in her big brown eyes.

"It's going to be okay." Kelly stroked their heads and cooed to them in a quiet voice. "Nothing to worry about."

Princess leaned against her chest and continued to quiver, while Poppy lay across her lap with a heavy sigh. For the duration of the standoff inside the house, Kelly continued to stroke their fur in an attempt to calm their fears. When a door slammed at the back of the house and the voices quieted, she figured the boys had come to an impasse. Before long the screen door opened. She looked up as James came out onto the porch. The dogs sat up and wiggled with excitement.

"Are you okay?" she asked him.

"I sent him to his room before I wiped the smirk from his face."

She tried to smile. He couldn't send Alex to his room forever. It wasn't a resolution, only a stalling tactic. One her own parents had used with Kate more times than Kelly could remember. In the end, they still had to find a solution.

"So, are you okay?" she repeated as he kneeled before her and stroked the little dogs' heads with his big hand.

He looked up at her, and she received her answer in the dark of his eyes. *No.*

"I'm really sorry about that," he said, "I should have taken you home so you didn't have to get in the middle of all this."

"I asked to be here." She stroked his cheek with her fingers, then reached up and tucked a lock of his hair back up into the style that looked like it had been pulled and yanked into place. "I want to be here. For you."

The dogs jumped from her lap. He captured her hand and kissed the backs of her fingers. "I'm going to have to stay up all night and watch him."

Imprison him. That wouldn't work. She knew. Not only from her own personal past experience, but from numerous perps whose parents had thought that locking up their troubled child was the ultimate answer. Understanding the situation was a start. Followed up by a number of tactics that all included love and patience. James was too steeped in emotion right now to want to hear any suggestions she might have. There would be time later.

"Don't you have to testify in Bozeman tomorrow?"

"Shit." He ran a hand through his hair. "I forgot all about that."

She smoothed her hand over his shoulder. "I'll stay with you so you can get some sleep."

"I couldn't ask you to do that."

"I didn't hear you ask me." She shrugged. "I don't have anything pressing to do in the morning. I can make a pot of coffee and keep the girls company." She reached down and stroked their silky heads. "Maybe I can trade out their bandanas for bows. Or those cute pink doggie dresses I saw at Target."

"Don't you dare. I already get enough crap because I have Yorkies and not Rottweilers." His gaze roamed from her forehead to her chin then back up to her eyes. With a smile he cupped her face with his hands, drew her mouth down to his, and kissed her with relief and gratitude on his lips. "Thank you."

How did she tell him it was nothing, when it was everything? That she'd do anything for him. That when she hadn't been paying attention she'd jumped into the pool and was drowning in the overflow of love that filled her heart whenever he looked at her. Touched her. Held her in his arms.

I love you.

The words tingled on her tongue. Threatened to leap out and make a fool of her.

She'd fallen in love with the man.

It had been so easy to do.

He'd made it easy.

CHAPTER SIXTEEN

At five o'clock in the morning, Kelly found herself trapped between the back of the leather sofa, a very large and wonderfully muscled male, and two little dogs. The male variety had his arm slung over her waist and was breathing the deep, even flow of sleep, while the furry females of the pack were using her shoulder and hip as pillows. They, too, were deep in la-la land. If Kelly wasn't mistaken, those were snores, not snuffles coming from Princess. Though she couldn't move an inch and her left side had completely fallen asleep, she figured it was a pretty good place to be.

Last night she had told James to go ahead to bed and she would take the graveyard shift of guarding Alex. He'd refused and somehow they'd become their current tangle of arms and legs. While he slept, she stroked his hair, studied the troubled expressions on his face, and tried to come up with some solutions to the issues he was having with his baby brother. Which, in and of itself, was a joke. What did she know about raising kids? She'd never even raised a hamster.

His sleep was restless, but each time he moved he managed to keep her against him, in his arms, like she was some kind of buoy to keep him afloat.

Around five-thirty she heard a car pull up out front. Matt and Kate had answered her plea to drop off the Buick so she'd have transportation after James left for work. She didn't think she had the skills to master his ATV or the Harley parked in his garage. Although on a different day she might welcome the challenge.

Carefully and slowly she extricated herself from the warmth of his arms and tangle of dog paws. The dogs gave her a sleepy-eyed look then snuggled up against James to fall back asleep. She tiptoed across the room, eased the front door open, and stepped out onto the porch. She met her sister and Matt down by the curb.

"Hey." She hugged Kate. "Thanks for bringing the car by."

"Everything okay?" Kate asked.

"I don't think so. They had a really ugly argument, and Alex has been in his room ever since."

"You sure he's in there?" Matt asked.

Kelly nodded. "James checked several times. I'm not sure how teen boys pout, but I'd say Alex is a pro."

"He's just like James." Matt shoved his hands into the pockets of his uniform pants.

"I know." Kelly folded her arms against the nip in the air. "That's why they can't find a way to communicate."

"James knows what he means to say, but sometimes his emotions get to his tongue first," Matt said.

"So what's it going to take?" Kate asked, zipping up her sweatshirt. "Aside from knocking their stubborn heads together."

"Hopefully not the catastrophic event it took for James to figure it out," Kelly said.

Matt looked away as if remembering what happened that day and how very close James came to dying. Then he looked back at Kelly, a grim look on his face. "You sure you want to get tangled up in this?"

"What else have I got to do with my time?" Kelly joked.

"A million other things," Kate interjected. "Like icing the baptism cake for Moira Kane's baby girl."

Kelly sighed. "Leave it and I'll take care of it after James comes home."

"Whoa." Kate held up her hand. "Totally kidding. Do *not* let Sister Serious back in this vicinity."

"I've got to get to the station." Matt gave Kelly a quick hug. "You call if you need us, okay?"

Kelly nodded.

Kate hugged her, too, and whispered, "James is lucky to have you, Kel."

"That's what friends are for, right?"

"Friends." Kate laughed. "Don't try to bullshit a bullshitter, Sis. I tried to play that game too." She looked up at Matt with love in her eyes. "And look what happened."

Matt laughed. "Took you damn long enough, too." He gave Kate a kiss on the forehead then wrapped his arm around her shoulders and led her to the sheriff's SUV.

With a sigh Kelly watched him open the door for his wife then help her up onto the seat. When they shared a brief kiss, Kelly turned away with a longing in her soul so deep it stole her breath.

Breakfast at the pissed-off, male-dominated Harley home was something Kelly had never experienced. Not that she didn't know how men behaved in the mornings with their foot shuffles and groggy half-conscious responses. Her dad and brother hadn't invented those. No, the difference came with two alpha males squaring off, lips pulled back in toothy snarls, claws extended. While she'd made some semblance of a meal with the sparse offerings from the refrigerator, the boys did their best to circle each other, bump shoulders in the hall, and sit down to eat holding their forks like weapons. The two little dogs at their feet stared up as if to say *"Come on, you guys, get it together. And feed us a snack, will ya?"*

If it wasn't so sad, she would laugh.

"So, how do you think your testimony will go today?" she asked James as she scooped some scrambled eggs onto his plate.

He lifted his cup of coffee, watched Alex over the rim, and lifted his broad shoulders in a shrug. "I'm guessing it will take all day. The prosecutor—no offense—is a by-the-book die-hard."

"No offense taken." She added several slices of toast to the plates. "And Alex, what are your plans for the day?"

"He's going to keep his ass in this house until I get home so we can finish our *discussion*," James said, sounding every bit the stern parent.

Alex's head came up, and he fixed his defiant slit-eyed teenage glare on his big brother. "You can't keep me locked up in this house." The power of his retort was diminished when he shoved a piece of toast in his mouth and a big glob of grape jelly hung from his bottom lip.

James returned the rebellious scowl. "Watch me."

"Okay." Kelly slid onto the referee's chair at the center of the table. "How about we all take a deep breath, finish eating, and take this conversation back up when you've both calmed down a little?"

James flashed a tight smile. "I'm calm."

Right. She was sure that's exactly what Jaws said just before he took a bite out of Quint's boat.

As they finished the meal in silence, Kelly's gaze darted between the two of them, wondering how on earth this conflict could be resolved. She knew from her profession that both would have to be open to discussion. Then they would need to find a way to communicate. Use a little logic. And then they would need to come to a resolution together. The clenched jaws told her all that might just be a dream. Still, she found she wanted to help.

Maybe some women would back away from the battle, but this is what Kelly had been trained to do. It's what she'd lived for. It's what she'd been good at. It's what she *was* good at. Only now she intended to focus that energy on people she cared about. Not total strangers.

When James got up to shower and get ready for work, Kelly cleared his dish and fed bits of scraps to the Yorkies at her feet. She watched Alex methodically stab his scrambled eggs and poke them into his mouth. When she slid her hand under the tub of margarine, he looked up.

"What? Are you going to jump all over me, too?"

She slipped the lid back onto the margarine. "Do you want me to?"

"No." He stabbed a clump of egg. "It's just what I'm used to."

An ache surrounded her heart as she watched him close himself off by burying his head in his hand. She sat back down, covered his hand with hers, and drew it away from his face. Dark eyes looked up, so much like the brother she had fallen in love with.

"Alex, I know you don't know me more than a passing hello or goodbye, and I can tell by the look in your eyes that you don't trust me. And that's okay. Trust has to be earned. But I hope you'll give me the chance. I'm going to hang around here today and—"

"Don't you mean he's forcing you to babysit me?"

"First thing you need to know about me?" She smiled. "Nobody forces me into anything. I'm a state prosecutor and—"

"Shit. That's as bad as *him* being a cop."

She laughed. "Worse. *He* only gets to arrest the bad guys. *I* get to put them in prison."

"You think that's fun?"

"Nope. Not fun at all. But I didn't make the choices to take from others. Or hurt people." *Or kill them.* "The criminals make those decisions themselves. Everyone is in control of their own destiny. Just depends on where you want to take it. What most people don't think about when they are in the moment is that their actions will have an effect on the rest of their lives. Other people's lives too. Not just for that day. Not just for a week or a year. But for their entire lifespan."

"That sucks."

"I'm pretty sure that's exactly what every criminal thinks as the prison door closes behind them. Well, at least for a few minutes." She lifted her coffee and sipped. "Some people, though, have no conscience whatsoever."

Alex nodded, stabbed another bite of egg and poked it into his mouth.

"Since I'm hanging around here all day," she said, lifting the veil off the heavy conversation, "How about you teach me how to play that video game?"

He lifted a dark brow. "You want to learn to play *Call of Duty?*"

"Sure." She grabbed his empty plate. "But don't be surprised if I kick your ass at it."

"I'm not worried." He gave her a genuine smile—teeth and all. He wagged his fork in the air for emphasis. "You're a girl."

"Do you know how many cases I've prosecuted? Hundreds. Want to know how many I've lost?" She grabbed his fork. "One." *And it was the biggest loss of her life.* Though with the sudden admiration warming Alex's brown eyes she wasn't about to feed him that bit of information. "So prepare yourself, my man, to surrender and weep."

When James opened the bathroom door and steam rolled out into the hallway, Alex slipped back into his bedroom to avoid another confrontation. Unwilling to add more kindling to the fire, James let him pass without comment. He secured the end of the towel at his waist and went in search of Kelly. He owed her an apology for getting her tangled up in this mess. Nobody besides him needed to suffer the teenage angst of his little brother. Not his mother. Definitely not Kelly. She was too good for that.

She was too good for *him*.

He didn't know how he'd allowed himself to get so wrapped up in her. That hadn't been his intention. But the more he'd come in contact with her, the more he'd seen her, touched her, and held her, he'd lost all control over simple reason. Hell, he was losing control all over the place.

His life was a big, fucked-up mess.

Again he asked himself why anyone in their right mind would choose to get involved with him.

He'd been smart until now to keep his relationships casual. One-night stands. Brief encounters. And then along came Kelly, and he'd thought back to all those times in school when he'd watch her go about her normal day. Watch her go back to her normal family. And he'd begun to crave a normal life. When she came back into town, those cravings intensified. But it wasn't just the normal life he desired; he wanted that life to include Kelly and her smile. Her quiet calm that soothed the beast inside him when he didn't know which way to turn. The sheer happiness she brought to his heart.

He was a selfish bastard to toss her into this mess.

But he needed her.

And he wanted her.

He just didn't know what to do with her.

A clatter of sound came from the other room, and he found her in the kitchen putting away the dishes. When he came up behind her and slid his arms around her waist, she turned and gathered him in close.

Rising to her toes she pressed her cheek against his. "Mmmm. Clean-shaven, and you smell good too."

"Too bad I couldn't talk you into taking that shower with me."

Her soft hand slid down his chest, and she smiled up at him. "I'll take a rain check."

Early morning sunshine poured through the window. With her in his arms, James realized he could stand there just like that all day. Unfortunately he had a long drive to Bozeman and a court process that would swallow any hopes he had for a quick return. He bent his head and gave her a long, slow kiss, tasting the coffee and sugar on her tongue.

He could totally get used to mornings like this.

He *wanted* to get used to mornings like this.

Minutes later, he'd put on his uniform and strapped on his gun. She met him at the front door.

"Thank you for staying with Alex today."

She smiled. "That's what friends do, right?"

"Friends." His heart thumped hard. "Right."

She smoothed the backs of her fingers down his cheek. "Have a good day in court."

He laughed. "Isn't that an oxymoron?"

"Is the prosecutor a male or female?"

"Female."

"Then make sure you smile and say *ma'am*."

"Always do." He laughed again, enjoying the tingle dancing through his veins. He wrapped her in his arms and lifted her up onto her toes. "I'm putting you in charge today, Counselor."

"Duly noted. I promise nothing will happen while you're

gone." She gave him another quick kiss. "Now get going before I hold you in contempt."

"Angelface, you can hold me any way you want."

Midway through Kelly's fourth failed attempt at *Call of Duty*, Alex teased her and asked if she wanted him to break out *Donkey Kong*. She liked him. He was fun and funny. Yet he always seemed to have something to say that remained cloistered at the tip of his tongue.

Kelly glanced at her watch. "It's almost noon. Are you ready for some lunch?" She dropped the game controls to the coffee table and moved the little dogs off her lap.

"You don't have to wait on me."

"True." She got up from the sofa. "But I could use the experience making a PB&J. My sister Kate is sucking me back into working at the bakery, and I need all the pastry-development skills I can get."

"Then give yourself a whole lot of experience and make it two sandwiches." Alex laughed. "If you don't mind."

She turned her head and looked at him.

"Please."

She smiled. It was hard to associate the rebellious bad boy she'd seen just last night for the charming and polite young man before her now. "Glass of milk, too?"

He grinned and nodded. "A big glass. Please."

At that moment, the telephone rang.

"I'll get it," Alex said and grabbed the wireless from the cradle.

Seconds later he held his hand over the mouthpiece. "I'm going to take this in the other room if that's okay."

"Sure." She hitched her thumb toward the kitchen. "I'll get on those sandwiches."

Kelly pulled down a loaf of bread from the cupboard and grabbed the jar of chunky peanut butter. The refrigerator gave her the choice of grape jelly or strawberry. Since they'd had grape that morning she chose the latter. While she evened the spread out and tried not to tear the bread, she couldn't help but think about what a nice change it was to be making a sandwich herself during the day and focusing on the simple task. As opposed to her butt being glued to her office chair and shoveling a tasteless fast-food meal into her mouth while she pored over evidence and testimonies.

As she screwed the lids back onto the peanut butter and jam, she called out. "Alex. Your sandwiches are ready."

She set both on a plate and placed it on the table. Then she grabbed the milk jug from the refrigerator and poured a large glass.

"Alex?"

No answer. Maybe he was still on the phone. She'd give him a few more minutes and keep herself busy by any of the numerous tasks that could be accomplished in the kitchen. No question, this place screamed bachelor pad. The house was cute and had potential, and she could tell James had put in the effort to make it a home. But neither James nor Alex seemed to be the *Home and Garden Television* type.

Several minutes later, when Alex still hadn't come to the table, Kelly walked into the hall to call for him again. Princess and Poppy followed, whining, and tapping their little dog toenails on the hardwood floor. Alex's bedroom door was open, and she poked her head inside the neat and tidy room.

"Alex?"

No Alex.

She looked down at the four brown eyes looking up at her then continued down the hall to James's room and opened the door.

Empty.

Shit.

She ran to the bathroom, almost tripping over the dogs, and knocked on the closed door.

No answer.

Shit. Shit.

She ran back through the house, looked pointlessly out the front door, then ran out into the backyard. Her eyes darted from corner to corner of the yard.

No Alex.

She scrambled across the grass to the garage and yanked open the side door.

No. Alex.

Shit.

Somehow when she hadn't been looking, Alex had disappeared.

Kelly sank to her knees on the concrete. Surrounded by power tools, power machines, and all things male, the little dogs perched their front paws on her thighs. She looked down at them through teary eyes and whispered, "Where did he go, girls?"

Their tailless little butts did not wag. That's when Kelly knew she was really in trouble.

An hour and a half later, Kelly stopped at the corner of Little Deer and Buckhorn to allow a very slow bandana-adorned goat to cross the road. Why the animals in this town wore articles of clothing was anyone's guess. Any other day she'd be amused.

She'd searched everywhere for Alex. Covered all the places she and James had checked the night before to no avail. He didn't have a car, which meant he couldn't have gone far. Desperate, she'd even called out to her mother to see if she could use her powers from beyond to find him. But her mother had not heeded the call, and Alex was still MIA.

She'd tried everything she could think of. Now she had no choice but to ask the help of the experts.

She had to find Alex . . . before James came home.

When the goat finally trotted to the other side, Kelly hit the gas on the old Buick and drove straight to the sheriff's station.

The parking lot of the old cinder-block building was nearly empty as Kelly swung the Buick into a space. She grabbed the keys from the ignition and ran toward the entrance. Just as she pushed open the glass door, Matt walked up to the woman behind the front desk. He looked up as Kelly came inside.

"I was just about to call you."

Kelly tried to calm her erratic heartbeat. "Why?"

"I solved your missing-person's case."

"How did you know he was missing?"

Her brother-in-law's dark brows lifted. "Because I found him?"

The urge to drop to her knees with relief rolled over her. "I'm sorry. I know that sounded dumb."

Matt smiled. "Nothing sounds dumb when you're in a panic. You want to see him?"

"Is he okay?"

"He's fine."

"Is he . . . locked up?"

"Not yet."

A rush of air pushed from her lungs. "Thank god."

"Come on. He's in my office."

Matt came around from behind the counter, and Kelly followed him, thanking whomever it was upstairs that had made Alex findable and in good health. Although she just might have to kill him herself for all the worry he'd put her through.

"Where'd you find him?" she asked.

"I think I'm going to let him explain that one himself." Matt reached for the knob on his office door. "Although in about five minutes he's going to have company to either corroborate his story or tear it apart."

Great. Didn't that just sound ominous as hell.

Kelly entered the room behind Matt and sighed with relief when she saw for herself that Alex was in one piece. While she expected defiance to be marring his young face, instead she found remorse.

She headed toward him, and he stood. She looked up into his dark eyes. "Are you okay?"

He nodded, those eyes searching her face as if to gauge

her intent. Then she just grabbed him into a hug and held on, even though his rigid body language said he wasn't exactly comfortable with her open display. "You scared the hell out of me, Alex. I was so worried."

His shoulders lifted with a sigh, and then his arms came around her in a shaky embrace. "I'm sorry."

"I know."

He leaned back and looked at her. "You do?"

She nodded. "Where did you go?"

He glanced away, and then his eyes went to Matt's. "That phone call I got? I just needed to see someone. And I knew you would tell me I couldn't go."

"Maybe if you'd talked to me about it we could have worked something out."

He looked at her like the idea was completely foreign to him.

"Communication, Alex. Believe it or not, it actually works."

He gave her a timid smile, as though he didn't actually believe her.

The front desk attendant buzzed Matt, and he told them to send the individuals to his office. Within seconds Chelsea Winkle and a man Kelly guessed to be her father entered the room.

"Chelsea?" Kelly glanced between the two teenagers. Guilt was graffitied across their faces. "What's going on?"

"I'm sorry, Kelly. I know you said I should leave him alone, but . . ." Chelsea looked at Alex with warmth and affection in her eyes. Alex looked at Chelsea in the same way.

A little shiver tickled the pit of Kelly's stomach. *If it's meant to happen it will,* she'd told the young girl. Looked like although it might be meant to happen, Chelsea was more than willing to give it a little push.

". . . I just couldn't," Chelsea continued. "I called him and told him I wanted to see him. So he agreed to meet me at the park."

"That's where I found them and called Sheriff Ryan," Chelsea's father said. Resentment tightened the corners of the man's mouth. "When she ran out the door without any explanation, I jumped in my car to go after her. It took me a while to track her down."

He'd done a better job of it than she had, Kelly thought.

"And then I found her with *him*."

"And what were they doing when you found them, Mr. Winkle?" Kelly asked.

"We weren't doing anything." Alex jumped to defend Chelsea. "We were just talking."

Kelly held up her hand and went into lawyer mode. "What infraction did Alex perpetrate to compel you to call the authorities, Mr. Winkle?"

"He . . . uh . . ."

"I'm sorry," Kelly said. "I didn't hear you."

"Yes, Mr. Winkle." Matt sat down behind his desk, reached into a drawer and pulled out some papers. "I need to know the charges, so I can fill out the forms."

Chelsea looked up at her father. "Dad. You know you can trust me."

"But I can't trust *him*."

"Yes, you can, Mr. Winkle," Alex said. "I promise I'd never do anything to hurt Chelsea. I know she's a nice girl."

Kelly's chest puffed out with pride. "If you intend to press charges," Kelly said, "you need to supply us with the offenses."

Mr. Winkle's gaze darted around the room and landed on Alex, where it held. "I'm just trying to protect my daughter."

Alex gave a quick nod. "I understand, sir. And for what it's worth, I'm on your side."

When Alex extended his hand to Chelsea's father, Kelly smiled. And melted. The older man looked at that outstretched offering of peace for a long breath before he reciprocated the gesture.

Matt shoved the papers back in his drawer and stood. "Are we good here?"

Mr. Winkle nodded and placed his hand at Chelsea's back to escort her from the office. She did not leave without a backward glance and a warm smile to Alex.

Though everything had been settled amicably in Matt's office, Kelly knew as soon as James came home the caca would hit the proverbial fan.

CHAPTER SEVENTEEN

Kelly had no knowledge of parenting, and while she steered the Buick toward James's house her intent was as far from adolescent-rearing as possible.

"Thank you," Alex said, staring out the side window.

Kelly studied him for a moment and sighed. "Alex, it's none of my business what happens between you and your brother, but I want you to know if you ever need to talk to anyone, I'm here."

He nodded slowly. "I can't believe you're not yelling at me."

"I'm not much of a yeller." She laughed. "That's my sister's job. I'm more of the give-an-individual-the-stink-eye-and-they'll-break-down-like-a-house-of-cards kind of person."

He chuckled. "You're awfully short to be so intimidating."

"Yeah? You ever hear about the mouse who roared?" She smiled. For a few minutes nothing but silence passed between them. "So . . . Chelsea, huh? You know you have to earn the respect of a girl like her."

"Yeah. She's pretty great."

"So are you, Alex."

"Could you try to convince James of that?"

"Uh-uh. That's your job."

"Never gonna happen. After mom got sick, he got stuck with me. That's why he's always pissed off."

"I don't think he sees it that way."

"Oh yeah. He does. Half the time he ignores me. The other half he's yelling at me."

"I know what it's like to be ignored, Alex. I had a big brother who was the golden boy and could do no wrong. And I had a baby sister who rebelled loudly about everything. Between the two of them I got lost in the shuffle. So I had to find my way. Find who I was and who I wanted to be. Because at the end of the day when the world is quiet and you have nothing but your own conscience, you have to be a person who can hold your head high and know you've done the very best you can."

"So then why did you leave your career to come back here?"

"Somewhere along the way I started wanting something different." Kelly shrugged. "I want someone to notice me for more than who I am in the courtroom. For more than how many criminals I can put away in a year. I just want to find someone who will love me. Unconditionally."

"Yeah." Alex sighed. "Me too."

Kelly reached across the seat and patted his hand. "I guess the need to be loved is a pretty strong force, isn't it?"

Alex nodded. "Can make you act pretty stupid, too."

"Give James a chance, Alex. Because even though he might get a little lost in translation, he loves you. Very much."

"You know, he used to be my big brother. I thought he was

awesome. He used to take me hiking and fishing . . . and we'd talk about everything from baseball to girls." His voice trailed off as he gazed out the window. "Now all he does is yell."

"You might try starting a conversation instead of acting out. More talking usually equals less yelling. I think James is trying to be a parent. And he's not sure how it all works."

Alex turned his head and looked at her with those soulful dark eyes. "I just want my big brother back."

Late afternoon, James pulled the truck into his driveway. He turned off the ignition, sat back, and looked at the house. A huge breath of frustration pushed from his lungs. After sitting in the witness chair for hours, he'd finally been able to leave the courtroom. As soon as he checked his texts, he saw the one from Matt about Alex's newest episode. Much to his surprise he'd received nothing from Kelly. He'd tried to call her. When she didn't answer he'd left her a message. He'd texted her, but she still didn't return his call.

The long drive home had been prolonged due to road construction at the West Fork Bridge. In the duration of the drive he'd run a gamut of emotions from pissed off, to worried, to frustrated. Eventually he'd done a three-sixty and ended up pissed off again.

After a few more moments of inner grumbling, he grabbed his cell phone and equipment bag off the seat and headed toward the house. When he opened the front door, Poppy and Princess greeted him with yips and wiggles like he'd been gone forever. The house looked spotless, like Mrs. Clean had come in and doused the place with a fire hose. Alex sat on the sofa, arms folded, scowl firmly in place. Kelly came out of the kitchen wiping her hands with a towel, looking like it was just any other day.

Sans smile, she looked up at him with those deep-green eyes. "Hi."

"Hi?" He tossed his phone on the table, and, before he could get a handle on all the emotions that had built up like a Yellowstone geyser, he opened his big mouth. "That's it? Alex disappears, and I get no phone call from you?"

She folded her arms. "Well, I—"

"What the hell happened?"

"It's kind of a long story," she said. "Why don't you have a seat, and we can all talk about it."

"I don't want to sit down. I want to know what the hell happened." He looked at Alex, who now stared up at him with defiance burning in his eyes. "What the hell were you thinking? I told you to stay put."

"You can't lock him up forever, James. In case you haven't noticed, that doesn't work."

James shot his gaze back to Kelly. "I wasn't talking to you."

"Wow." At the force of his words, she took a step backward. "Okay, I realize you're upset—"

"*Upset?*"

Alex came up off the sofa and took a step. "Don't yell at her."

Kelly rushed to intervene with a hand on his brother's chest. "It's okay, Alex."

His brother was defending her? What the hell?

"Go to your room, Alex. And don't come out until I tell you to." James pointed a finger at Alex and waited until he stormed from the living room. Then he turned back to Kelly. "How could you let this happen?"

"Are you blaming *me*?"

"*You* promised nothing would happen while I was gone today."

"I didn't plan for—"

"You know what? Maybe you should just go. I think you've interfered enough for one day." Those weren't the words James intended to use, but they leaped from his mouth before he could corral the emotion wound tight in his chest. What he really needed was some time to process everything.

"*Interfered?*" Kelly shook her head. "Is that what I've done here? If so, I apologize. But if you didn't want me to *interfere* you shouldn't have left me in charge, James. Because that's what I do. It's what I've done for a living for the past seven years. I weigh the evidence and I take charge. Right or wrong. When Alex disappeared I did what I felt I needed to do. I saw no reason to send you into a panic with a voice message when you were stuck in court and had a long, arduous drive home."

"I called you and left a message. I sent a text. You couldn't at least return my call?"

"I didn't get a message *or* a text."

James grabbed up his phone to prove her wrong. That was when he saw the red exclamation mark next to the text he thought he'd sent. Indicators that his message hadn't gone through. "Shit." He tossed the phone down. There was a section with bad reception in a long stretch of the canyon. That must have been when he'd tried to reach her.

"If I hadn't found him," Kelly said, "or if a real emergency had occurred, I would have called you immediately. Alex didn't mean to cause any trouble."

"How do you know? You think after just a few hours you know him better than I do?"

"Of course not. I know because I talked to him. Based on that, I don't think this is a situation that should bring about more yelling or more bad feelings. You have to choose your battles, James. Define your role in his life. Who are you to him? His brother? His parent? His watchdog? If *you* don't know, then how is *he* supposed to know?"

Everything in James's gut tightened and twisted. His emotions were getting in the way of what he really wanted to say, but he couldn't seem to get a handle on them and just express the relief he'd felt when he'd learned his brother was safe. He'd entrusted Alex into her care, and he felt she'd let him down. And now she was telling him what to do? "I know how to handle my brother."

"I don't think so." Her beautiful mouth flattened. Her eyes narrowed. "I think you still see yourself as that fifteen-year-old boy who walked away when Alex was a baby. Kids want and need rules. Guidelines. Even if they break them once in a while. I think you're so afraid of doing the wrong thing with him, you won't do anything at all."

"I don't do anything?" he barked. The dogs barked back. "You have no idea what I do or don't do."

"I have a pretty good idea. Look, we all fail at things. Sometimes it helps to admit when you've failed, admit you're human. It really comes down to what you do with the lesson you learned that counts."

"Fine. I get it." James's head spun. It was easy for her to come in and save the day, to point out his failures. She was a temporary fixture in Alex's life. Hell, she was temporary in *his* life for all he knew. He'd asked her to stay, but she'd never committed. And that bothered the hell out of him more than he wanted to admit. What would he do when she went back to Chicago? She wouldn't be around to help him fix things. Then again, it wasn't her responsibility to rescue him from his own errors in judgment. But that didn't make the finger she pointed in his direction feel any better.

"What about you?" he jabbed back. "Did you learn from your failures in the courtroom?"

"Nice attempt at redirecting the message." She gave him a tight smile. "But since you asked . . . Yes, I have. I learned that failure can make you stronger. If you'll let it."

"Then maybe you're right. Maybe I've failed at doing anything for him because I've been spending too much time with *you*." He shoved his hands through his hair, realizing it might be easier to push her away now than for him to bawl like a baby if she walked on her own. "Shit. I knew better than to take you on."

"*Take me on?*" Her brows pulled together, and her eyes darkened. "What does that mean?"

"I already had more responsibility on my plate than I could handle. But then *you* came back, and you looked so damned lost. Like you needed someone to show you how to loosen up. To have some fun. And I—"

"You what?" Her jaw clenched. "Felt sorry for me?"

"That's not what I was going to say."

"But it's what you meant." She reached for her purse,

which sat on the floor near the front door. Princess hopped inside the leather bag, as if she thought she would go along for the ride.

James's stomach churned, and a streak of dread burned through his heart. This conversation had turned into a disaster, and he had to put a stop to it. To put a stop to her walking out that door.

As she gently lifted Princess from her purse, he took a step toward her. "Kelly, I—"

"I don't want to hear it." He expected her to come up with a look she'd use in the courtroom. Instead she had an expression of utter disappointment—a look that registered much worse in his book.

"For your information," she said, hitching her purse strap over her shoulder, "I'm not a charity case. I know how to have fun. I *am* fun. I don't need a teacher. And I don't want or need to be yours or anyone else's responsibility."

Before he could tell her what an ass he'd been and beg her forgiveness, she had her hand on the door. She paused, and hope sparked deep in his heart. He had to find the words to make everything better. But when she turned, he saw that the glimmer in her eyes had died.

"By the way, *Deputy*, if *anyone* in this house is lost, it's *you*. You can resent me all you want, but until you forgive yourself you will never move forward. No one can believe in you until you believe in yourself. And I sincerely hope you find yourself before its too late." She pushed open the screen door and walked out.

The door closed with a bang. A clear signal that it was already too late. Panic moved in his chest while her footsteps took her out of his life. He wanted to go after her, but his feet wouldn't move. Anger, defeat, and guilt froze him in place.

"Way to go." Alex—obviously eavesdropping—stormed through the living room, pushed open the screen door, and followed her outside.

James dropped to the sofa and tried to catch his breath. How could it be that everything he'd meant to say had come out wrong? He didn't know what the hell he was doing anymore. Everything he tried to do right he completely fucked up.

He loved that girl. He respected her. Yet his behavior just now had shown none of that. And like a total dumbass he'd just let her walk out the door. He rubbed his hand against the growing ache in his chest. He'd told himself he couldn't get involved. That he had nothing to offer. That his life was just too screwed up to include her. But he'd gotten involved anyway. And then he'd committed the real crime. He'd pulled her into his mess of a life. The more he'd pulled, the more he'd realized how much he needed her. And that just plain scared the hell out of him. His gut and his brain swirled together in a tornado of confusion.

At that moment Alex came back into the house. He stood inside the door, arms folded, with a glare so dark James suddenly felt like their roles had been reversed.

"You screwed up, Bro." Alex walked farther into the room, stopping in front of James with a lift of challenge to his chin. "She's the best thing that ever happened to either of us."

"What do you mean *us?*"

Alex pointed at the door. "She's the only one who's ever been straight up. Tells it like it is. And asks for nothing in return. I left the house today because Chelsea wanted me to meet her. That's who I went to see last night, too. And when I explained it to Kelly, she seemed to understand that Chelsea is important to me and that I want to spend time with her. Just like you want to spend time with Kelly."

Hard to fault that logic.

"When Kelly came to the station today, I thought she'd rip into me the way you always do. But she didn't," Alex said. "Do you know what she did instead? She hugged me. Told me I'd scared her and that she'd been worried about me. And that made me feel bad. It made me understand how scared you must get when I disappear or do stupid things. It made me understand how bad I've hurt Mom."

Alex shook his head. "I had to wonder if I could make someone I barely knew feel that way, what have I been doing to the people who cared about me."

"Alex, I—"

His little brother held up his hand. "Let me finish before you go stomping all over me."

James pulled his words back, while guilt grabbed him by the throat. "Go ahead."

"Kelly set me straight today," Alex said. "She told me how much you love me and that you've just been trying to figure things out."

"She did?"

"Yeah. She also told me that at the end of the day I had to be happy with who I am. I didn't do anything wrong today except leave this house to go talk to a girl who I'm crazy about. Just like you're crazy about Kelly. Is that so wrong?"

"Alex, I'm—"

"You should be happy. You should be hugging her instead of tearing her head off. You know why? Because she loves you."

James's heart jumped. "Did she say that?"

"God." Alex jammed his fingers into his too-long hair. "You are so lame. No, she didn't say it. She didn't have to. But when I was dissing on you she protected you."

A smile tickled James's lips. How was it that the *little* brother had just taught the *big* brother a lesson in life? "When did you get so smart?"

Alex shrugged. "Always been smart. Just never had anyone explain things so clearly to me before like Kelly did."

The ache in James's chest intensified. "Alex, we need to talk. I don't know what I'm doing with you," he admitted. "And I apologize for that. I didn't have any role models, and I thought I was doing my best. I know I've failed, but . . ." James stood and found himself almost eye-to-eye with the little boy his mother had once brought home bundled in a fuzzy blue blanket. "I want you here with me. You're my little brother. And I love you."

"Then just be my big brother and trust me. Talk to me. Guide me." A smile eased across Alex's mouth. "If you can do that, I promise I'll be the person you want me to be."

"I'll try."

"There is no try. Only—"

"All right, I get it." James laughed. "No need to quote Yoda."

"Good. Then stop yelling so much. You give me a headache." Alex chucked him on the shoulder. "I apologize for being such a pain-in-the-ass. And . . . I love you, too."

"I'm sorry," they both said simultaneously and wrapped each other in a hug.

James fought back tears. He'd once walked away from Alex when he'd cried out for help. James now realized his own rebellious behavior had been a cry for help, as well. And Alex had followed in his footsteps. The revolving door on this behavior needed to close. Kelly was right. Love, understanding, and communication would open a new one.

Poppy and Princess danced and yapped at their feet as if they knew reconciliation was in the air. And maybe a Scooby snack, too.

"So what are you still doing here?" Alex asked with a final pat to James's back. "Go after her. Because if you don't, I might go after her myself. I kind of think I'm a little in love with her."

"Yeah." James's heart tightened and swelled all at once. "Me too."

Chapter Eighteen

W hat did a clown do to overcome heartache? Put on more face paint? Add an extra flower to their costume? Sprinkles allowed herself to have a really good cry, then she added sparkly tassels to her pink boots. Though in her heart she didn't believe a truckload of sparkles would lift the ache that weighed heavy in her chest.

As an awful afternoon edged toward dinnertime, Kelly stood in her room while the phone on the dresser vibrated. She glanced at the incoming text from Daniel. Two words.

Time's up.

Great. As if she didn't have enough on her plate.

She shot a glance to the mirror.

Showtime.

Time to make some decisions.

She sipped a cup of orange spice tea, careful not to mess her make-up, and came to the only conclusion that made any sense. It was risky but she had no other real choice.

In less than an hour's time, she'd completed the phone call that threw her new life into motion. It had gone easier than she thought and had lifted the burden from her shoulders if not from her heart.

With a flip of her petticoats, she grabbed her new supply of balloons from the dresser and stuffed them into her bag of tricks. Then she grabbed her keys and went out into the living room.

"Well now." Her father grinned up at her from his recliner, where he'd been watching a particularly buttery episode of Paula Deen. "I see Sprinkles has added some new bling to her outfit."

"Dad," Kelly laughed. "It's a little weird to hear you use the word *bling*."

"Hey, I can be hip and cool."

"Well, don't try too hard." Kelly crossed the room and kissed him on his balding head. "I love you just the way you are."

"Are you heading off to the hospital?"

"Yeah. I thought I'd check in with Charity to see how she's doing. Maybe read a story or two to anyone I can lasso into listening to me."

He reached up and took her hand. "No more tears?"

"I'm not sure. But at least a bright pink nose hides the evidence."

"You know," he smoothed his thumb over the top of her hand, "I'm always here if you need me, but I won't interfere if you don't ask. You're a grown woman, and you're smart, and I always trust you to know what you're doing."

She only wished James would trust her, too. Kelly leaned

down and hugged her dad. "Oh, Daddy, never trust that I know what I'm doing when it comes to matters of the heart. I'm new at this love stuff."

He chuckled. "Sometimes things aren't always so clear. And sometimes even when you love someone, your thoughts go in separate directions. You just have to know what to fight for and what to let go. Your mother and I used to have some knock-down-drag-out arguments over things that now seem so silly. I can guarantee you that arguments like which freeway off-ramp to take or which color to use for the icing on someone's birthday cake are definitely worth letting go."

"So how did you and Mom work things out?"

"Sometimes I slept on the couch till she'd forgive me. But most of the time we just realized our love was bigger than misspoken words."

"How do you know when your love is bigger?"

He poked her in the chest. "That right there will tell you. And don't ever ignore it. It's an old saying but worth repeating: Life's too short."

Kelly thought of her mom and how lost her dad had been since she died. She wished he was able to see her and talk to her like the rest of them, but maybe there was a reason for that. Maybe her mom and dad didn't have any unspoken words between them. Nothing left undone.

"Dad? Can I ask you a really personal question?"

"Sure."

"What was the last thing you and Mom said to each other that morning?"

Her father's chest lifted in a stuttered sigh, and for a moment he looked as if he couldn't bear to remember that day. Then a slow smile curved his mouth as the memory came back.

"I told her I was thinking of taking her on a bakery tour of Europe for our anniversary. She laughed. Patted me on the cheek, looked up at me, and said, 'You're a good man, Bobby, and I love you.' And then she died in my arms." He looked up with tears in his eyes. "That's really something special, isn't it? To hear those words? To know that you're the last thing the one you love saw before they passed on?"

Tears pooled in Kelly's eyes too. "It really is." She hugged him, placed her hand on his chest, and felt his heart skip. In that moment Kelly realized that love wasn't always easy, and sometimes it broke your heart. But in the end, love was truly all that mattered.

A warm wind blew across the stretch of pines that led to the Clear River Lodge as James drove toward the house and parked near the veranda. His boots thudded up the steps of the wraparound porch, and he lifted his fist to knock on the door. When it swung open, Dean stood there instead of Kelly. For a man who'd just spent time in the tropics, he looked tanned, but he did not look happy and relaxed.

"How nice of you to come all the way over here so I could kick your ass."

Nope. Not happy.

"I came to see Kelly."

Dean folded his arms. "She's not here."

"Where is she?"

"I told you not to make my sister cry." Dean stepped

through the door and out onto the porch. "You did. So do you honestly think I'm going to tell you where she is?"

"Yeah."

"Why?"

"Because I love her. And because I fucked up. And because I need to apologize."

Emma, holding their kitten, Lucky, snuck beneath Dean's arm. "Pull in your claws, honey," Emma said to Dean, not the cat.

Dean looked down into his wife's face. "He made my sister cry."

She looked up at her new husband and laughed. "*You* made *me* cry. But you still got your opportunity to apologize. And look where we are now. Don't you think James and Kelly deserve that same happiness?"

Dean's wide shoulders lifted with a sigh, and for the moment James knew he wouldn't get his face smashed in by the ex–football pro.

"Fine. But if you make her cry again—"

"I won't," James promised. "The last thing I ever want to do is hurt her. Do you know where she went?"

Dean shook his head. "She gave us a hug, grabbed her stuff, and left."

"Thanks."

"Good luck," Emma called as he ran down the steps. "You'll need it."

Like he didn't know? Kelly pissed-off he could deal with. Disillusioned would be tougher to handle.

On the way to the hospital, Kelly stopped to see Kate and reveal her alter ego. She'd been prepared for her sister to laugh. She'd not been prepared for Kate to cry and tell her how proud she was. They'd had a talk, and Kelly revealed her plans, which made Kate cry even harder. You could say what you wanted about Kate—that she was over-the-top or unpredictable. Kelly only knew she was glad Kate was her baby sister.

Since the Buick had consumed every last drop of gas, Kelly barely made it into the Gas and Grub before it gave its last cough. Of course, she couldn't actually blame the car for running out of gas, but for the moment it was a quick deterrent from all the other thoughts boggling her mind.

With the sun shifting toward the horizon, the heat of the summer day finally abated. She hoped she wouldn't need to do any further makeup repairs. The tears she'd shed with her father had done enough damage. Then there was the whole sob fiasco with Kate. Kelly was lucky her pink nose had stayed in place.

While she waited for the tank to fill, she leaned back in the seat and on the radio listened to "Happy Together." Halfway through the chorus, a cool breeze floated over her shoulder.

"I always loved that song."

"Mom! Are you crazy to show up here?" Kelly turned to look at her mother. With the sun still shining, she could only see a faint blue glow. "People are going to drive by and think I'm nuts talking to myself. Can they see your glow too? Or are they going to think I'm cooking meth in the backseat?"

"Whoa." Her mother's voice sounded amused. "Back up

the truck, sister. No, they can't see me. And no, they aren't going to think you're a crack dealer. However, the part about them thinking you're a little squirrelly is a good possibility."

"Well, won't that just be a great addition to my not-so-perfect day."

"About that. I must admit I was quite surprised by young Alex. Once you get past all that bluster and gruff, he is a very nice boy."

"Yes, he is. His big brother, however—"

"Needs you."

"I don't think so. He just needs someone to yell at."

"Yelling is good for the soul. It clears out all the clogs and makes way for something really incredible."

"It makes me cry," Kelly said, thinking back to just a few hours ago when she'd left James's house and felt like her heart had snapped in two.

"Yeah." Her mother's pale lips slid into a smile. "Good stuff."

"Crying is good stuff?"

"Crying lets you know you have a sensitive heart beating in your chest. It lets you know you're alive." Her smile turned wistful. "I miss that."

Kelly's stomach twisted. How could she sit there and be so selfish when her mother had lost everything? "I'm sorry, Mom. I guess when you get so wrapped up in your own misery it's easy to forget how it affects others."

"Exactly."

The gas nozzle clicked off, and Kelly got out to complete the transaction. When she grabbed the gas receipt and climbed back inside the car, her mother's glow had brightened a little and changed to purple. Kelly turned on the ignition and pulled away from the gas pump.

"I do like that outfit, dear." Her mother chuckled. "It reminds me of when you were about four years old. Kate had hit the terrible twos—which seemed to last well into her teens—and she'd taken to pitching a hissy fit whenever she didn't get what she wanted. One day you decided to try to shut her up by playing dress-up and putting on a show. But before you got your costume all together, Kate had cried herself to sleep. So you performed a very cheeky rendition of 'Goldilocks and the Three Bears,' in which the bears were interpretations of Kate at various temperaments."

Kelly gasped. "I did not."

"You sure did." Her mother laughed. "I always thought you made a fabulously innocent point about your baby sister and her numerous dispositions."

"Some things never change." Kelly turned the car into the hospital parking lot. "She's still pretty fiery."

"Yes. And you're still the patient big sister."

The air shifted within the car and when her mother spoke again it was right over her shoulder.

"I apologize for taking advantage of that, honey. I never meant to shut you out. Your sister was just a handful. And your brother, well, he wasn't much easier. But that doesn't mean your daddy and I didn't love you just as much. Or that we didn't get just as excited for you. We're very proud of the woman you've become. And I know, on good authority, that the life you are about to live will be as wonderful as you've always wanted."

"I appreciate that, Mom. But I know there are no guarantees. And I've long passed the fairy-tale stage of believing in happily-ever-afters."

"Well that's a bunch of crap."

"It's the truth." Something flicked her ear. "Ouch. Did you do that?"

"Yes. Don't you dare stop believing." Her mother's tone took on the same gruff quality she used when any of her kids got out of line. "Your daddy and I proved that we could do anything—we could make magic—as long as we did it together. Love is out there waiting for you. Don't you dare give up on him. You grab hold of that happiness with both hands, and you'll find that together there's nothing you can't do. You love him, don't you?"

"Are you talking about James?" Kelly glanced into the rearview mirror to find her mother's glow had turned hot pink. "You think he's the one?"

"Don't you?"

Kelly stopped the car and shifted around. The backseat was empty. Her mother had disappeared. And Kelly was left to answer the question all on her own.

Second stop on James's list was Matt and Kate's lakeside cabin. When no one answered the door, he jumped back in his truck. As he drove toward town, in his head he played over and over the rotten things he'd said to Kelly. He thought of what she'd said in response. And he thought of what his suddenly wise little brother had said. James didn't know if he'd ever be enough for a woman like her, but if she'd give him the chance, he'd do his best to be the man she wanted him to be.

He certainly planned to choose his words more carefully in the future.

On Main Street he drove toward the Sugar Shack. Hopeful, he pulled around to the alley but was disappointed when he discovered Matt's company car and Kate's minivan. Not the old Buick. He knocked on the back door to see if his friends knew where he could find her.

When the door opened, Matt stood there with a bemused look on his face. "You sure you want to come in here, buddy?"

James peeked over Matt's shoulder. "Kelly in there?"

"Nope."

"Kate?"

"Yep."

"She loaded for bear?"

"She's loaded for you."

Shit.

Matt moved aside, and James stepped into the line of fire.

"Well, well. Look who's here." Kate dusted her hands on her pink apron and strolled toward him.

Judging by the look on her face, he wasn't sure whether to move backward or run. Kate scared him more than Dean.

"How are you, James?" Kate patted his shoulder. "Broken any hearts lately?"

Obviously. "Do you know where your sister is?"

"Hmm." She tapped her chin. "Let me think. She could be at my dad's house. Or she could be at Dean's."

"I already went by there."

"Or . . . she could have bought a one-way ticket back to Chicago. How much of a guessing game are you willing to play?"

Since he was the one usually doing the razzing, he knew the time had come for him to get a taste of his own medicine. But when his entire future was at stake, he wasn't much in the mood to accommodate. "I take your sister very seriously, Kate. So joke all you want, but I'd really like to find her."

"Why?" Kate folded her arms and studied his face intently. "Because you love her?"

"Yeah. I do. And now I've told you *and* Dean, so I'd really like to find Kelly and tell *her*."

"Check Mercy."

"The hospital?" His heart squeezed.

Kate nodded.

"Is she okay?"

"Why don't you go find out for yourself?"

Seconds later he put the truck in gear and exceeded the speed limit to reach Mercy Hospital. Still, the wheels didn't turn fast enough.

Why was she at the hospital? And why wouldn't Kate tell him? Jesus, he knew he could be a dumbass once in a while, but he tried to be a good guy most of the time. He might have fallen short in recent days, but he could still prove himself. If Kelly would only give him the chance.

He pulled the truck into a parking space near the hospital entrance. Visiting hours were almost over, and the lot was nearly empty. But there, at the end of the aisle, sat Letty Silverthorne's bomber of a Buick.

As he passed through the hospital's sliding doors, he discovered the information desk was empty, as were the carpeted halls. No one to ask to have Kelly paged. Where would he look for her? The building may only be three-stories high, but what if he was looking for her on the second floor while she went down to the first floor?

He ran a hand through his hair.

The elevators.

He'd just park himself between the lobby and the elevators on the first floor. There would be no way he could miss her.

If there had been anything wrong with Kelly, he knew Kate would be at her side. Which meant she had to be here as a visitor.

Anticipation rattled through his nervous system as he leaned back against the wall and waited. When an elevator door slid open, he perked up, only to be disappointed when an elderly couple exited. He gave them a smile and wished them a good night, then went back to his watch.

Over the intercom, a voice announced that visiting hours were over. He saw that as a good sign. Well, for him anyway. If Kelly was there visiting someone, she would be leaving soon. The elevator doors slid open several more times while occupants unknown to him exited and made their way to the parking lot. He glanced at his watch, sighed, and leaned back against the wall to continue the wait.

When a half hour had passed, he walked to the window and looked out into the parking lot to see if she'd somehow slipped past him. The Buick remained in the same space, so he headed right back to his command station. He heard the elevator doors whoosh open. His head came up, surprised when a clown, pre-occupied with searching the bag slung over her shoulder, exited and began to walk toward him.

Beneath a lavender top hat adorned with a purple feather,

a red-and-white dress that flared out from the waist with layers and layers of petticoats, torn jeans, and pink cowboy boots, the jester was hard to miss. Around her slender throat, a carnival-colored necklace flashed and jingled as she walked toward him. The sparkly tassels on her boots swayed.

He'd seen this clown before and thought back to the day a whole Volkswagen full of painted faces passed by him when he'd been on patrol. *This* clown had thrown him a kiss.

At that moment she looked up. Her dotted pink nose wrinkled. Her smile slipped.

No. Way.

"Kelly?"

Kelly forgot to breathe. Her heart slammed into her ribs when she looked up, surprised to see James standing there. She wasn't ready to talk to him. But by the determined look on his face, it didn't appear she would have a choice.

The points of the car keys pressed into her palm as she marched past him. "I'm sorry you've mistaken me for someone else."

"Then tell me your name." He followed her down the hall.

"My name is Sprinkles." She stopped, turned, and dug into her bag again. "Would you like me to make you a balloon animal? Perhaps a dog? I'm very good at making poodles."

"I like your name, *Sprinkles*." He took a step toward her, and her heart gave another hard knock. "It reminds me of a very special night in the Sugar Shack."

"I don't know anything about that." Her hand came out

of the bag holding several long colorful un-inflated balloons. "I'm really only good at a few animals, but I'm learning to make hats."

He took her hands, curled his fingers over hers, and held on before she could make an escape.

"I'll pass on the poodle, Sprinkles. But I do have a request."

She lifted her gaze to his dark, soulful eyes, and any remaining chill in her heart melted.

"Forgive me?"

"Why should I?" To her surprise her voice remained steady, even while everything inside her rattled.

"Because back at the house I acted like a total ass. Instead of thanking you for your help with Alex, I got tangled up in the emotion and said all the wrong things." He squeezed her fingers.

"I know I'm not very good with words, but one thing is very clear. I love you," he said. "And I need you. You're the calm in my storm. You fill the emptiness in my heart. You bring the smile to my face." He sighed. "I didn't know what I wanted until I found you. And when I thought I lost you I couldn't bear it. I'd never resent you. I respect you. I think you're an amazing woman."

His big hands slid up her arms to cup her face. "I want more than a one-night stand with you. More than a few stolen moments. I want to wake up every morning with you in my arms. I want to hold you until I'm old and gray and crotchety because I can't hook up my suspenders alone." He inhaled a big breath. "I'm so sorry. Please, Angelface, say you forgive me."

The smile in her heart burst up to her lips. "You love me?"

"Yeah. I do."

"Then I think you're doing just fine expressing how you feel."

His smile equaled her own. "I can make you happy, Kelly. If you'll just give me the chance."

"This isn't just about me. Or you. Or even us. What about your brother? If we're going to be together, he's a part of it, too. And I'm not sure I can stand to see you two going at it all the time."

He nodded, took a breath. "Alex and I have traveled a tough road together. You were right. I made a huge mistake when he was a helpless baby, and I've felt guilty ever since. I didn't know what to do with him, and I didn't know how to overcome all that guilt. I didn't know where I fit in his life. So I ended up yelling. A lot. After you left, he and I talked."

"You did?"

"Yes. He told me you were the best thing that ever happened to me. To *us*. And I couldn't agree more. Everything is going to be okay between him and me from now on. No more yelling. Better communication. I know where I fit in his life now."

"You promise?"

"I promise."

"Then I forgive you."

A rush of thankfulness pushed from his lungs. "Alex told me something else too."

"What's that?"

"He told me that you were in love with me."

"Alex is a pretty smart kid."

"Yeah. He is." A smile burst across his beautiful mouth. He wrapped his arms around her and lowered his forehead to hers. "Say you love me."

She hummed a little sigh. "I love you."

"Even though I can be really difficult at times and often stick my foot in my mouth?"

"Yes." She chuckled. "Even though."

"Then will you please stay here in Deer Lick? Because I'm not sure I could stand it if you went away. If you do need to go back to—"

"Shhhhhh." She pressed her fingers against his soft lips. "Why would I want to go anywhere when my heart is happy right here? I love you. And you don't just run out on someone at the first sign of trouble. I contacted the state attorney's office this afternoon and resigned."

"You're kidding."

She shook her head. "That's not who I am anymore. I like it here. I like being near my family. Being a part of the community. Enjoying life instead of letting it pass me by. I like being with you."

"Then don't just stay. Marry me."

"Marry you?"

He took her hand and pressed it against his heart. Beneath her fingers she felt the strong, steady beat.

"I know a hospital hallway isn't the most romantic place to pop the question," he said. "But I love you. And I really don't want to imagine what my life would be like without you. I've been waiting all my life for somebody like you."

Her shoulders lifted. "Then why would I want to go any-where else?"

"Does that mean you'll marry me?"

"Yes. That means I'll marry you. We can be a family—you, me, and Alex. Poppy and Princess, too."

"That would make me very happy."

She sighed. "Me too."

When he lowered his head and kissed her, hope and hap-piness swelled in her heart. Everything he put into that kiss verified he was a man she could count on. He may not always have the right words, but he was a man who would protect her. A man who would love her through thick and thin. In that kiss Kelly discovered that they could make magic—do anything—as long as they did it together.

More than just falling in love with the town and commu-nity, she'd fallen in love with the man who'd taken the time to open her eyes. And her heart.

When the kiss ended, he lifted his head and his dark eyes glittered with pleasure. "So what's with the clown thing?"

"It's my hidden talent." She looked down, fluffed out her petticoats, and grinned. "You challenged me to do something that makes me and others smile. So I invented Sprinkles. She reads to the kids upstairs. She makes them laugh and forget their pain for just a little while. She gives me a feeling of ac-complishment. She makes me smile."

His long fingers caressed her cheek. "She makes me smile, too."

She grinned. "Hey wait a minute. Didn't we make a bet on that?"

"Doesn't matter. I already won. I got you." His strong

arms curled around her, and he held her close to his heart. "I love you, Kelly."

Kelly's heart swelled.

I love you.

Only three little words. But for Deer Lick's newest funny girl they were three words that took all the wonderful things she believed about life and made them even better.

EPILOGUE

---

18 months later

On Valentine's Day, Kelly had planned for a romantic candlelight dinner with champagne, flowers, chocolate syrup, and her hunky husband. To bring in an extra dollop of fun, she'd bought a sequined heart bra and ruffled thong panties. *And* an aerosol can of whipped cream to cover all those special places the bra and panty didn't hide.

On Valentine's Day, Kelly had *never* planned on being sardined into her mother's rusty Buick alongside her siblings and their spouses on the way to Mercy Hospital. With Dean at the wheel and Matt riding shotgun, a very expectant Kate sat in the middle puffing through a contraction. Beside her, Matt held her hand and sweetly talked her through it, even when she threatened to withhold sex for the next fifty years.

In the backseat, with their mother's quilting materials and pastry cookbooks removed, Kelly was sandwiched between James and an also-expectant Emma, who thankfully still had a few months to go. Outside the fogged windows, a light snow drifted from the sky while inside the car heavy winter coats made the ride even less comfortable. The radio blasting an old tune from The Supremes didn't help.

"Are you sure you're okay, Kate?" Emma asked. "I mean, it is awfully crowded in here and any one of us has a bigger SUV we could have driven."

"No worries. I'm going to get us all there safely," Dean said as he turned the corner at Reindeer and Mule Deer. "You and my baby girl okay back there, honey?"

Emma shook her head and chuckled. "We're just fine."

Between contractions, Kate laid her head on Matt's shoulder. "I wanted us *all* to be together in *this* car. It's important."

James took Kelly's hand in his and gave it a knowing squeeze. They'd had a conversation on their Disney honeymoon, where the entire family, including Alex and her father, had joined in the fun after a few private days. With his near-death experience, Kelly had felt safe in telling James about her mother's ride-along visits and her preoccupation with her Tom Jones grand-entrance theme. Kelly knew that Kate had wanted them all together for a very important reason—for a very important person whose visits had become almost non-existent in recent months.

Kelly gripped James's hand, hoping their mother wasn't too busy earning her wings to come pay a quick visit. "Alex is going to be disappointed he missed this," she said.

James kissed her forehead. "He'll be home for spring break."

Life with the Harley men had smoothed out, and Kelly found herself fiercely protected by both until Alex graduated from high school and went off to college in Idaho. She missed him. The dogs missed him. And James, who'd taken back his big-brother position, seemed a little lost without him. With any luck, after college Alex would move back to Deer Lick. If not, there was a great big world out there for him to conquer. Then again, wherever Chelsea Winkle settled, Kelly had a feeling Alex would settle there, too.

They'd found a wonderful facility for James's mother, where she was able to play cards and eat meals with three other ladies the staff had nicknamed the Golden Girls.

With one empty house and one that was a bit too small, Kelly and James sold both houses and had recently moved into a four-bedroom log cabin. Big enough, with room to grow.

Two blocks from the hospital, Creedence Clearwater abruptly stopped chooglin' and Tom Jones began to wail "It's Not Unusual." Mid-contraction, Kate puffed out a "Yes!," which garnered an odd look from Matt and Emma, who apparently had never been apprised of Leticia Silverthorne's delayed journey to the other side.

Moments later Dean stopped the car in front of Mercy's entrance, and everyone piled out. Their father, who had semi-retired, and Edna Price, who continued to create mischief amongst the community, met them at the door with a nurse and a wheelchair.

Kate looked at them like they were crazy. "I'm walking," she announced.

Matt's dark brows slid together with concern. "Are you sure?"

"Of course I'm sure." Hand on her stomach, Kate turned

back and looked at the Buick with a huge grin. "My mom didn't raise no wussies."

Several hours later when delivery time arrived, everyone except Matt had been ushered from Kate's room. They now all stood outside in the hall, waiting. Kelly smiled at James, who leaned with one shoulder braced against the wall. She gave him a wink, took him by the hand, and led him around a corner for a few moments of privacy.

"Not exactly how we planned to spend Valentine's Day," she said.

He brushed a lock of her hair aside and curled his warm fingers inside the collar of her sweater. "The day doesn't end until midnight." He bent his head and kissed her.

"Mmmm. I have something really special for you, too." She wiggled her eyebrows. "A *new* hidden talent."

"Yeah?" His grin lit her up from the inside. "You know I can't wait. Tell me what it is."

"Do you know where we are?"

He laughed. "I believe we are standing in the hospital hallway."

"Do you remember what happened in the hallway downstairs?"

"I asked you to marry me."

"So this hallway seems like the perfect place for good things to happen."

"With your sister in there giving birth, I would have to agree."

She slipped his hand from her collar and guided it down to her belly. "Happy Valentine's Day, Daddy," she whispered.

He drew his head back and looked at her with complete and utter surprise brightening those beautiful dark eyes.

"Are you serious?"

She nodded.

The smile she loved so much spread wide across his handsome face. "Then we really do have something to celebrate."

As he wrapped her in his arms and lifted her off her feet, the husky cry of newly born Madeline Leticia Ryan got the party started.

Farther north, amid gossamer wings and heralding trumpets, Letty Silverthorne looked down at her happy, expanding family and smiled. "My work is done."

"Not so fast."

Letty turned toward the deep voice, expecting another scolding from the *Him* in charge. She lifted her hands. "I promise. I haven't broken any rules."

"Lately." His silver brows lifted. "I've not come to reprimand, but to offer you a new challenge. You seem to have done so well with your last."

Her shoulders lifted with pride. "I promise I won't let you down."

"We'll see."

Letty grinned. "So what's my new job? Dusting clouds? Shining rainbows?"

He chuckled. "Nothing quite so . . . quaint. You've earned your wings, Leticia. Now you will use them as a guardian."

"A guardian! To who?"

A swift wave of His hand parted the clouds, so Letty

could see her family gathered below. "Your granddaughters. And I can guarantee they will be an even bigger challenge than your own offspring. Do you accept?"

Letty cast her gaze over those she loved the most. She'd not only received a second chance, she'd gotten more. She nodded. "Happily."

If you loved SOMEBODY LIKE YOU
and want to see where it all began,
read on for a peek at Kate and Dean's stories in
SECOND CHANCE AT THE SUGAR SHACK
and ANY GIVEN CHRISTMAS,
available from Avon Books
wherever e-books are sold

An Excerpt from
SECOND CHANCE AT THE SUGAR SHACK

Chapter One

Kate Silver had five minutes. Tops.

Five minutes before her fashion schizophrenic client had a meltdown.

Five minutes before her career rocketed into the bargain basement of media hell.

Behind the gates of one of the trendiest homes in the Hollywood Hills, Kate dropped to her hands and knees in a crowded bedroom *In Style* magazine had deemed "Wacky Tacky." Amid the dust bunnies and cat hair clinging for life to a faux zebra rug, she crawled toward her most current disaster—repairing the Swarovski crystals ripped from the leather pants being worn by pop music's newly crowned princess.

Gone was the hey-day of Britney, Christina, and Shakira.

Long live *Inara*.

Why women in pop music never had a last name was a bizarre phenomenon Kate didn't have time to ponder. At the end of the day, the women she claimed as clients didn't need a last name to be at the top of her V.I.P. list. They didn't need one when they thanked her—their stylist—from the red carpet. And they certainly didn't need one when they signed all those lovely zeros on her paychecks.

Right now she sat in chaos central, earning every penny. Awards season had arrived and her adrenaline had kicked into overdrive alongside the triple-shot latte she'd sucked down for lunch. Over the years she'd become numb to the mayhem. Even so, she did enjoy the new talent—of playing Henry Higgins to the Eliza Doolittles and Huck Finns of Tinsel Town. Nothing compared to the rush she got from seeing her babies step onto a stage and sparkle. The entire process made her feel proud and accomplished.

It made her feel necessary.

Surrounded by the gifted artists who lifted their fairy dusted makeup brushes and hair extensions, Kate brushed a clump of floating cat hair from her nose. Why the star getting all the attention had yet to hire a housekeeper was anyone's guess. Regardless, Kate intended to keep the current catastrophe from turning into the Nightmare on Mulholland Drive.

Adrenaline slammed into her chest and squeezed the air from her lungs.

This was her job. She'd banked all her worth into what she did and she was damn good at it. No matter how crazy it made her. No matter how much it took over her life.

After her triumph on the Oscars red carpet three years ago, she'd become the stylist the biggest names in Hollywood demanded. Finally. She'd become an overnight sensation that had only taken her seven long years to achieve. And though there were times she wanted to stuff a feather boa down some snippy starlet's windpipe, she now had to fight to maintain her success. Other stylists, waiting for their star to shine, would die for what she had. On days like today, she would willingly hand it over.

In the distance the doorbell chimed and Kate's five minutes shrank to nada. The stretch limo had arrived to deliver Inara to the Nokia Theatre for the televised music awards. With no time to spare, Kate plunged the needle through the leather and back up again. Her fingers moved so fast blisters formed beneath the pressure.

Peggy Miller, Inara's agent, paced the floor and sidestepped the snow-white animal shelter refugee plopped in the middle of a leopard rug. Clearly the cat wasn't intimidated by the agent's nicotine-polluted voice.

"Can't you hurry that up, Kate?" Peggy tapped the Cartier on her wrist with a dragon nail. "Inara's arrival has to be timed perfectly. Not enough to dawdle in the interviews and just enough to make the media clamor for more. Sorry, darling," she said to Inara, "chatting with the media is just not your strong point."

Inara made a hand gesture that was far from the bubble gum persona everyone in the industry tried to portray with the new star. Which, in Kate's estimation, was like fitting a square peg into a round hole.

"Kate?" Peggy again. "Hurry!"

"I'm working on it," Kate mumbled around the straight pins clenched between her teeth. Just her luck their wayward client had tried to modify the design with a fingernail file and pair of tweezers an hour before showtime.

"Why do I have to wear this . . . thing." Inara tugged the

embossed leather tunic away from her recently enhanced bustline. "It's hideous."

The needle jabbed Kate's thumb. She flinched and bit back the slur that threatened to shoot from her mouth. "Impossible," she said. "It's Armani." And to acquire it she'd broken two fingernails wrestling another stylist to the showroom floor. She'd be damned if she'd let the singer out the door without wearing it now.

"Inara, please hold still," the makeup artist pleaded while she attempted to dust bronzer on her moving target.

"More teasing in back?" the hair stylist asked.

Kate flicked a gaze up to Inara's blond hair extensions. "No. We want her to look sultry. Not like a streetwalker."

"My hair color is all wrong," Inara announced. "I want it more like yours, Kate. Kind of a ritzy porn queen auburn." She ran her manicured fingers through the top of Kate's hair, lifting a few strands. "And I love these honey-colored streaks."

"Thanks," Kate muttered without looking up. "I think." Her hair color had been compared to many things. A ritzy porn queen had never been one of them.

"Hmmm. I will admit, these pants seriously make my ass rock," Inara said, changing gears with a glance over her shoulder to the cheval mirror. "But this vest . . . I don't know. I really think I should wear my red sequin tube top instead."

Kate yanked the pins from her between her teeth. "You can *not* wear a *Blue Light Special* with Armani. It's a sin against God." Kate blinked hard to ward off the migraine that poked between her eyes. "Besides, the last time you made a last-minute fashion change you nearly killed my career."

"I didn't mean to. It's just . . . God, Kate, you are so freaking strict with this fashion crap. It's like having my mother threaten to lower the hem on my school uniform."

"You pay me to threaten you. Remember?"

"I pay you plenty."

"Then trust me plenty." Kate wished the star would do exactly that. "Once those lights hit these crystals, all the attention will be on you. You're up for the new artist award. You should shine. You don't want to end up a fashion tragedy like the time Sharon Stone wore a Gap turtleneck to the Oscars, do you?"

"No."

"Good. Because that pretty much ended her career."

Inara's heavily made-up eyes widened. "A shirt did that?"

"Easier to blame it on a bad garment choice than bad acting."

"Oh."

"Kate? Do you want the hazelnut lipstick?" the makeup artist asked. "Or the caramel gloss?"

Kate glanced between the tubes. "Neither. Use the Peach Shimmer. It will play up her eyes. And make sure she takes it with her. She'll need to reapply just before they announce her category and the cameras go for the close-up."

"Kate!" Peggy again. "You have got to hustle. The traffic on Sunset will be a nightmare."

Kate wished for superpowers, wished for her fingers to work faster, wished she could get the job done and Inara in the limo. She needed Inara to look breathtaking when she stepped onto that red carpet. She needed a night full of praise for the star, the outfit, *and* the stylist.

Scratch that. It was not just a need, it was absolutely critical.

Inara's past two public appearances had been disasters. One had been Kate's own oversight—the canary and fuchsia Betsey Johnson had looked horrible under the camera lights. She should have known that before sending her client out for the fashion wolves to devour. The second calamity hadn't been her fault, but had still reflected on her. That time had been cause and effect of a pop royalty temper tantrum and Inara's fondness for discount store castoffs. It may have once worked for Madonna, but those days were locked in the fashion vault. For a reason.

Kate couldn't afford to be careless again. And she couldn't trust the bubble gum diva to ignore the thrift store temptations schlepping through her blood. Not that there was anything wrong with that for ordinary people. Inara did not fall into the *ordinary* category.

Not anymore.

Not if Kate could help it.

As soon as she tied off the last stitch, she planned to escort her newest client right into the backseat of the limo with a warning to the driver to steer clear of all second-hand clothing establishments along the way.

"This totally blows." Inara slid the shears from the table and aimed them at the modest neckline. "It's just not sexy enough."

"Stop that!" Kate's heart stopped. She grabbed the scissors and tucked them beneath her knee. "Tonight is not about selling sex. Leave that for your music videos. Tonight is about presentation. Wowing the critics. Tomorrow you want to end up on the best-dressed list. Not the *What the hell was she thinking?* list."

Inara sighed. "Whatever."

"And don't pout," Kate warned. *Or be so ungrateful.* "It will mess up your lip liner."

"How's this look?" the makeup artist asked, lifting the bronzer away from one last dusting of Inara's forehead.

Kate glanced up mid-stitch. "Perfect. Now, everybody back away and let me get this last crystal on."

"Kate!"

"I know, Peggy. I know!"

Kate grasped the leather pant leg to keep Inara from checking out the junk in her trunk again via the full-length mirror. She shifted on her knees. A collection of cat hair followed.

Once she had Inara en route, Kate planned to rush home and watch the red carpet arrivals on TV. Alone. Collapsed on her sofa with a bag of microwave popcorn and a bottle of Moët. If the night went well, the celebration cork would fly. If not, well, tomorrow morning she'd have to place a *Stylist for Hire—Cheap* ad in *Variety*.

Kate pushed the needle through the leather, ignoring the hurried, sloppy stitches. If her mother could see her now, she'd cringe at the uneven, wobbly lengths. Then she'd deliver a pithy lecture on why a career in Hollywood was not right for Kate. Neither the Girl Scout sewing badge she'd earned as a kid nor the fashion award she'd recently won would ever be enough to stop her mother from slicing and dicing her dreams.

Her chest tightened.

God, how long had it been since she'd even talked to her mother? Easter? The obligatory Mother's Day call?

In her mother's eyes, Kate would never win the daughter-of-the-year award. She'd quit trying when she hit the age of thirteen—the year she'd traded in her 4-H handbook for a *Vogue* magazine.

Her mother had never forgiven her.

For two long years after high school graduation, there had been a lull in Kate's life while she waited anxiously for acceptance and a full scholarship to the design school in Los Angeles. Two years of her mother nagging at her to get a traditional college degree. Two years of working alongside her parents in their family bakery, decorating cakes with the same boring buttercream roses, pounding out the same tasteless loaves of bread. Not that she minded the work. It gave her a creative outlet. If only her mother had let her shake things up a little with an occasional fondant design or something that tossed a challenge her way.

Then the letter of acceptance arrived.

Kate had been ecstatic to show it to her parents. She knew her mother wouldn't be happy or supportive. But she'd never expected her mother to tell her that the best thing Kate could do would be to tear up the scholarship and stop wasting time. The argument that ensued had led to tears and hateful words. That night Kate made a decision that would forever change her life.

It had been ten years since she'd left her mother's unwelcome advice and small-town life in the dust. Without a word to anyone she'd taken a bus ride and disappeared. Her anger had faded over the years, but she'd never mended the damage done by her leaving. And she'd never been able to bring herself to come home. She'd met up with her parents during those years, but it had always been on neutral ground. Never in her mother's backyard. Despite her mother's reservations, Kate had grown up and become successful.

She slipped the needle through the back of the bead cap and through the leather again. As much as she tried to ignore it, the pain caused by her mother's disapproval still hurt.

Amid the boom-boom-boom of Snoop Dog on the stereo and Peggy's non-stop bitching, Kate's cell phone rang.

"Do *not* answer that," Peggy warned.

"It might be important. I sent Josh to Malibu." Dressing country music's top male vocalist was an easy gig for her assistant. He'd survived three awards seasons by her side. He could walk the tightrope with the best of them. But as Kate well knew, trouble could brew and usually did.

Ignoring the agent's evil glare, Kate scooted toward her purse, grabbed her phone and shoved it between her ear and shoulder. Her fingers continued to stitch.

"Josh, what's up?"

"Katie?"

Whoa. Her heart did a funny flip that stole her breath. *Definitely not Josh.*

"Dad. Uh . . . hi. I . . . haven't talked to you in, uh . . ." *Forever.* "What's up?"

"Sweetheart, I . . . I don't know how to say this."

The hitch in his tone was peculiar. The sewing needle between her fingers froze midair. "Dad? Are you okay?"

"I'm ... afraid not, honey." He released a breathy sigh. "I know it's asking a lot but ... I wondered ... could you come home?"

Her heart thudded to a halt. "What's wrong?"

"Katie, this morning ... your mother died."

CHAPTER TWO

A hundred miles of heifers, hay fields, and rolling hills zipped past while Kate stared out the passenger window of her mother's ancient Buick. The flight from L.A. hadn't been long, but from the moment she'd received her father's call the day before, the tension hadn't uncurled from her body. The hour and a half drive from the *local* airport hadn't helped.

With her sister, Kelly, behind the wheel, they eked out the final miles toward home. Or what had been her home a lifetime ago.

They traveled past the big backhoe where the Dudley Brothers Excavation sign proclaimed: We dig our job! Around the curve came the Beaver Family Dairy Farm where a familiar stench wafted through the air vents. As they cruised by, a big Holstein near the fence lifted its tail.

"Eeew." Kelly wrinkled her nose. "Gross."

Kate dropped her head back to the duct-taped seat and closed her eyes. "I'll never look at guacamole the same again."

"Yeah. Quite a welcome home." Her sister peered at her

through a pair of last season Coach sunglasses. With her ivory blond hair caught up in a haphazard ponytail, she looked more like a frivolous teen than a fierce prosecutor. "It's funny. You move away from the Wild Wild West, buy your beef in Styrofoam packages, and forget where that hamburger comes from."

"Kel, nobody eats Holsteins. They're milk cows."

"I know. I'm just saying."

Whatever she was saying, she wasn't actually saying. It wasn't the first time Kate had to guess what was going on in her big sister's beautiful head. Being a prosecutor had taught Kelly to be tight-lipped and guarded. Though they were only two years apart in age, a world of difference existed in their personalities and style. Kelly had always been on the quiet side. She'd always had her nose stuck in a book, was always the type to smooth her hand over a wrinkled cushion just to make it right. Always the type to get straight A's and still worry she hadn't studied enough.

Kate took a deep breath and let it out slowly.

It was hard to compete with perfection like that.

"I still can't believe it's been ten years since you've been home," Kelly said.

Kate frowned as they passed the McGruber farm where someone had planted yellow mums in an old toilet placed on the front lawn. "And now I get the pleasure of remembering why I left in the first place."

"I don't know." Kelly leaned forward and peered through the pitted windshield. "It's really spectacular in an unrefined kind of way. The fall colors are on parade and snow is frosting the mountain peaks. Chicago might be beautiful, but it doesn't compare to this." Lines of concern scrunched between Kelly's eyes ruined the perfection of her face. "I know how hard this is for you, Kate. But I'm glad you came."

The muscles between Kate's shoulders tightened. Right now, she didn't want to think about what might be difficult for her. Others were far more important. "I'm here for Dad," she said.

"You know, I was thinking the other day . . . we all haven't been together since we met up at the Super Bowl last year." Kelly shook her head and smiled. "God. No matter that our brother was playing, I thought you and Mom were going to root for opposing teams just so you'd have one more thing to disagree about."

"I did not purposely spill my beer on her."

Kelly laughed. "Yes, you did."

The memory came back in full color and Kate wanted to laugh too.

"That's why Dad will be really glad to see you, Kate. You've always made him smile. You know you were always his favorite."

At least she'd been *somebody's* favorite. "I've missed him." Kate fidgeted with the string attached to her hoodie. "I didn't mean to . . ."

"I know." Kelly wrapped her fingers around the steering wheel. "He knew too."

The reminder of her actions stuck in Kate's throat. If she could do it all over, she'd handle it much differently. At the time she'd been only twenty, anxious to live her dreams and get away from the mother who disapproved of everything she did.

The interior of the car fell silent, except for the wind squealing through the disintegrating window seals and the low rumble of the gas-guzzling engine. Kate knew she and her sister were delaying the obvious discussion. There was no easy way to go about it. The subject of their mother was like walking on cracked ice. No matter how lightly you tip-toed, you were bound to plunge into turbulent waters. Their mother had given birth to three children who had all moved away to different parts of the country. Each one had a completely different view of her parental skills.

Her death would bring them all together.

"After all the times we offered to buy her a new car I can't believe Mom still drove this old boat," Kate said.

"I can't believe it made it to the airport and back." Kelly tucked a stray blond lock behind her ear and let out a sigh. "Mom was funny about stuff, you know. She was the biggest 'if it ain't broke don't fix it' person I ever knew."

Was.

Knew.

As in past tense.

Kate glanced out the passenger window.

Her mother was gone.

No more worrying about what to send for Mother's Day or Christmas or her birthday. No more chatter about the temperamental oven in their family bakery, or the dysfunctional quartet that made up the Founder's Day parade committee, or the latest gnome she'd discovered to stick in her vegetable garden.

No more . . . anything.

Almost a year had passed since she'd been with her mother. But even that hadn't been the longest she'd gone without seeing her. Kate had spent tons of time with Dean and Kelly. She'd snuck in a fishing trip or two with her dad. But an entire five years had gone by before Kate had finally agreed to meet up with her mother in Chicago to celebrate Kelly's promotion with the prosecutor's office. The reunion had been awkward. And as much as Kate had wanted to hear "I'm sorry" come from her mother's lips, she'd gone back to Los Angeles disappointed.

Over the years Kate had meant to come home. She'd meant to apologize. She'd meant to do a whole lot of stuff that just didn't matter anymore. Good intentions weren't going to change a thing. A knife of pain stabbed between her eyes. The time for could have, should have, would have, was history. Making amends was a two-way street and her mother hadn't made an effort either.

She shifted to a more comfortable position and her gaze landed on the cluttered chaos in the backseat—an array of pastry cookbooks, a box of quilting fabric, and a knitting tote where super-sized needles poked from the top of a ball of red yarn. Vanilla—her mother's occupational perfume—lingered throughout the car.

Kate inhaled. The scent settled into her soul and jarred loose a long-lost memory. "Do you remember the time we all got chicken pox?" she asked.

"Oh, my God, yes." Kelly smiled. "We were playing tag. Mom broke up the game and stuck us all in one bedroom."

"I'd broken out with blisters first," Kate remembered,

scratching her arm at the reminder. "Mom said if one of us got the pox, we'd all get the pox. And we might as well get it done and over with all at once."

"So *you* were the culprit," Kelly said.

"I don't even know where I got them." Kate shook her head. "All I know is I was miserable. The fever and itching were bad enough. But then you and Dean tortured me to see how far you could push before I cried."

"If I remember, it didn't take long."

"And if I remember," Kate said, "it didn't take long before you were both whining like babies."

"Karma," Kelly admitted. "And just when we were at our worst, Mom came in and placed a warm sugar cookie in each of our hands."

Kate nodded, remembering how the scent of vanilla lingered long after her mother had left the room. "Yeah."

The car rambled past Balloons and Blooms, the florist shop Darla Davenport had set up in her century-old barn.

"Dad ordered white roses for her casket." Kelly's voice wobbled. "He was concerned they wouldn't be trucked in on time and, of course, the price. I told him not to worry—that we kids would take care of the cost. I told him to order any damn thing he wanted."

Kate leaned forward and peered through her sister's sunglasses. "Are you okay?"

"Are you?" Kelly asked.

Instead of answering, Kate twisted off the cap of her Starbuck's Frappuccino and slugged down the remains. The drink gave her time to compose herself, if that were even possible. She thought of her dad. Simple. Hard-working. He'd taught her how to tie the fly that had helped her land the derby-winning trout the year she turned eleven. He couldn't have been more different from her mother if he'd tried. And he hadn't deserved to be abandoned by his youngest child.

"How's Dad doing?" Kate asked, as the iced drink settled in her stomach next to the wad of guilt.

"He's devastated." Kelly flipped on the fan. Her abrupt action seemed less about recirculating the air and more about releasing a little distress. "How would you be if the love of your life died in your arms while you were tying on her apron?"

"I can't answer that," Kate said, trying not to think about the panic that must have torn through him.

"Yeah." Kelly sighed. "Me either."

Kate tried to swallow but her throat muscles wouldn't work. She turned in her seat and looked at her sister. "What's he going to do now, Kel? Who will take care of him? He's never been alone. Ever," she said, her voice an octave higher than normal. "Who's going to help him at the Shack? Cook for him? Who's he going to talk to at night?"

"I don't know. But we definitely have to do something." Kelly nodded as though a lightbulb in her head suddenly hit a thousand watts. "Maybe Dean will have some ideas."

"Dean?" Kate leaned back in her seat. "Our brother? The king of non-relationship relationships?"

"Not that either of us has any room to talk."

"Seriously." Kate looked out the window, twisting the rings on her fingers. The urge to cry for her father welled in her throat. Her parents had been a great example of true love. They cared for each other, had each other's backs, thought of each other first. Even with her problematic relationship with her mother, Kate couldn't deny that the woman had been an extraordinary wife to the man who worshipped her. The chances of finding a love like the one her parents had shared were one in a million. Kate figured that left her odds stretching out to about one in a hundred gazillion.

"What's wrong with us, Kel?" she asked. "We were raised by parents the entire town puts on a pedestal, yet we all left them behind for something *bigger and better*. Not a single one of us has gotten married or even come close. As far as I know, Dean has no permanent designs on his current bimbo of the moment. You spend all your nights with a stack of law books. I spend too much time flying coast-to-coast to even meet up with someone for a dinner that doesn't scream fast food."

"Oh, poor you. New York to L.A. First Class. Champagne. And all those gorgeous movie stars and rock stars you're surrounded by. You're breaking my heart."

Kate snorted. "Yeah, I live such a glamorous life."

A perfectly arched brow lifted on Kelly's perfect face. "You don't?"

While Kate enjoyed what she did for a living, every day her career hung by a sequin while the next up-and-coming celebrity stylist waited impatiently in the wings for her to fall from Hollywood's fickle graces. She'd chosen a career that tossed her in the spotlight, but she had no one to share it with. And often that spotlight felt icy cold. "Yeah, sure. I just get too busy sometimes, you know?"

"Unfortunately, I do." Kelly gripped the wheel tighter. "You know . . . you could have stuck around and married Matt Ryan."

"Geez." Kate's heart did a tilt-a-whirl spin. "I haven't heard that name in forever."

"When you left, you broke his heart."

"How do you know?"

"Mom said."

"Hey, I gave him my virginity. I call that a fair trade."

"Seriously?" Kelly's brows lifted in surprise. "I had no idea."

"It wasn't something I felt like advertising at the time."

"He was pretty cute from what I remember."

"Don't go there, Kel. There's an ocean under that bridge. So mind your own business."

Matt Ryan. Wow. Talk about yanking up old memories. Not unpleasant ones either. From what Kate remembered, Matt had been very good at a lot of things. Mostly ones that involved hands and lips. But Matt had been that boy from the proverbial wrong side of the tracks and she'd had bigger plans for her life.

Her mother had only mentioned him once or twice after Kate had skipped town. Supposedly he'd eagerly moved on to all the other girls wrangling for his attention. Good for him. He'd probably gotten some poor girl pregnant and moved next door to his mother. No doubt he'd been saddled with screaming kids and a complaining wife. Kate imagined he'd still be working for his Uncle Bob fixing broken axles and leaky transmissions. Probably even had a beer gut by now. Maybe even balding. Poor guy.

Kelly guided their mother's boat around the last curve in the road that would lead them home. Quaking aspens glittered gold in the sunlight and tall pines dotted the landscape.

Craftsman style log homes circled the area like ornaments on a Christmas wreath.

"Mom was proud of you, you know," Kelly blurted.

"What?" Kate's heart constricted. She didn't need for her sister to lie about their mother's mind-set. Kate knew the truth. She'd accepted it long ago. "No way. Mom did everything she could to pull the idea of being a celebrity stylist right out of my stubborn head."

"You're such a dork." Kelly shifted in her seat and gripped the steering wheel with both hands. "Of course she was proud. She was forever showing off the magazine articles you were in. She even kept a scrapbook."

"She did not."

"She totally did."

"Go figure. The night before I boarded that bus for L.A., she swore I'd never make a living hemming skirts and teasing hair."

"No, what she said was, making a living hemming skirts and teasing hair wasn't for you," Kelly said.

"That's not the way I remember it."

"Of course not. You were so deeply immersed in parental rebellion she could have said the sky was blue and you'd have argued that it was aqua."

"We did argue a lot."

Kelly shook her head. "Yeah, kind of like you were both cut from the same scrap of denim. I think that's what ticked you off the most and you just didn't want to admit it."

No way. "That I was like Mom?"

"You could have been identical twins. Same red hair. Same hot temper."

"I never thought I was anything like her. I still don't."

"How's that river of denial working for you?"

"How's that rewriting history working for *you*?"

Kelly tightened her fingers on the steering wheel. "Someday you'll get it, little sister. And when you do, you're going to be shocked that you didn't see it earlier."

The remnants of the old argument curdled in Kate's stomach. "She didn't believe in me, Kel."

"Then she was wrong."

For some reason the acknowledgment from her big sister didn't make it any better.

"She was also wrong about you and your financial worth," Kelly added. "You make three times as much as I do."

"But not as much as Dean."

"God doesn't make as much as Dean," Kelly said.

Their big brother had always been destined for greatness. If you didn't believe it, all you had to do was ask him. Being an NFL star quarterback did have its perks. Modesty wasn't one of them.

"Almost there," Kelly announced.

The green highway sign revealed only two more miles to go. Kate gripped the door handle to steady the nervous tension tap-dancing on her sanity.

Ahead, she noticed the swirling lights atop a sheriff's SUV parked on the shoulder of the highway. The vehicle stopped in front of the cop had to be the biggest monster truck Kate had ever seen. In L.A., which oozed with hybrids and luxury cruisers, one could only view a farmboy-vehicle-hopped-up-on-steroids in box office bombs like the *Dukes of Hazzard*.

The swirling lights dredged up a not-so-fond memory of

Sheriff Washburn, who most likely sat behind the wheel of that Chevy Tahoe writing up the fattest citation he could invent. A decade ago, the man and his Santa belly had come hunting for her. When she hadn't shown up at home at o'dark thirty like her mother had expected, the SOS call had gone out. Up on Lookout Point the sheriff had almost discovered her and Matt sans clothes, bathed in moonlight and lust.

As it was, Matt had been quick to act and she'd managed to sneak back through her bedroom window before she ruined her shaky reputation for all time. Turned out it wouldn't have mattered. A few days later she boarded a bus leaving that boy and the town gossips behind to commiserate with her mother about what an ungrateful child she'd been.

As they approached the patrol vehicle, a deputy stepped out and, hand on gun, strolled toward the monster truck.

Mirrored shades. Midnight hair. Wide shoulders. Trim waist. Long, long legs. And . . . Oh. My. God. Not even the regulation pair of khaki uniform pants could hide his very fine behind. Nope. Definitely *not* Sheriff Washburn.

A double take was definitely in order.

"Wow," Kate said.

"They didn't make 'em like that when we lived here," Kelly noted.

"Seriously." Kate shifted back around in her seat. And frowned. What the hell was wrong with her? Her mother had been dead for two days and *she* was checking out guys?

"Well, ready or not, here we are."

At her sister's announcement Kate looked up at the overhead sign crossing the two-lane road.

Welcome to Deer Lick, Montana. Population 6,000.

For Kate it might as well have read *Welcome to Hell*.

Late the following afternoon, Kate stood amid the mourners gathered at the gravesite for Leticia Jane Silverthorne's burial. Most were dressed in a variety of appropriate blacks and dark blues. The exception being Ms. Virginia Peat, who'd decided the bright hues of the local Red Hat Society were more appropriate for a deceased woman with a green thumb and a knack for planting mischief wherever she went.

No doubt her mother had a talent for inserting just the right amount of monkey business into things to keep the town blabbing for days, even weeks, if the gossips were hungry enough. Better for business, she'd say. The buzz would catch on and the biddies of Deer Lick would flock to the Sugar Shack for tea and a sweet treat just to grab another tasty morsel of the brewing scandal.

Today, the Sugar Shack was closed. Her mother's cakes and pies remained unbaked. And the lively gossip had turned to sorrowful memories.

Beneath a withering maple, Kate escaped outside the circle of friends and neighbors who continued to hug and offer condolences to her father and siblings. Their almost overwhelming compassion notched up her guilt meter and served as a reminder of the small-town life she'd left behind. Which was not to say those in Hollywood were cold and unfeeling, she'd just never had any of them bring her hot chicken soup.

Plans had been made for a potluck gathering at the local Grange—a building that sported Jack Wagoner's award-winning moose antlers and held all the community events—

including wedding receptions and the Oktober Beer and Brat Fest. The cinder block structure had never been much to look at but obviously it remained the epicenter of the important events in beautiful downtown Deer Lick.

A variety of funeral casseroles and home-baked treats would be lined up on the same long tables used for arm wrestling competitions and the floral arranging contest held during the county fair. As far as Kate could see, not much had changed since she'd left. And she could pretty much guarantee that before the end of the night, some elder of the community would break out the bottle of huckleberry wine and make a toast to the finest pastry chef this side of the Rockies.

Then the stories would start to fly and her mother's name would be mentioned over and over along with the down and dirty details of some of her more outrageous escapades. Tears and laughter would mingle. Hankies would come out of back pockets to dab weeping eyes.

The truth hit Kate in the chest, tore at her lungs. The good people of Deer Lick had stood by her mother all these years while Kate had stood off in the distance.

She brushed a speck of graveside dust from the pencil skirt she'd picked up in Calvin Klein's warehouse last month. A breeze had cooled the late afternoon air and the thin material she wore could not compete. She pushed her sunglasses into place, did her best not to shiver, and tried to blend in with the surroundings. But the cost alone of her Louboutin peep toes separated her from the simple folk who dwelled in this town.

Maybe she should have toned it down some. She could imagine her mother shaking her head and asking who Kate thought she'd impress.

"Well, well, lookie who showed up after all."

Kate glanced over her shoulder and into the faded hazel eyes of Edna Price, an ancient woman who'd always reeked of moth balls and Listerine. The woman who'd been on the Founder's Day Parade committee alongside her mother for as long as Kate could remember.

"Didn't think you'd have the gumption," Edna said.

Gumption? Who used that word anymore?

Edna poked at Kate's ankles with a moose-head walking stick. "Didn't think you'd have the nerve," Edna enunciated as though Kate were either deaf or mentally challenged.

"Why would I need *nerve* to show up at my own mother's funeral?" *Oh, dumb question, Kate. Sure as spit the old biddy would tell her ten ways to Sunday why.*

The old woman leaned closer. Yep, still smelled like moth balls and Listerine.

"You left your dear sweet mama high and dry, what, twenty years ago?"

Ten.

"It's your fault she's where she is."

"*My* fault?" The accusation snagged a corner of Kate's heart and pulled hard. "What do you mean?"

"Like you don't know."

She had no clue. But that didn't stop her mother's oldest friend from piling up the charges.

"Broke her heart is what you did. You couldn't get up the

nerve to come back when she was breathin'. Oh, no. You had to wait until—"

Kate's patience snapped. "Mrs. Price . . . you can blame or chastise me all you want. But not today. Today, I am allowed to grieve like anyone else who's lost a parent. Got it?"

"Oh, I got it." Her pruney lips curled into a snarl. "But I also got opinions and I aim to speak them."

"Not today you won't." Kate lifted her sunglasses to the top of her head and gave Mrs. Price her best glare. "Today you will respect my father, my brother, and my sister. Or I will haul you out of this cemetery by your fake pearl necklace. Do I make myself clear?"

The old woman snorted then swiveled on her orthopedic shoes and hobbled away. Kate didn't mind taking a little heat. She was, at least, guilty of running and never looking back. But today belonged to her family and she'd be goddamned if she'd let anybody drag her past into the present and make things worse.

Great. And now she'd cursed on sacred ground.

Maybe just thinking the word didn't count. She already had enough strikes against her.

It's your fault . . .

Exactly what had Edna meant? How could her mother's death be any fault of hers when she'd been hundreds of miles away?

Kate glanced across the carpet of grass toward the flower-strewn mound of dirt. Beneath the choking scent of carnations and roses, beneath the rich dark soil, lay her mother.

Too late for good-byes.

Too late for apologies.

Things just couldn't get worse.

Unable to bear the sight of her mother's grave, Kate turned her head. She startled at the sudden appearance of the man in the khaki-colored deputy uniform who stood before her. She looked up—way up—beyond the midnight hair and into the ice blue eyes of Matt Ryan.

The boy she'd left behind.

An Excerpt from
ANY GIVEN CHRISTMAS

CHAPTER ONE

Game time.

Nothing in NFL quarterback Dean Silverthorne's career of media blitzes, celebrity propaganda, and general mayhem had prepared him for the wedding-day brouhaha in which he found himself immersed.

His formula for a happy marriage?

Stay single.

Not that he didn't believe marriage worked. His parents proved it did with a thirty-six-year union.

He just didn't believe marriage would work for him.

Ever.

He'd been smart enough to figure out that mystery of life at the age of fourteen. While his seventeen-year-old cousin had stood inside the smallest chapel in Deer Lick, Montana, and pledged his life to a girl he'd knocked up but barely knew, Dean had been rolling in the hayloft of Old Man Wilson's barn. One hand firmly on third base beneath Cathy Carlisle's pretty pink tank top, the other sliding into home beneath her grass-stained 501s.

The misery Dean witnessed that day on his cousin's face had compelled him to make himself two promises. Never get suckered, lured, conned, or tricked into exchanging the dreaded *I Do's.* And never, ever let anything or anyone stand in the way of his dream to become a star NFL quarterback.

At thirty-four he could claim success to both.

For twenty years he'd played it smart *and* safe. Touchdown passes and reliable condoms. Victorious teams and supermodels more intent on landing magazine covers than putting a *Mrs.* before their names.

In his book, weddings and all the froufrou crap they entailed were more trouble than an intercepted pass on the final play of the game. For years he'd avoided such occasions. Yet here he was, smack-dab in the heart of matrimony central, stuffed into the monkey suit he only hauled out for awards banquets.

As he stood inside Deer Lick, Montana's local Grange he glanced around the spacious room and almost laughed. Someone with a very twisted sense of humor had transformed the plain white cinder block walls he'd known as a kid into some kind of girly circus tent with twinkling fairy lights. The long-deceased masters who'd built this farmers' fortress must have turned in their overalls.

Though an early December snowstorm blew a bitter cold wind outside the big metal doors, inside the corners were draped with autumn bouquets wrapped in gold ribbons that swirled toward the concrete floor. Dinged-up folding tables had been covered by white cloths and mirrored centerpieces reflected the glow of tapered white candles. The entire display was an outrageous departure from the usual sparseness of the women's Friday-night Bingo games or the annual Texas Hold 'em tournament that stunk up the place with stale beer and cheap cigars. Even Kate's big-pawed pup, who sat perfectly humiliated near the gift table, had been bedecked with a pink satin tux.

The redhead who'd bullied him into attending the event waltzed by on the arm of her new husband. The bride—a.k.a. his baby sister—had the balls to wink at his obvious discomfort.

"How's the shoulder, Dean?" Edna Price clamped an arthritic hand over his good shoulder and smiled. Her weathered face crinkled like an old dry chamois.

"Great." Thankful for ditching the arm sling that labeled him as weak, Dean rotated his shoulder slightly. A simple movement to prove he wasn't in agony for the pain pills that would temporarily numb the ache.

"Bull pucky." His mother's dearest friend shook her blue-haired coif. "The minute that Denver tackle drilled you into the turf, I told your daddy you was gonna be in a big hurt."

Dean's lips compressed so tightly the blood drained from them. *Big hurt* didn't begin to describe the pain that had sliced through him after that hit—the pain that had twisted in his shoulder like a dull-edged razor. The air had been sucked from his lungs and he'd barely managed to get up off that field. In a haze of agony he'd lifted his hand in a wave to his team and to the stadium of fans, before they carted him away to the locker room for a series of x-rays and MRIs.

He smiled now at Edna, and the blood flowed back into his lips. He refused to display an ounce of weakness. Whining was for pussies. "Just another day at the office, Mrs. Price."

The sympathy in the older woman's faded eyes told Dean he couldn't fool someone who'd had her own share of pain. "Well, we're real proud of you, son. And we're sure lookin' forward to the Stallions winnin' a spot in the Super Bowl this year."

"Yeah," Dean grumbled. "Me too." Only he wouldn't be there to participate. And didn't that just piss him off.

Last year he'd let his team down. The coveted Lombardi had been within their reach. But in the final forty seconds of the game he'd stayed too long in the pocket. The defense had been fast and his feet hadn't been quick enough to buy time for his receiver to get in position. He'd overcompensated. The pass flew over the receiver's head and into the gloves of the opposing team, who took the ball in for the winning touchdown. A rookie mistake. And he'd been no damn newcomer to the game.

The vicious sack he'd received during the Thanksgiving Day game last month had drilled his already-ravaged shoulder into the unforgiving turf. As a result, he'd been placed on the "injured" list for the remainder of the season—or longer, if he listened to the bullshit they tried to feed him in rehab.

His team had lost that day and now his guys had to rely on the backup QB to take them to the show. He'd failed them twice. No way in hell would he fail them again. No. Way.

A few of the boys had visited him after the surgery—his third within four seasons, on the same shoulder. They'd apologized for not having his back. And they'd sworn they didn't blame him for the loss that day. But anyone with eyes could see their disappointment. Hell, it burned in his gut.

While the guilt blazed, he returned his attention to the

present, determined to sail through the remainder of the matrimonial festivities and get back to the real world.

After a few quick anecdotes about life on the NFL Superhighway and a hug that smelled faintly of moth balls and Listerine, Edna Price moved on. Dean downed his crystal flute of champagne.

The doctors were wrong.

Damned wrong.

He'd prove it to them and everyone else of little faith.

"Well, well. The hometown hero returns."

Fawn Derick, the first girl in junior high he'd managed to educate on the finer points of "Show me yours and I'll show you mine" sauntered toward him in a little black dress and pearls.

Fawn no longer possessed the long, lithe body she'd once flaunted in tank tops, tight Wranglers, and strappy little sandals. Now she had an excess of curves. Some natural, some man-made. As she leaned in for an air kiss, she pressed herself close enough for him to decide which was which. Even more impressive than Fawn's after-market assets? The huge diamond on her finger she'd received from a rich Californian who played rancher.

"And you've just become more beautiful in my absence."

Obviously flattered, Fawn leaned in for a full-breasted embrace. "Are you staying long?" she whispered against his ear.

Though Fawn had once been tempting and it might be fun to reminisce, for him, married women were more forbidden than women who salivated over a possible future trip to the altar.

He gave a shrug that fired a spike of pain through his shoulder. "Once they break out the hokey-pokey or the chicken dance, I'm outta here."

Coffin-black cat claws drifted down the sleeve of his Hugo Boss. "I meant, are you staying long . . . in town."

Not if he could help it. He had a life to get back to—one where a good time did not come with rules and attachments. Besides, he'd only be good for a day or two in his hometown before he became bored out of his mind. Or a target for females with big ideas.

The women in Deer Lick, God bless them, subdivided into three categories: single, married, and single again. They came in all shapes and sizes but they all had the same ambition: a band of gold around their finger and a ring through their intended's nose. Being a wealthy NFL star quarterback made him a prime target.

Fawn wasn't the first tonight to let him know she might be open to a little action down at the Cottage Motel. As much as he hated to disappoint them, he didn't do groupies, strangers, or anyone who may have a jealous significant other. He didn't want to end up like the Ravens' former running back who'd taken up with a groupie and ended up gut-shot like an opening-day buck. So to preserve his unrivaled reputation among the townsfolk and not to come off as a total ass, Dean turned on his *aw-shucks* charm.

"Sorry, gorgeous, it would be great to get together like old times. Unfortunately I've got to get back to the team."

Her hopes disintegrated with her smile. "But I thought—"

"Hey, big brother, they're playing our song."

With an exaggerated look of apology, Dean turned away from Fawn and her thinly veiled invitation toward his baby sister, who gave him a smug smile that proclaimed she knew she'd just rescued his sorry ass. No doubt she intended to collect her reward later. So while Sinatra serenaded them, Dean swept his sister into his arms and out onto the dance floor. He'd deal with the painful repercussions later.

His heart gave a proud stammer when he looked down into her green eyes. Marriage may not be for him, but it already seemed to be sitting well with her. "Has anyone mentioned how breathtaking you are?"

"Just the man I married, you, and maybe a few dozen others. Who's counting?" She gave him a wide grin and smoothed her hand over his injured shoulder in a motherly gesture. "You don't look so bad yourself. A tux looks *so* much better on you than that stinky old football jersey."

He chuckled to cover his flinch at even her softest touch. "That stinky old jersey generates million-dollar contracts."

"Happiness is not always about money, you know."

"Is that how you convinced yourself to give up your glamorous Hollywood career?"

"*Au contraire*, big brother, I didn't have to *convince* myself of anything. My career appeased me, but it never brought me deep satisfaction. You know, the kind that makes you go, 'Oh yeah. *This is it.*' But that man right there . . ." She tilted her bridal veil toward her new husband as he waltzed by and twirled his seventy-year-old partner in her orthopedic shoes. "*He* definitely gave me my *aha* moment."

"Uh-huh." Dean let his gaze drift so he wouldn't insult

her with an eye roll. "You were surrounded by the Spielbergs, DeNiros, and Madonnas of the world. What could possibly make one small-town deputy stand out above the rest?"

"Oh, that's easy. Honesty. Heart. Compassion. Not to mention the toe-curling sex."

His gaze snapped back. "TMI, Kate."

Her laughter rang as light as Christmas bells. "Someday you'll find the right woman and fall in love. Then you'll know what I'm talking about."

"I don't fall in love." He grinned. "Lust . . . is another matter."

"Well, *Mr. Perfect*, I hate to be the bearer of bad news, but you *will* fall in love. And when that happens, you will be shocked down to your jock strap. Because nothing else in this world will be more important to you than every breath she takes."

The catered hors d'oeuvres in his stomach dive-bombed at his sister's use of the nickname he'd earned after his first flawless season at USC. *Mr. Perfect*. He couldn't claim to be perfect anymore. Far fucking from it. "I doubt it. There are still too many long-legged blondes out there."

"Silly me. By the tabloid covers I see at the Gas and Grub, I'd have thought you'd already sampled them all."

"Nope. Still a few left. When I'm done with them I'll move on to the brunettes."

"You can talk smack all you want, big brother. But I know the real you. And that party-all-the-time playboy image you portray isn't the real you."

"Says who?"

She laughed. "Says me. Because Dad would kick your ass if you were truly that disrespectful."

Dean smiled. Kate was right. He had a deep appreciation for women. He didn't expect to have any woman he wanted, but he didn't mind it. And he certainly never took advantage. But where baby sister was concerned, he had no intention of letting down his guard. Otherwise the next thing he knew she'd have him set up in some cozy little cottage with a white picket fence, a wife, and 2.5 kids. Family meant everything to him. But appreciation didn't mean he had to have one of his own.

While Sinatra sang about flying off to far Bombay, their sister Kelly, middle child and kick-ass prosecutor, twirled and wobbled by in the arms of the best man. James Harley's wild reputation spanned the Rockies. Not exactly Kelly's brand of testosterone. Kelly tilted her head back and giggled.

Giggled? Sister Serious? No way. "Our sister appears to be drunk," Dean said. "And flirting."

Kate glanced over her shoulder. "She's having fun. Leave her alone."

"You're not worried she might do something stupid?"

"She's a big girl," Kate said. "And she deserves to have a little fun. The case she's on is ugly and tragic. She's not eating and she's losing sleep. So if she lets her hair down for a night, who the hell cares?"

"Not me?"

"Correct. Not you. And not me."

After another quick check on their tipsy subject, he conceded. "I guess a little happiness never hurt anybody."

Concern wrinkled Kate's forehead. "I want you to be happy too, Dean. With something more than throwing a football."

"Careful, you're starting to sound like Mom."

"Really?" Her smile brightened. "Maybe that's not so bad."

"*This* from the daughter who believed our mother out-wickeded the Witch of the West?"

"Maybe I've changed my mind. We women are allowed to do that, you know." She gave his hand a squeeze. "And the first thing Mom would tell you would be to stop pushing yourself so hard."

The look she gave him was all-knowing. But Kate didn't know half of what she thought she knew. No one did. And no one would find out, either.

Everything in his life was trashed. And for a moment, the tremendous losses stole his breath. He glanced away at the festive decorations. They reminded him of what his mother would create. Only this time she hadn't. She hadn't even been there to see her last-born walk down the aisle.

Their mother had died suddenly a few short months ago. No warning. No goodbye. Just *bam!* She was gone.

His eyes stung and he blinked.

He missed her.

She'd been his biggest fan. And more times than not, his best friend. And it seemed as though Kate intended to pick up the baton now.

"If that new husband of yours ever gets out of line, you better come to your big brother," he said, steering the conversation away from himself.

"No way." Kate tilted her head back and laughed. "If he gets out of line, *I* get to use the handcuffs."

Go figure. Kate had found her paradise in a town with a population of six thousand. His paradise, however, was a thousand miles south in the Lone Star state on the deep green field of football dreams.

"Now, what's this about Mom?" he asked.

"Mom is . . ." Kate paused and looked over his shoulder. Then she gave him a faint smile.

Her odd comment snapped his attention back to the present and he found they'd waltzed toward the edge of the dance floor. "Mom *is?*"

"Never mind." Kate stopped in front of two women who appeared to be in the midst of an entertaining conversation. One of them happened to be the little blonde he'd escorted down the aisle just a few hours earlier. She turned toward them with laughter still playing at the corners of her mouth.

"Dean, this is my very good friend, Emma Hart." Kate slipped his hand from her waist. "Why don't you two dance and get to know each other better?"

Dean whispered against her ear, "Do *not* play matchmaker, Kate."

As though she didn't hear, Kate embraced the blonde dressed in a strapless chocolate gown that hugged some pretty knockout curves. "If he's not nice, I give you permission to sack him."

A smile and a wink later, Kate glided away, leaving him alone with a too-short woman who looked too intellectual, seemed much older than the models he dated, and by the lack of gold on her finger, was most likely single and man-shopping. Still, his sister would never forgive him if he didn't display uber-politeness. He had no choice but to turn on the charm he usually reserved for the media after an opposing team had opened up a can of whoop-ass.

As Frank Sinatra faded away, the DJ put on a country ballad. What was it with all the hokey slow dances? Dean took his cue and extended his hand. "Well, Emma, very good friend of my sister Kate, would you care to dance?"

She looked up at him and sparks flashed deep in her unique Mediterranean-blue eyes. Lips that looked marshmallow-soft parted slightly and revealed the slightest space between her two front teeth. In an instant, studious turned to sexy and a deluge of testosterone flooded Dean's system that he couldn't have held back if he'd been the Hoover Dam.

She hesitated.

He held back a laugh.

Like she'd really turn him down?

She tilted her head and silky hair draped across her bare shoulder. He took that as a yes and reached for her hand.

"Thanks." She tucked her hand behind her back. "But no thanks."

Emma looked up at Deer Lick's golden boy and found bewilderment shading his green eyes.

He'd never been turned down before.

Poor baby.

In the space of a heartbeat he recovered as smoothly as the pro who commanded the football field, and he surprised her when his sensuous lips curled into a smile.

Too bad the gesture was wasted. She didn't plan to stick around and wait to be dazzled. She turned away from the man who was paid millions to repel gigantic ogres in gladiator garb, and who apparently possessed some kind of magic that caused women all over America to drop their panties like coins in a wishing well.

As a bridesmaid she had duties to attend to. Especially since it appeared the maid of honor seemed a bit too tipsy to handle the task.

Emma curled her fingers into the dupioni silk of her dress and lifted it so she wouldn't fall on her face as she walked toward the bar in her borrowed high heels. As much as she hated to admit it, even to herself, coming face-to-face with Dean Silverthorne had rattled her composure. When he'd walked her down the aisle at the wedding, she hadn't looked up and he hadn't looked down. Their eyes had never met. When she'd stood on the altar, she'd focused solely on the beautiful vows being exchanged between the loving couple. But now, standing an arm's length away with his penetrating gaze focused on her? That had been an entirely different matter.

"Champagne, please," she told the rent-a-bartender, who promptly popped the cork on a fresh bottle. While Emma waited for her drink, Carrie Underwood's passionate vocals filled the room. The sweet rhythm of the music poured through Emma's bones and she started to hum along. As she accepted the fluted glass from the bartender, she became aware of a large tuxedoed presence taking up space to her left. He leaned an elbow on the rented bar, and the luxurious scent of pricey aftershave and warm male settled over her like a seductive web.

"So, you come here often?" The deep timbre of his voice was tinged with humor.

Emma smiled into her glass of champagne and sipped. The bubbles tickled her nose. She looked up, a smirk still on her lips. "Actually, I do. On Wednesday nights I meet here with the ladies' auxiliary and once a month we hold a Mommy and Me crafting class."

Her own attempt at humor was met with the imaginary sound of crickets.

"Oh." She gasped dramatically. "I'm sorry. Was that a pick-up line?"

His smile slipped and his dark brows pulled together.

"And that works for you?"

"No." A burst of amusement rumbled in his broad chest. "But I try at least once a day to put my foot in my mouth. How'd I do?"

"I'd give you an A+."

"Perfect." He leaned toward the bartender and ordered a glass for himself. Champagne in hand, he turned his back to the bar and lifted his glass as if to toast her.

Hmmmm. She thought she'd made herself clear. *Not interested.* So why didn't he go away?

Intent on discouraging further conversation, she turned her attention to the dinner tables across the room to see if the disposable cameras were in use. One of her bridesmaid duties was to make sure everyone had a good time, and Emma always took her responsibilities to heart. The man beside her, however, appeared not to be deterred.

She looked up. "Is there a problem?"

"No problem." He shrugged his non-injured shoulder. "Just curious."

"About?"

"Why you didn't want to dance." His head tilted. "Don't you know how?"

"Of course I know how." Was he kidding? She knew how to bust a move. Poorly. Alone in her living room with only her cat watching. "I simply choose not to."

His *Sexiest Man of the Year* smile widened to a grin as if he'd been challenged. Emma looked away. She took a sip of her champagne and scanned the room again, searching for any excuse to politely escape his overwhelming presence. He was a gorgeous man who, in his tux, would put a red carpet George Clooney to shame. She could clearly understand how women would fall prey to his kind of drug. But she'd sworn to never put herself in that position again. Once had been enough.

His dark brows lifted. "You don't like me, do you?"

"Don't be silly." She kept her attention across the room and wiggled her fingers in a wave to Dean's father, who was doing his best to avoid the attention of man-eater Gretchen Wilkes. Poor man. "I barely know you."

"You know . . ." He took a long sip of his champagne. "I believe I like this kind of dance much better."

She looked up. The lingering grin on his face clearly said he was quite entertained for some odd reason. "I'm afraid I don't know what you mean."

"This banter." He waved his hand between the two of them. "You know, verbal dodge ball."

"Really? Well now *I'm* curious," she admitted.

"About?"

"Why you're wasting your time talking to me. I'm not a supermodel or a movie star. I don't even mud wrestle."

"Well, that works out great." Charm oozed from every virile pore in his body. "Because I much prefer Jell-O wrestling."

She shook her head. "Why is it that men are always drawn to women who don't mind humiliating themselves?"

"Guess I've never regarded a friendly little Jell-O tussle as humiliating."

"Well, of course not. Because men like you always see the end game."

"Which is?"

"Meaningless sex. A one-nighter, nooner, or whatever time of day you manage to find a willing body."

"So, from your point of view," he responded, pointing a long, masculine finger at her, "that's all *men like me* are looking for? A quickie?"

"Isn't it?"

"Absolutely not."

"Right." *And sunflowers grow on Mars.* "You don't remember me, do you?" she blurted out in a choked laugh.

He looked down at her, studied her face. Then his mouth slid into a cautious smile. "Don't take it personal."

Emma held his gaze. Men like Dean Silverthorne gobbled up women like her. Men who used women, ruined their reputations, then moved on without a sprinkle of apology.

Love 'em and leave 'em.

Been there. Done that.

Didn't need to make a return trip.

"I wouldn't dream of taking it personal." Emma set her half-empty glass on the bar. "If you'll excuse me." As she scooted around him, his big hand touched her arm.

"Wait a minute." Concern tightened his brow. "*Should* I remember you?"

"I have to go. Your sister is about to throw the bouquet." She shot him an exaggerated look of regret. "But don't worry. Men like you never remember women like me." She tapped her chest. "We're completely forgettable."

CANDIS TERRY was born and raised near the sunny beaches of Southern California and now makes her home on an Idaho farm. She's experienced life in diverse ways, from working in a Hollywood recording studio to scooping up road apples left by her daughter's rodeo-queening horse to working as a graphic designer. Only one thing has remained constant: Candis's passion for writing stories about relationships, the push-and-pull in the search for love, and the security one finds in their own happily-ever-after. Though her stories are set in small towns, Candis's wish is to give each of her characters a great big, memorable love story, rich with quirky characters, tons of fun, and a happy ending. For more, please visit www.candisterry.com.

Be Impulsive!

Look for Other
Avon Impulse Authors

www.AvonImpulse.com